The Su

Their perfect world is torn apart at the

hands of the Japanese.

Will love, friendship and determination

be enough to survive…?

By

Jo Price

Book Bubble Press

Published in the United Kingdom by

Book Bubble Press

First printed October 2017

A CIP record of this book is available from the British Library.

ISBN: 978 1 912494 00 2

Visit: www.bookbubblepress.com

This Book is dedicated to my Gran and all of

the brave QA's who suffered so much but

complained so little.

And to my children, Luke and Alyssa, for

whom I wrote the story so that this little part

of our history would not be forgotten, and

their promise that they *might* read it.

A note from the Author

I have come to know the characters in this story very well. Out of respect for those who lived and fought during the period, many of the names are factual.

Their characters and personalities however, are not.

Sadly, most have now passed away and therefore were unable to give their thoughts or opinions, therefore the book is loosely based around diaries and actual events, but is a fictional depiction of their experiences.

Don't they say that a picture can say a thousand words? Well, it's true, it can. When I first opened the suitcase that is what I found. Hundreds of stories just waiting to be told. Adventures and disasters, love stories and tragedies. Where did I start? As I picked through all of the memories, so carefully placed and treasured, I uncovered the story of two people thrown together by circumstance and bound by a deep, passionate, enduring love. But it was also a story of horror, brutality, of unimaginable sacrifice and humiliation, a story of such adversity that it is difficult for us to comprehend today. Those two people were my Grandparents, and this is the story of how they survived the Japanese occupation of Hong Kong in World War 2. Growing up, I thought about the story often and when I asked, nobody knew much about it. Even as a young child, every time I went to visit, I would ask to look in the suitcase and every time I became more fascinated and more admiring of the characters within. I used to ask my Gran about it, hoping that she would open up and share her stories of how it had really been. She never did. She would tell the same witty anecdotes that would make us all laugh but then would soon close down and change the subject.

"Don't be silly," she would say. "Nobody is interested in all of that."

But I was. I wanted to ask more. I wanted to ask about the people she had known, the things she had seen, how my Grandparents had met. The pain behind her eyes stopped me every time. She was clearly trying to forget much of what I was so curious to know.

Then, after suffering with dementia and living in her own happy world for a number of years, she died. Joan Whiteley was, like so many of her generation, a lady so unassuming you would never know what she had survived. A lady who both inspired yet sometimes terrified me, with her stern, no nonsense glares. One look could render any of us silent within seconds. On the other hand she was the smiling, cheery white-haired Granny who would always walk around singing or whistling to herself, usually carrying a faded rolled up carrier bag instead of a handbag - unless she was wearing her Sunday best for church or special occasions. She lived to the ripe old age of 86 and died with dignity and not much drama, which is what she would have wanted. She disapproved of any kind of fuss.

When she was gone, I again asked if I could look through the suitcase. Once I opened it, the smell conjured up the memories, and the curiosity returned. I wanted to know more. I wanted to know how it been for girls so young, so full of life and adventure to be thrown into situations so awful that it made the strongest, bravest man weep. I wanted to know how they had survived years as Japanese Prisoners of War and come through it smiling and with humour. I wanted to know how they could put their experiences behind them and go on to lead normal, happy lives. Deep down I knew the answer. Because they had to. The generation demanded it. They were made of strong stuff and without their grit, determination, and bravery; our world would look much different than it does today.

There were so many memories within that little, faded suitcase. There was nothing special about it, it was small and textured, a faded brown with rounded edges and a bright red satin lining. On either side of the handle there were two brass locks, not that I ever remember them being closed, the fear being we would never get the case open again as the little key had long since been lost. Lifting the lid I could see that at some point my Gran had written her name and one of her many addresses in the top left corner on the inside of the lid in black felt tip pen.

There were two diaries in the suitcase, neatly placed side-by-side, and a small leather case holding a passport and other official documents. In another small folder there are more photographs, notes and letters from patients, friends and colleagues that she had known during the time that she was a POW in Stanley Internment Camp. The notes and pictures showed the sense of humour and solidarity that must have been needed to get them through the worst period of their lives. The pencil drawings and coloured sketches paid tribute to their creators as immensely talented artists. And there was a photo album.

I reached in and pulled out the photo album. Everything in that suitcase had always been arranged in the same order. The photo album was always on top. It was black leather and heavy and had obviously been looked after and treasured, showing few outward signs of ageing. I traced my fingers over the lovely, embossed cover design which showed a traditional Chinese junk within a typical Far Eastern scene of clouds, a temple and cherry blossom all around. It was beautiful. It smelled of old leather and paper and thick black blotting paper pages had delicate flower-patterned tissue paper were stuffed between each page, protecting the precious, decades-old, photographs. The pages were held in place by two black metal pins, which could be unscrewed to add or remove leaves.

The photographs were held in place with photo corners that had long since yellowed. Underneath the photographs, descriptions written in white pencil crayon faded with age. The images showed happier times, young friends full of hope, setting out on their adventures and sharing experiences that they could never have dreamed of being part of during wartime.

So much care had been taken in presenting the photographs; all the images laid out in order, the little captions so neatly written to make sure the memories would never be forgotten. My Gran had painstakingly set them out to tell a story, to remind her of the happier times that she spent in Hong Kong, and maybe try to block out some of the bad.

Time and time again, I would thumb through the pictures, trying to imagine the stories from those happy times. A postcard image was on the inner cover, labelled 'Hong Kong by night.' The landscape looked different then, but it was just as impressive as it is today. The photographer had captured all of the lights of the boats in the harbour and their reflection in the water. Even before the war, Hong Kong was a beautiful and vibrant city.

The first collection of photographs in the album is of a grand cruise ship, The Viceroy of India. They showed the deck, the games room, the swimming pool, the writing room, and an excited group of young nurses about to set sail. How thrilling it must have been for a girl from Crumpsall, a small suburb of Manchester, to begin her adventures as a member of the Queen Alexandra's Imperial Military Nursing Service (QAIMNS) in such grand style.

Pages of photographs show her voyages across the globe. They map out Gibraltar and Cape Town, and even the rescue of hundreds of Canadian women and children from the SS Ceramic which had been involved in a collision with a tanker one night in the Atlantic. It is incredible that those pictures of near disaster were simply tucked in between the happy snaps. Just another sign of war, and what people took in their stride.

Then, followed a series of pictures of trips taken by my Gran and her QAIMNS colleagues once they had arrived in Hong Kong, to Lantau Camp and Silvermine Bay. The same small group of friends, now familiar, looking tanned, happy, and carefree. It was 1940 and the world was at war. Hitler was on his march, but Hong Kong, for now, was free.

The diaries became my prized possessions. The first tells the story of 1941. My Grandparents and their friends had a wonderful year. It was a golden time of carefree, high living and offered a stark contrast to the second diary; a little red autograph book that held accounts of cruelty, starvation, death, and a desperation to keep life as normal as possible. It told of music lessons, grand performances and concerts, and the Snake and Staff newsletters that were written with great humour to keep the camp entertained and spirits high. The friendships formed during this time bound these people together for life, in a way that no other experience ever could. When reading this diary, I feel immense pride, not just in my Gran, but in the Great British 'stiff upper lip' and get on with it attitude displayed not by all, but by many.

I carefully turned the pages of the second diary, small, red, and unassuming. Its mottled leather cover had the word '*Autographs*' written in silver filigree across the front in the style of a signature. Faded with age, the little book looked like it could probably tell many more tales than were chronicled within. The edges were worn and there were deep creases in the cover where it had been folded in attempts to hide it. The pages inside, once cream, beige, and dusky pink, faded to sepia. The silver edging rubbed away by years of handling. The pages delicate, and crumbling. Some of them had already become detached, some only barely attached by cotton stitching that was holding them together by a thread. As I turned the first page out fell a folded, aged sheet.

It read:

Ward	1 left arm
Cafford	2 left leg
Pilfold	Head
Spendelow	Right leg amp
Wanstall	Left leg amp

And so it went on, the young nurse had recorded 17 names of men and their injuries, presumably on one of her ward rounds. It was almost shocking to read how matter of fact my Gran was about the poor

men who'd lost limbs or suffered other, life changing traumas. Another

sign of the strength of character of the nurses who cared for the soldiers

and civilians suffering from horrific injuries.

As I carefully turned the pages, little cryptic notes that my

Grandad sent to her from his POW camp fell out from between the

pages. They said very little as the Japanese vetted all correspondence that

left the camps. Most of them simply stated 'Keep cheery my dear'. I can

only imagine how she must have felt when these brief notes of hope

arrived, confirming that he was alive and thinking of her.

The red *'Autograph'* diary started after the surrender, Black

Christmas 1941. The first entries were brief and must have been written

to just mark the significant dates of the events leading up to the surrender.

It is hard to imagine the chaos and how she must have felt at that time.

Together, the diaries tell a story of hardship that was repeated throughout

the Far East during World War 2.

To me, she was my Gran, but here in front of me was just one

of the many chapters of the extraordinary life of Joan Whiteley. She went

on to have three children, five grandchildren, and five great grandchildren,

two of whom she managed to meet before she passed away. Who, as a

young nurse, had decided to join the QAIMNS, an elite nursing corps who worked alongside the soldiers on the frontline during World War 2. The 24 year old woman was driven by a need to serve her country alongside her brothers/friends and countrymen. Like so many of her generation, she took pride in being part of the noble effort to fight the Axis powers. They possessed a sense of duty that sustained them through the arduous and painful times to come.

I needed to piece together the fragments, to puzzle out the story of Joan's experience during the war. Once I researched the era, the people, and the events, I realised just what a huge undertaking it was. I had discovered, and became part of, a period in time that so many were still trying to commemorate, to make sure it was never, ever forgotten. Keeping these memories alive, so that the fight and sacrifice of a generation had not been in vain became paramount.

This is her story.

And theirs.

The battle for Hong Kong has been widely written about, but largely forgotten in the western world. Apart from those who were there and those passionate enough to research and write some incredible accounts of the attack that seemed to have taken everyone by surprise. Nobody in the colony thought that the Japanese would dare, or even be capable of attacking the mighty British Empire. It was a catastrophic underestimation of an army that had become hardened warriors during their battles across China. There were even some Chinese who had taken refuge on Hong Kong Island from the ravaged mainland of China, seeking protection under the British flag. The rich and powerful 'peakites' within the British expat community were appalled. The more astute and wealthy Chinese left in their boatloads to Macao and other points along the coast.

In the meantime, whilst the Japanese were getting ever closer, the colony continued to live the high life. In the shadow of war, business was booming, and a social whirl of parties, tennis, picnics at the beach, dinners at The Gripps and The Parisian Grill, bridge clubs and golf with the odd bit of sailing thrown in, all part of daily life. Hidden in plain sight, the Japanese spies had long since made themselves part of the local landscape, as had intelligence agents from Taiwan. No-one seemed to care. In 1937, Taiwanese agents were already set up at various points in the New Territories with radio transmitting equipment. By 1939, the

Japanese had enough intelligence to issue its troops maps of the defence installations 'protecting' Hong Kong. Thousands of Chinese triads, holding grudges against Imperial Britain, fed information back to Major Okada Yoshimasa, the man responsible for the Asia Development Agency or 'Koa Kikan.'

Their task was to de-stabilise and undermine the British rule from within the colony by feeding propaganda to the non-European community and paving the way for the attack. The triads were the bus boys, the rickshaw pullers, the cooks and the barbers. All passing information back to the Japanese. It was one of the most well-planned, well-informed attacks ever executed, and the British were in the main, completely oblivious.

Chapter 1

"Penny for them."

"Pardon?"

"A penny for your thoughts?" Brenda asked, as she lay on the grass outside Leeds General, a huge, modern building standing six stories high. At one end, there were semi-circular balconies designed for patients to sit out in the fresh air as they convalesced. Brenda Morgan was watching some of these patients being fussed over by her colleagues as she and her best friend, Joan Whiteley, took a well-earned break after a busy morning on Ward 8.

They had met on the first day of midwifery training and were inseparable ever since. One was rarely seen without the other, to the point where Matron called them Tweedledum and Tweedledee. Together, they made a striking pair; both brunette with short pin curled hair, as was the style, although Brenda always complained that she had more of a struggle to tame her unruly curls.

Brenda rummaged in her bag and triumphantly presented Joan with a small square of chocolate. Joan smiled as she took it from her and rolled onto her back.

"Have I mentioned that you're the best friend a girl could have, tweedledee"

"I'm also the best friend a man could have," Brenda said. "Gosh, have you seen Jack Fuller down in 17b?"

Joan rolled her eyes. "I haven't."

Brenda was desperate to get married and called dibs on every somewhat decent looking man under the age of 30 who crossed their paths.

"You're going to mess up your hair if you lay back like that, you know? You'll have to reset it again." Joan ignored her and picked up her sketch pad. Brenda had asked Joan to sketch her and make sure that she emphasised her best features. She wanted to send it to a soldier she had been writing to since he had left the hospital following a minor operation. She smiled as she handed the pad over to Brenda, "What do you think?"

"Oh my days! You've made me look short and dumpy with crazy hair! And what is that slightly mad smile all about?"

"Have you ever thought that might be what you actually look like, my dear?" Said Joan, taking the pad back and admiring her handywork. "I actually think I've got you down to a tee." Brenda pulled a face and said,

"Well I clearly won't be sending that down to Dorset, will I?"

"I think you should, men like a woman with a sense of humour."

Brenda picked up some grass cuttings and threw them at Joan.

"Well, we can't all have perfect hair, a perfect figure and huge baby blues now can we?" She said, her eyes twinkling with mischief. Joan snorted. "Hardly! I would give anything for your curves. You can keep the crazy hair though." She rolled back onto her front. "And you know full well that men always prefer the girls with the big, brown doe eyes."

Joan loved working with Brenda. They always had such good fun together; it didn't really seem like work at all. Joan was the slightly more reserved and sensible of the two. She had been raised with two older sisters and a brother, so had learned to look after herself from a young age. Her mother was of the children should be 'seen and not heard generation' and so, as the youngest of four, she was often left to amuse herself.

Brenda and Joan shared the same duty roster and made a great team on the ward. Both were hard workers and took their duties seriously, balanced with times they laughed so hard that they couldn't breathe. The last 12 months were the most fun that Joan had ever had. They were working together as Staff Midwives, and today was their last shift before both going home to see their families for two weeks before their new duty rota started. Brenda had been born and bred in Leeds and Joan was from Manchester. That was the only downside, Brenda was only around the corner from the hospital and Joan had a train ride ahead of her, which she never looked forward to.

Despite the journey, Joan was so excited to be going home this time; she couldn't wait to see her brother Bill. He was home briefly before heading off to North Africa with his regiment in June. As the youngest, they were very close and as children had often got themselves into trouble, especially with their older sisters, Alice and Edith. Bill was kind and funny and always had such good stories to tell. He had the unfailing ability to make her laugh and bring her out of the darkest of moods. It was hard to believe that she would be seeing him the next day.

The two nurses were enjoying the sun on their faces on the unusually bright and warm March afternoon, happily relaxing and each lost in her own thoughts, until Brenda had broken the silence.

"I was just wondering what it will be like when we join up," said Joan.

She turned towards Brenda, propping herself up on her elbow. "I was talking to Teresa in the canteen and both her and Rose are going to London next week for their interviews."

"Are they? I haven't had a letter through yet have you?" said Brenda, sitting up.

"No not yet, but Matron said that we should be getting them any day now. Apparently, they are desperate for newly trained nurses so I can't imagine that we will have to wait long." Joan smiled.

It was 1940 and the wheels of war were turning once more. They had been talking about joining up for some time now and had both been drawn to the idea of joining the Queen Alexandra's Imperial Military Nursing Service, or QA's for short.

Brenda had been attracted by the uniform, a distinctive scarlet and grey, but for Joan the QA's history was her main reason for joining up. Lady of the Lamp, Florence Nightingale, and her brave team of nurses had inspired Joan become a nurse.

During the Great War, the military had only accepted experienced nurses. But a year into what looked like a second global war, the War Office had decided that newly qualified nurses could join up straight away. It had worried Joan slightly, so little seemed to have happened since war broke out nine months earlier, and yet the Army was already relaxing the rules for the recruitment of its nursing staff. Regardless, as a qualified nurse, Joan felt it was her duty to join up, and she couldn't wait.

"Blimey Joan, can you imagine sailing over to France in the fancy grey and scarlet?" Brenda said glancing across at her friend. "We will look so grand."

Joan nodded and smiled as she lay back down on the grass.

"I can't wait to wear the uniform either. It's about time they realised that we lower classes might actually make good nurses too!" she teased, chuckling as she waited for Brenda's inevitable reaction. It was a subject guaranteed to rile her. It was only a recent development, but the Army was now recruiting nurses straight into the position of Sister, equivalent to a Lieutenant. At last, it was less about the nurses' social background and more about their ability as a nurse. Brenda let out an exaggerated sigh and gave her friend a playful nudge as she lay down again beside her.

"Don't get me started again, Whiteley!" she warned, retaliating by calling Joan by her surname, an Army habit she knew that she hated. "I do wonder how different it will be as an army nurse though."

"I doubt it will be any different at all after working with our Matron. The Army couldn't be any more particular about their hospital corners than she is!"

They both laughed before falling back into a comfortable silence and their own thoughts of the prospects of joining the QA's. It was all so exciting. Joan's thoughts strayed back to the coveted grey and scarlet uniform. It could only be bought at Harrods in London, made to measure. Matron had said that this was likely to change with rationing and fabric becoming scarce, but for now they could hope to feel like nursing royalty, assuming they passed their entrance interview and could get their uniforms before the regulations changed again. The trademark grey, elbow length cape with the scarlet trim made the QA's the most respected and sought-after nursing corps in the Army. Joan had heard rumours that the cape might go as it was becoming more impractical and depending on where nurses were being stationed, it was no longer

compulsory to have one. Joan, however, was more impressed by the grey woollen greatcoat and beret. She had always admired the nurses when they had worn them.

They reluctantly left the peace and quiet of the gardens and returned to the ward. The rest of the shift went by in a blur and, before they knew it, they were saying their goodbyes as Joan caught the last train back to Manchester.

"See you in a couple of weeks, Joan," said Brenda, waving as the train pulled out of Leeds Central station.

"You will indeed." Joan replied as she leaned out of the window. "Have a wonderful break and let me know as soon as your letter arrives."

"Oh I will! I just can't wait!" Brenda shouted, just as she disappeared from view in a cloud of steam.

Joan settled into her seat. A woman's shadow passed the blurred window of her carriage and footsteps slowly faded away down the corridor. The train shunted and clanked its way through the darkness of the blackout. Joan squinted, trying to get her bearings, but could see virtually nothing out of the train's window. Every so often, the shadow of a town or village would appear during the brief moments that the moon shone through the clouds. Her thoughts soon turned back to the war, and her hope of becoming a military nurse. The Army seemed to have stepped up its recruitment campaign in a bid to enlist as many nurses as possible to 'do their duty.' 5000 by June, Matron had said. The adverts and posters painted a picture of a wonderfully glamorous lifestyle and a 'unique opportunity to see the world'. Before the war, the images of pretty nurses wearing pristine uniforms in exotic and far off locations had only been found on hospital notice boards, but now, Joan saw them on every billboard, and in every newspaper she opened, laden with phrases like 'I serve' and 'Your Country Needs You!' appealing to a nurses' sense of duty.

The more she saw and read about the QA's, and the lives that they were living abroad, the more thankful she was that her Matron convinced her to interview at the War Office to join the elite team of nurses.

By the time she had reached Manchester Victoria station, and caught the bus back to Crumpsall, Joan was exhausted. It had been a long day. As she walked in through the front door, her gaze fell on the little brown envelope perched pointedly on the table. She immediately rushed over to tear open the envelope. The letter within told her that her application had been accepted and she was to go to London that same week for an interview. Clutching the letter to her chest, she smiled, hardly believing it was finally happening. She read the letter again slowly, absorbing every word. This was the first step of a new adventure. She could hardly wait. She had to let Brenda know, and hoped a letter had been waiting for her too.

Chapter 2

Within days, Joan made travel arrangements and before she knew it, she was in London's famous Underground for the first time. Struggling to figure out the huge maps hanging on tiled walls, she finally worked out that the military hospital was straight down to Charing Cross and one stop across to Westminster. The heat trapped within the unventilated corridors was suffocating, and the smoke of a million cigarettes hung in the air. She could not wait to get out.

All of that was forgotten the moment she stepped outside again, confronted by the Houses of Parliament and the River Thames flowing beside. The sight took her breath away. In awe, a deep sense of pride filled her as she walked down Abingdon Street along the length of the Palace of Westminster, wondering where the House of Commons ended and the House of Lords began. A carefully-tended park soon gave way to an uninterrupted view of the Thames to her left before she reached her destination; Queen Alexandra's Military Hospital, known as Millbank hospital. She arrived at the imposing Edwardian red brick building and saw the now-familiar sandbags outside the front entrance. Almost every building she had walked past had been the same: sandbags and bored looking soldiers guarding the doorways. Once inside, she was directed to the Army Matron's office. Joan sat and waited her turn, nervously twisting her handkerchief in her hands.

She had spent hours going through all the possible questions that she might be asked with Brenda while they were in Leeds and she had spent the whole train journey down trying to remember them all. The interviews were renowned for being tough. As her own Ward Sister had repeatedly reminded them; the Army only accepted the finest nurses to join their boys on the frontline; it seemed everyone was becoming more patriotic by the day, getting 'behind the boys'.

Joan was finally called through, directed to sit opposite the stern looking Matron perching behind an enormous desk. As she listened to the Matron talking, she drew a long deep breath to try to compose herself, conscious of appearing too nervous. The words went slowly around her head: *keep calm and listen, this is your only chance, so do not blow it!* She was going to be part of the Queen Alexandra's Imperial Military Nurses Service with officer status. How grand that sounded. Little Muriel Joan Whiteley from Crumpsall was going to be in the Queen's Army! Who'd have thought it?! If accepted, she would be sent for Army training before being posted to serve as an army nurse looking after wounded soldiers - who knows where?

Her mind was racing with the possibilities and the fact that she had yet to answer a single question on her nursing skills from the

notoriously formidable Army Matron. *Concentrate, Joan,* she said to herself.
She had so far been interrogated on her parents' social standing in the
community and seemed to have said all the right things, or at least she
hoped it had been enough. *When are you going to ask me about nursing?* Joan
thought to herself. *When are you going to ask me why I want to join the QA's? I
had prepared for those questions!*

"Are you any good at tennis?" the Matron asked. Joan quickly
snapped back into the conversation, wondering why on earth she was
being asked about tennis. The office was dark and unbearably hot, making
it difficult to focus on the questions being fired at her. The only sounds
were the whirring of the overhead fan and the scratching of the matron's
pen as she scrawled all over Joan's application. Every so often there were
the sounds of hurried footsteps outside the Matrons office, reminding her
that she was in a working hospital. Joan had to concentrate hard on not
letting her mind wander. She looked at all the certificates and photographs
that covered the wall behind the Matron's back, wondering what they
were all for. Despite all that she had heard about the recruitment criteria,
Joan was still surprised at how much of her interview had been based on
her background and her parents' respectability. It was probably not
surprising; Florence Nightingale herself was from the upper classes, as
were her team of nurses. Florence had only managed to get to the Crimea
because of a lifelong friend who just happened to be Secretary of State for

War at the time. Joan was bright enough to recognise the emphasis still being placed on this and had managed to build her modest, working class background into a respectable middle-class family where 'one was expected to know how to ride, play tennis and boules'. Joan cleared her throat: "I was brought up playing tennis Matron. I was practically born with a tennis racket in my hand. My father was keen that we are all competent players."

She gave her best smile, hoping that she had sounded convincing.

"Good. Excellent." Matron replied as she began shuffling through paperwork and ticking boxes on the many forms spread across her desk.

The excitement and anticipation of the adventure that lay ahead made it hard for her to sit still in her seat. Matron stood and without smiling, shook her hand and handed her a sealed envelope.

"Congratulations, you are now a Queen's Army nurse. You will receive further instruction. Do not open until you are instructed to do so."

Joan slowly took the envelope from her, and realised that her mouth was open but no words came to mind. She quickly grabbed her bag and nodded, aware that she must look like a complete halfwit.

"Thank you," she stammered. "Do you know where I might be posted?"

"Possibly the Far East, but probably France." Said the Matron matter-of-factly, sitting back down in her seat.

"Oh!" exclaimed Joan, surprised at the mention of the Far East. That had not even occurred to her. Was there even a war going on in the Far East? She had no idea. The Matron looked up and half smiled.

"I expect that it will be France, but you are likely to be mobilised quickly, so make sure you are ready. We will make the necessary arrangements with your Matron in Leeds."

"Yes, of course." replied Joan standing there holding her breath as though waiting for the Matron to speak again. But Matron had already moved on to the next application and without looking up said,

"That will be all, Whiteley."

Joan practically ran out of the office. *Blimey,* she thought. That was not what at all what she had expected. What had she let herself in for?

As she sat on the train home, she wondered how on earth she was going to tell her family that she could be leaving so soon. Her father and Bill would be supportive; they always were. But her mother and sisters, Edith and Alice, would be far from thrilled if she were to be posted to the Far East. It gave her a headache just to think about- she would miss them all so much. The enormity of what she had got herself into filled her with trepidation. Far more than the pride she thought she would feel at being accepted to join the QA's was her own fear of a new unknown. She tried not to think too much. Instead, she focused on the fields and trees as the train thundered by, clutching her bag with the sealed envelope inside tightly to her chest. She was half tempted to open it, the other half not wanting to know what it contained. Dear Lord! She raised her eyes to the ceiling and shook her head slowly. The fear was returning. She would have to write to Brenda and tell her. She prayed that Brenda had received her letter too. She hated not knowing. Neither families were wealthy enough to have a telephone, she would just have to write and let her know.

Dinner that evening was much the same as it had ever been. It was so lovely to have Bill home, and Edith was also there, which had been a pleasant surprise. She had been living in Cornwall with her husband Les but had returned to see Bill before he went on active duty again. Joan smiled to herself at how quickly they all just settled back into the routines they had before the war had started, when the five of them sat like this every mealtime. It was as if nothing had happened outside the four walls of their very respectable Victorian town house on Rectory Road. But Joan, sick with nerves, was struggling with her meal. She knew they were all waiting for her to tell them what had happened at the interview. They were aware that she had joined up, but they had also assumed that she would be receiving full army training first before being posted somewhere in the UK. She had confided in Bill about Matron's mention of the Far East. He had laughed and said. "That's the army for you. I wouldn't worry, that could change a hundred times before you receive your orders."

Joan did not feel reassured, and knew her mother and sisters would not share Bill's light-hearted reaction. She took a deep breath.

"Well," she announced, "it looks like I've been accepted into the QA's and will get my orders soon."

There was the briefest of silences before her father clapped her on the back.

"Really well done, Joan," he said, "they'd have been fools not to have accepted you." He was always so proud of his youngest daughter. For her to be awarded the same rank of Army Lieutenant was something he could never have imagined. Bill was smiling, as expected, and to her surprise, her sisters were also nodding in agreement. Joan had imagined them to be upset that she would be going away and leaving them to look after their parents but could not have been more wrong. A wave of relief washed over her.

"I am thrilled for you Joan," said Edith, "you have worked so hard, you deserve it. You must be so excited!" Alice was trying to force down a mouthful of hotpot, desperate to get a word in.

"Any idea of where you will be going?" She finally managed to blurt out before coughing. Joan swallowed and looked at Bill. It was the one question she was dreading, but her brother just raised an eyebrow in amusement. Joan flashed him a look that said, 'not helpful' and turned to Alice.

"Well, they said it was most likely to be France," she looked down at her plate of food, "or possibly the Far East." She said quietly.

"Gosh really?" said Alice. "I didn't even know that we had troops in the Far East?" She said, looking at Bill.

Bill shrugged. "The last I heard was that we were pulling our troops out of Shanghai but maybe they'll send you to Outer Mongolia." Joan stuck her tongue out at Bill, but then saw that her mother, until now silent, was looking alarmed.

"Just ignore him mother," she said reassuringly. "They are not going to send me to Outer Mongolia! It is most likely to be London or France." She reached out and held her mother's hand, "Mother? Please say something."

"I just don't know what to say to you my dear," her mother finally whispered. "I am so pleased for you and I know that whatever I say will not stop you. You are proud and stubborn and I am torn between being completely terrified for you and being immensely proud."

She looked at her youngest daughter with tears starting to well in her eyes.

"You have my blessing but I wish with every fibre within me that you weren't going anywhere - home or abroad."

Joan sighed with relief, and felt a lump in her throat. It was going to be difficult for her parents, but having her mother's blessing meant the world to her. She had never been rebellious, if anything she had always gone out of her way to make sure that she did the right thing and caused her family no distress, but she had always secretly craved adventure. She needed to do more than stay in Manchester and wait out the war. She looked over at her father who smiled warmly at her.

"I have never been so proud, my dear," He beamed. Bill caught Joan's eye and winked before launching into a story about one of his new Army buddies who had set off a manhunt within half an hour of arriving at the barracks. He hadn't gone and done a runner, Bill was saying, he'd just wandered into the village for a packet of woodies.

They all laughed, but Joan could see it was a bit forced from her mother. Her sisters saw it too. Bill and his father were getting on as they always did; best friends. Joan's thoughts drifted and she wondered whether Brenda had been for her interview yet.

Chapter 3

The next few weeks flew by and, before she knew it, Joan was instructed to open the manila envelope that she was given in London. The letter simply confirmed that she was now officially a Queen's Army Nurse, and that she must report to the Military Hospital at once to receive further instruction.

Joan was back at Manchester Piccadilly the following morning and spent the train journey south going through every possible scenario. She admired the way Bill seemed so laid back about Army orders, and she understood there was a logic to just doing what you were told without asking questions. But how difficult would that be? She thought of *The Charge of the Light Brigade* and the famous lines in Tennyson's poem: 'theirs not to reason why, theirs but to do and die'. Joan realised so little had changed since the Crimean War.

So, if it was to be the Far East, then where? She kept thinking about Singapore and Hong Kong, but did the British have other interests there? She imagined a world map, remembering the pride everyone shared because so much of it was coloured pink. She also thought of the Army training and when and where that would be taking place. She wasn't entirely sure what it would involve but thought it would emphasise things like ranks and the due deference to be given to each, perhaps even explain to her the kinds of behaviour she should expect from other soldiers given she was the equivalent to a Lieutenant. She thought about the Geneva Conventions and whether that would form another part of her training. God forbid that it might include learning to fire a gun, or rifle as Bill insisted on calling it. All this and more whirred around until she felt dizzy from so many unanswered questions.

The train arrived in London and Joan made her way along the same route back to Queen Alexandra's Military Hospital. Her stomach tightened, every building entrance seemed to have more sandbags than last time, and the soldiers looked less cheerful. The war was coming closer to Joan Whiteley. The atmosphere in the hospital had changed as well. It no longer seemed calm and quiet– there was now a loud and constant hum of hundreds of people going about their business.

It didn't take long to realise the nurses were, as the Matron had said, being mobilised. As she had feared, her concerns about the lack of army training they had been promised were confirmed.

After chatting with a few of the nurses who were milling around, no one seemed to have received any training at all, and yet they were expected to travel anywhere from Normandy to Africa, to Southeast Asia and, of course, the Far East. The prospect of travelling to somewhere so exotic was both incredibly exciting and utterly terrifying. Panic rose further in her throat as she contemplated the idea of being sent away without any of the military training she had expected to receive. Things must be getting serious if the army were sending nurses to the frontline with nothing but their nursing skills. *Ours not to reason why, Joan.* The enormity of what was happening started to dawn on her.

She had found her way to the Matron's office, and again sat nervously outside, waiting to be called. She watched everyone walking to and fro along the corridor, hearing doors slamming and the general bustle of activity. Staring at her hands, she smiled inwardly as she realised she was again playing with a handkerchief the same way she had been the last time she was here. It was at that moment that a familiar voice rose above the background noise and let out that unmistakable laugh. A door was ajar further down the corridor and the chatter continued as Joan approached, pushed open the door and stood there smiling. Brenda's eyes widened as she realised her best friend was stood feet away.

"Joan!" she squealed and almost bowled her over with the force of her embrace.

"I am so pleased to see you; I didn't know whether I would." Brenda continued, hugging Joan until she had no more breath in her. "Here we are, and it's finally happening! This is so exciting. I can't believe I found you so soon. Have you been told where you are being posted yet? I've been told the Far East! That can't be right surely?"

"Calm down," Joan laughed. "I suppose we'll find out where we're going today. I certainly hope so—the suspense is killing me!"

"Somewhere hot and sunny I hope," Brenda said. "I just can't wait. It will be so much fun to get away from here; it's all just too depressing for words!"

Joan didn't care where she went. This is what she wanted more than anything and her need for fulfilling her duty was greater than the need for a jolly somewhere hot, although she had to admit that aspect was very appealing too. She knew that it wasn't going to be easy, no matter where they were sent, but she was prepared to work hard. After her nursing training, she was used to that and wouldn't want it any other way. Despite the beaming giddiness of Brenda, Joan again felt the now familiar nervous tingling in her stomach; they could be sent anywhere in the world in just a matter of days.

There was a real sense of urgency in the air, nurses and officers rushing around carrying an air of utmost importance. But did they all feel the same as she did – a bit panicked, a bit excited but mostly with a sense of not having the foggiest notion of what was going on. It was as though everyone else in the hospital knew the situation apart from her. And Brenda of course, not that she seemed to care as she continued to chatter 10 to the dozen while Joan quietly sat in silence for a moment trying to push away the familiar feeling of trepidation. *Had she done the right thing?*

What on earth had she been thinking signing up for the Army? She sat and crossed her fingers, silently praying that they would be posted together.

She looked over at Brenda, admiring the fact that nothing seemed to faze her or get her down; she had a boundless energy that was, sometimes, quite exhausting. Joan, on the other hand, was feeling nervous enough for both of them. They had their fair share of fun while they had been training in Leeds but Joan had been brought up to think that you can only play hard if you have worked doubly hard. Brenda was a hard worker herself, but it was a motto that she found infuriating.

When Joan finally got in to see the Army Matron, the meeting was the opposite of her previous experience when she went for her interview in the same room. There was none of the previous nonsense about social standing or being able to play tennis. This time Matron was efficient in a way that only the Army could instil in a person; Joan was in an out in less than five minutes. As anticipated, she was indeed to be sent to the Far East and, no, she would not be given any more detail than that. Matron's final statement was that, as far as friends and family were concerned; she was to tell them she was going on a holiday cruise. Joan felt a fresh jolt of panic. Why would they not tell people where they were going? Dear God, what would her mother say? What sort of threat was a group of nurses to anyone that this information should be kept secret? She dismissed her troublesome thoughts. As she always did, Joan started to make a mental list of the things she had to do before she set sail on the biggest adventure of her life.

She waited impatiently in the building's main entrance hall, again with her fingers crossed that they would be given the same posting. It would be so much easier to be away from home if the two of them were together. Joan thought again about the posters and the glamorous lifestyle that they promise, and couldn't help being excited by the idea. Matron had made sure that she was aware the QA's were expected to be the best of the best and as new recruits, all the eyes of the Army would be on them.

The sight of Brenda bounding down a flight of stairs, waving a piece of paper, attracting the attention of everyone who saw her, interrupted Joan's thoughts.

"I got the Far East—tell me you did too!" Joan couldn't help but smile at her friend. Her relief was immense.

"Yes, I did" she replied.

"I just can't believe it, can you?" said Brenda, out of breath from the excitement of it all. "Did you get any detail on whereabouts in the Far East we will be going? Matron said, as we were Year 1s, we would be sent somewhere low risk. She said we had to go pick up our kit and we would be told then. What do you think she meant by 'low risk'?" Brenda paused for breath and looked like she was considering the possible risks that could be ahead of them for the first time. She almost shook them from her head and laughed; continuing to babble excitedly about the cruise and the places they would see.

"It will be enough to just get away from the daily drudgery and greyness of Leeds! I can't wait!" she said.

Ever the more sensible, Joan, was thinking ahead. *Singapore? Malaya? Burma? Or maybe Hong Kong?*

When she arrived back in Crumpsall, hot and weary after another long day's travel, she was taken aback by her parents' response to her news. Despite her mother having given her blessing, now that she had had a bit of time to think things through, she had made it very clear that she thought Joan already had a good job at the hospital and that she would be letting her friends and colleagues down by disappearing off to 'Lord knows where and for Lord knows how long'.

Her father had remained silent as usual, but afterwards took her to one side to tell her how proud he was of her. Despite her protestations, he told Joan that he knew his wife could not wait to tell their friends and neighbours that their little Joan was now a Queen's Army Nurse and about to serve her country. She would never admit they were her real thoughts, he had said, adding that he had given up trying to understand his wife years ago. As Joan argued her case to her mother, she became aware of her father standing by, watching on, with a broad smile on his face. When his wife eventually retreated to the sanctuary of her kitchen,

Joan looked at her father beseechingly, she found her mother infuriating at times. Her father said nothing; he simply pulled his daughter close and kissed the top of her head. A simple gesture from a father to his daughter, but Joan had to wipe away a tear afterwards. They were not the kind of family who often showed affection, so her father's small gesture meant the world to her. Thankfully, the atmosphere in the grand Victorian Terrace in Manchester had softened by the following morning.

At breakfast, Bill brightened the mood with his incessant joking and chatter. If ever there was a crisis, Joan thought, she'd want him right beside her; he even managed to get their mother on side, and the four of them passed the time thinking about where Joan might end up and when. Bill refused to take any of it seriously.

Within a couple of days Joan had received orders to go to Liverpool. Brenda, she discovered, had received the same orders and they'd arranged to travel together. It was all so new; it was a great comfort to have each other as support even if it was only to collect their kit and instructions on where they were being posted.

Liverpool proved easier than they thought to get around. Stepping out of Lime Street Station, it didn't take long to get their bearings and head towards the docks where they had been told they would find the Army surplus office. When they got there, it was complete chaos. They were herded into a huge room full of servicemen and women all collecting their kit for their various assignments. Both the noise and the heat were unbearable and only added to the confusion. Eventually, they found where they were supposed to be and made it to the front of the queue. They were unceremoniously handed a pack that kitted them out for desert warfare. They looked at each other in complete confusion and utter horror.

"Desert warfare?" Brenda had blurted out. "This has got to be a mistake. Joan, we need to make sure this is right."

"Excuse me," Joan said to the officer handing out the kit. "I think you have given us the wrong equipment. We have a posting to the Far East." Her voice trailed off as the officer, clearly in no mood for answering any of their concerns and without looking up from his list, simply pointed a finger in the direction of a desk where a harassed female officer was being bombarded by questions from a crowd of confused looking young nurses.

After what seemed like an eternity of waiting around, they were eventually told that they were not being sent to the desert after all, but to the Far East as they had thought all along.

"It's an easy posting. Nice expat community there. Bloody hot though." The female officer had said before turning to another confused looking nurse. Their orders were, as the Matron had stated, that they were not allowed to tell their friends or family of their destination. As far as everyone was concerned the two of them were heading off on a holiday cruise following months of gruelling nursing training and exams. The unlikeliness and impracticality of this white lie seemed not to concern the Army. Joan, on the other hand, had thought it ridiculous and knew that she would have to tell her family where she was going and why. As for her friends, they would surely wonder what on earth she was doing swanning off on a holiday cruise in wartime and, of course, where would she say she had got the money from? It would seem so completely out of character that no one would believe it. She decided there and then that she wouldn't tell anyone apart from her family where she was going. She would just have to leave it to her mother and father to deal with any questions.

Brenda and Joan had emerged from the army surplus building hot, bothered, and completely exhausted after more than two hours of shuffling along in queues. They were fully loaded up with their kit and itinerary, and discovered they had strict instructions on what they needed to take as well as what wasn't allowed. The list of forbidden items was extensive and basically boiled down to the fact that they were only to take essentials. No luxurious or expensive items. Brenda had been slightly perturbed at the luxuries that she would have to go without, but Joan was more relieved that all basic equipment would be provided. She was glad for all the guidance she could get.

"Oh my goodness!" Brenda exclaimed. "Joan, come and look at this!" While Joan had been trying to work out exactly what she had in her new bundle of kit, Brenda had been scanning her documents and gave out a loud yell when she finally got to their itinerary. They sat down on a nearby bench and Brenda began to read through what the next few months had in store for them.

"Just listen to this," she said, she smiled and then put on her best BBC English accent. "Now, are you sitting comfortably? Good, then I shall begin. We leave Liverpool on Sunday for Gibraltar, then sail to Cape Town, then Mombassa, Bombay, Colombo, Penang, and Singapore before finally arriving in Hong Kong on Wednesday 11th September - my goodness, Joan, I've not heard of half of those places." She looked at the page a little more, "and we are then due to report for duty on Friday 13th September. Oooh, Friday 13th, not a good omen!"

Brenda was like a child on Christmas morning and continued to read out all their instructions, getting more excited by each sentence. Joan, on the other hand, was painfully aware of the fact that they were obviously not going to see their families for an awfully long time. She took the sheet of paper from Brenda and started to read through it for herself.

"At least we're not going to Outer Mongolia!" she joked, but soon shook her head when she saw Brenda looking at her in confusion. "Never mind," she chuckled and continued to scan the orders.

"Jeepers! I'm glad that we are not allowed to take much with us. This itinerary is a wardrobe and packing nightmare!" They both laughed and then fell silent, trying to take in the rest of the information. Joan shook the doubts from her mind. The upshot, she had told herself, was that they were about to become fully-fledged QA's and join the boys on the frontline, where their skills and resilience would be tested to the limit. If only she could tell her friends of the trip, this so-called luxury cruise, she was meant to be going on, they would all be sick with jealousy.

Chapter 4

A week passed before Joan received new orders to report to Liverpool, ready to set sail on the 'magnificent' SS Viceroy of India.

Well, here she was, Brenda again by her side, both ready to board what they had been told was the flagship of the P&O line. Sailing from Liverpool for Hong Kong would be the biggest adventure of their lives. She could barely take it all in. Yet again, they were surrounded by chaos and confusion.

"I wonder if this is what Florence Nightingale had in mind?" Joan said, half to herself, half to Brenda who was rummaging around in her bag.

"What do you mean?" said Brenda looking up squinting at her in the early morning sun.

"Well," replied Joan nodding towards the gathering of QA's that had formed at the dock, "'wherever the Army goes, the QA's will follow' and all that? Do you think that she would ever have envisioned this?"

Brenda stopped rummaging for a moment, "Yes Joan, I think she probably did and I'm jolly glad she did too, what would our boys do without the QA's mopping their fevered brows and plumping up their pillows?"

"What are you looking for anyway?" asked Joan distracted from her thoughts and aware that Brenda had practically emptied her entire kit bag onto the dockside.

"I can't find my spare woollen cape," said Brenda, impatiently unloading the contents of her bag onto the floor. "I'm certain that I packed it."

"I doubt that you'll be needing it in Hong Kong my dear," Joan laughed. "It is permanently hot and humid and probably about 40 degrees! Hey, what are these?" she asked, bending down to pick up two small notebooks that Brenda had unceremoniously dumped on the floor. One was a red leather-bound Autograph book and the other a matching blue leather-bound diary.

"Oh, mother gave me those before I left." Brenda said without looking up. "She said I should keep a diary of our adventure and to make sure that I get the autograph of any famous or interesting people that we may meet along the way, which is highly unlikely I would have thought." Brenda took the notebooks from Joan and seemed to be weighing them in her hands.

"You have one," she said, handing back the red autograph book. "It might be fun to compare notes. You never know, it might come in handy one day."

Joan smiled and took the small book from her friend. It smelled of new leather and its cream and white pages lay bare, just waiting to be brought to life with their adventures. Joan tucked the book away in a pocket on the front of her kit bag and, once more, was grateful to be making this journey with Brenda.

She looked at the mess Brenda had made of her kitbag, and all the equipment strewn about. She herself had packed the army 'whites' that would be pressed and starched and were much more suitable to the Far Eastern conditions. She loved the grey and scarlet cape but unlike the impractical Brenda had decided that this would be an unnecessary and heavy addition to her kit bag. Unlikely to need a pure woollen cape in the tropics, Joan had packed the red beret and grey greatcoat. She wanted to look the Sister very much 'ready for action' when she arrived in Hong Kong.

"You know, Brenda, this is all a bit daft, isn't it? Our final orders say, 'no communication with family and no obvious sign of Army to be seen', but just look around us." They had all been given the same kit and it was obviously army issue. They were in the midst of hundreds of people all dressed exactly the same. But inside her kit was the prestigious QA uniform. Matron had told them that the distinctive grey and scarlet was the 'signature of the Queen's Army Imperial Military Nursing Service and they should wear it with pride'. She had even given a little speech to explain what the uniform meant. It was said to have brought grown men to tears at the mere sight of their saviours in grey and scarlet, there to tend to their wounds and provide comfort as they lay there helpless, in agony, feeling at their most vulnerable and homesick. Most of them would be mere boys, and the QA's would give them a mother's love. Joan smiled to herself, lost in the memory. She had looked around at the other QA's in the room and could see there was more than a few with tears in their eyes. Joan had clenched her jaw – pride swirled inside at what she was doing, but she understood wounded soldiers needed more than a sentimental nurse. She would keep her emotions in check and do her job.

The ship left Liverpool on the evening of Sunday 21st July 1940, first stop: Gibraltar. Joan could barely contain her excitement. As they set sail she stood on deck with Brenda, watching Liverpool and England slowly get smaller and smaller. Her last view was of the famous three Graces, so symbolic of Liverpool, fading in the distance as night fell. On a hillside behind, she could just make out the outline of the city's huge new cathedral. Joan felt that she couldn't move until she could no longer see any sign of land. Brenda stood beside her, happily chatting to some pleasingly handsome servicemen who were about to do a reccie of the ship and try to get their bearings. It had been a warm day on land, but the air had cooled rapidly and she was suddenly cold.

"Are you coming then, Joan?" said Brenda. "I want to take a look at that pool properly!"

Once again, Joan was glad of Brenda's happy-go-lucky attitude and allowed herself to be dragged along and introduced to the Naval Officers, Mickey Holliday and Dickie Arundel. Despite them all having the same orders not to divulge whether they were servicemen or not, it wasn't difficult to work out those who were not on a holiday cruise. They were both Royal Engineer 2nd Lieutenants and the girls liked them immediately. They were full of fun and seemed to know everyone on the ship already.

As the four of them set out on their exploration of the ship they were again reminded of its sheer size and lavishness. It was easy to see how it had become the 'flagship'.

"She's got turbo-electric engines," Dickie was saying, "which means she uses electric generators to convert the mechanical energy of a turbine into electric energy." Dickie's voice trailed off as Brenda shot him an unimpressed look. Joan and Mickey smiled at one another.

"Come on Dickie, you'll bore the girls rigid at this rate!" All of them smiled, except Dickie, who put on a hurt expression seemed to be sulking. "It means that she can do 19 knots," he said just loud enough to be heard by the others who all burst out laughing.

As they walked down seemingly endless corridors and poked their heads around any number of doors, Joan and Brenda were increasingly amazed by the luxury of the Viceroy of India. They soon discovered the indoor swimming pool. The four of them stood on a balcony looking down at the water. Behind them a staircase took them down a floor to the pool itself. Joan took it all in, the moulded ceiling, the ornate benches, even the Royal-red rope that hung at the water's edge to give swimmers something to hold on to. It all seemed incredibly up-market and beyond anything any of them had ever seen before.

"It's the only indoor pool in the P&O fleet," Dickie offered nervously, acutely aware that he didn't want to say anything boring for fear of more ridicule.

"Imagine, Brenda," Joan said. "We're at sea but the water in that pool is barely rippling." Mickey shot a warning glance at Dickie, just in case his friend was about to say something else on the dull side.

"It's not bad," Brenda offered trying to effect nonchalance. "We have something similar at our house." Joan pushed her hard and Mickey smiled, but Dickie looked as though he was trying to work out if she was being serious.

Turning yet another corner, the four of them came across the First Class dining room, which was a very grand affair. It was like being in a country mansion with wooden panelling everywhere. They didn't dare enter; the room had obviously already been set up for dinner the following evening. Instead, they all peered in from the doorway.

"Apparently there's a separate dining room for breakfast," Dickie said.

"Pull the other one," said Brenda, wide- eyed and not quite sure whether to believe him or not. Despite the dimmed lights due to the lateness of the hour, everything seemed to glisten. The round tables had been set with white linen and a silver dinner service. The chairs were padded pale green velvet that matched the swags and tails of the long cream coloured curtains. Joan's eyes were drawn to the intricately moulded ceiling, which had been trimmed with gold leaf and in the centre, was the most spectacular chandelier. It was like something from a film. If it hadn't been for the motion of the sea as they sailed into open water, she could have sworn she was in some royal palace, rather than on a cruise ship. As an officer, she had been allocated a First Class cabin, which meant she could use this First Class dining room. *What on earth should I wear for dinner if not my QA uniform?* She wondered.

Mickey had gone on ahead and not noticed his companions had stopped behind him. "I've managed to find the smoking room Dickie. No ladies allowed, I'm afraid." He said, making his way back to the group. He winked at Brenda when he saw she was possibly about to launch into a protest about women's rights. When he caught sight of the impressive dining room he whistled and marched right in.

"Shhhh!' Brenda hissed. "You can't go in there."

"I'm just going to look at what is on the menu for tomorrow. And I don't know why you are all being so absurd, no one is going to tell us that we can't be in here." He picked up a menu from the nearest table and began reading it out loud. "Vegetable soup, prawn salad or ham and melon for starters…"

"Good evening, Sir."

Mickey nearly jumped out of his skin and dropped the menu. One of the stewards had appeared from the back of the room and greeted Mickey as he started to lay napkins on a nearby table. It was Mickey's turn to be the butt of the jokes as the others broke out in peals of laughter. Mickey decided that he would wait until the following evening to find out what was for the main course and hurried out of the room.

"I think that's enough exploring for one night, I'm done in. I'm going to turn in for the night." he said quickly, still red faced.

Dickie patted him on the back. "Well done, mate," he said chuckling. "I think that's a good idea."

Joan and Brenda were still giggling when they got back to their First Class cabins, which were connected by adjoining door. The four had agreed to seek each other out the following day, after they had had a good night's rest and got their sea legs. Joan and Brenda were also exhausted, and decided the rest of the ship would have to wait. They fell into bed and slept soundly.

They were woken the next morning by a sharp knock at the door. Joan rolled over to see her clock said it was a little before seven. She darted out of bed to find a note had been slipped under the door advising them that they were to attend a briefing session at 0800. *Welcome to the Army* Joan thought as she dragged herself into the shower room.

The early morning meeting was a debrief on what they should expect whilst on board. The Matron-In-Chief introduced herself as Catherine Hargreaves. Although petite, she commanded immediate respect. She was in her early forties with a sharp looking face that seemed to be constantly pulled into a disapproving frown. She was in sole charge of the girls on this voyage and began the meeting sternly.

"This is not a holiday cruise, and you are not on holiday. Whilst we are able to enjoy the facilities that the ship has to offer, you are to remember that you are Queens Army nurses and are on active duty with immediate effect. You are to report to the main drawing room each morning at 0800. You will have plenty of opportunity to get to know each other on this trip, and I expect that you have already noticed that we are sharing the ship with many Army and Navy personnel. Again, I will remind you that you are representatives of the QA's and you are to behave in a professional and dignified manner. There will be no fraternising with the married men and I would suggest that you do not do anything to let me, or yourselves, down. Any insubordination will be not be tolerated and will result in disciplinary action. Now, there are 55 of us on board. Most of you will be leaving us at Singapore. I have drawn up a list of who is going where, so please have a look to make sure that there have been no changes to your original orders"

Hargreaves paused and looked around the room at the group of young women who were all looking a bit shell-shocked.

"Bloody hell," whispered Brenda. Joan gave her a sharp dig in the ribs.

"I would suggest that today you familiarise yourselves with the ship," the Matron continued. "Tomorrow I will hand out an exercise sheet, which you are to follow each morning. There will then be lectures until lunch. The afternoons you will have to yourselves. That is all. You are dismissed."

With that she walked out of the room leaving the young nurses looking around at one another.

Brenda looked over at Joan, "Oh my days! She is tougher than I thought!" Joan just nodded. No one seemed to know what to do next, until a pretty nurse with a broad Scottish accent spoke up.

"Well I'll not be crossing that one, that's for sure."

Laughter broke the tension, and the room full of nurses burst into chatter. They crowded around the list that Matron had left for them and it confirmed that some were heading to Singapore, and some South Africa. In fact, out of the 55 nurses, only three others had been assigned to same destination as Brenda and Joan: Hong Kong. Freda Davis, Gwendoline Colthorpe and Daphne Van De Wart. Freda Davis said it was because there was not much going on there. Freda was tall and thin. She seemed to Joan to be all arms and legs with a long slender neck, she reminded her a bit of a giraffe. Freda was more attractive than pretty and was following the trend with her perfectly pin curled hair. Her accent, strong cockney, immediately grated on Joan. Brenda, seeing that Joan was getting fed up with the gregarious cockney, suggested that they headed for breakfast before it was all gone. A few nodded in agreement and started to make moves to leave. Freda spoke up again and suggested that they all meet on deck that evening for a 'gin fizz and a gossip'. Joan rolled her eyes; Brenda grabbed her arm and moved her towards the door.

"We'd love to, see you at seven." She shouted over her shoulder as she pushed Joan out of the room.

"Joan Whiteley, you are so funny. Don't ever take up poker – your face tells a thousand tales!" She laughed.

That evening, as promised, they arrived on the highly polished deck to find there was already quite a gathering. Freda walked over and greeted them as though it was her own party.

"Glad you could make it ladies, come on over and grab yourselves a drink." Joan raised her eyebrows at Brenda as if to say 'see, I told you she was annoying', but they dutifully followed her over to a couple of tables next to the bar. Brenda gave Joan a light pinch when she noticed that their new friends Mickey and Dickie had also joined the group. She headed straight over to them and sat down.

"Since when were you two invited for girlie drinks?" She said playfully. Mickey smiled back at her and said, "Well this is where the most beautiful girls on the ship are—where else would we be?"

Dickie gathered drink orders and headed to the bar to fetch cocktails. Brenda nudged Joan again and raised her eyebrows.

"Good grief woman, we've not even been on board for 24 hours! Do you not remember what Matron said this morning?"

"It's ok, I've already checked for a wedding ring!" Brenda said with a wink, before turning her attention back in Mickey's direction.

The evening was turning into a great night. The conversation flowed, and Joan and Brenda were having a lovely time getting to know their new friends. Dickie, in particular, seemed a lot more relaxed than he had been last night when he kept blurting out the facts and figures of shipping. But then again, Joan had thought, he was an engineer – he was bound to be interested in such things. She'd made a mental note to be more tolerant of him. As it was, she hadn't needed to. Mickey and Dickie were much more of a double act tonight, and they all got on well.

It had been ages since Joan had had such a night out. Wartime rationing was already pinching at the British way of life, and nights on the town had been particularly rare recently, and especially during her nursing training. She decided that she was going to make the most of every minute. The conversation inevitably turned to war and she was listening with interest to Dickie and another officer talking about the Dunkirk evacuation two months earlier, and what it meant for the Allies without a functioning army in Europe anymore. Dickie and the other officer disagreed about the importance of the Americans joining the war. Joan didn't have much of an opinion and wished that she had paid more attention to what was going on in Europe but had found it all too depressing. It seemed obvious that Hitler needed to be stopped by troops on the ground, but the recent news was that he had apparently invaded Russia and all three of them agreed that that would keep the Germans busy. She felt a tug at her arm and turned to see Brenda leaning towards her looking a little tipsy.

"I wonder how many of us will be on the journey back?" She was smiling but Joan could see that reality may well be hitting Brenda. The talk of war and a rumour mill in full turn was seeing to that.

"Don't be so ridiculous! Get all of those thoughts out of your head— we haven't even got there yet!" Joan tried to play down the situation, but Brenda's remark had irritated her. Some things were better left unsaid. Now she couldn't help but wonder that some of the people she was with, right at that moment, may not ever see Britain again. They were all so young and were being thrown into the unknown. How would any of them would cope with it all? She tuned into the conversation that Mickey was having with another naval officer who had joined them. They were discussing the fact that there had been much speculation about Italy joining the war and what that meant for the British Fleet in the Far East.

News had also reached them about the pro-Nazi French government that had set up in somewhere called Vichy. Not many had heard of Mers el Kabir either, but they were now aware that it as the Algerian port near Oran where the British had sunk most of the French fleet moored there, because their crews had refused to join the Allies. The young officers were talking about the possible repercussions and what that would mean for Britain. Joan still found it difficult to comprehend the realities of war but was beginning to realise that soon she would be very much aware, and needed to keep herself up to speed. Luckily, it sounded like Hong Kong was fairly low key in terms of war activity, which was obviously a relief. She was relieved, in retrospect, they hadn't been sent to France, things sounded much worse there than she had ever thought.

Chapter 5

The next few days were calm and relaxing as they headed for Gibraltar. Real war, for the moment, still seemed a long way away. After their lectures in the morning, they spent most of their afternoons sat on the large, highly polished deck drinking gin fizzes and trying to decide what planned activities they would take part in the next day. Joan wasn't sure if Brenda was bored or secretly afraid of what danger might be around the corner, but Brenda constantly tried to turn the conversation around to more light-hearted subjects.

They didn't have to wait long for a stark reminder that there was a war raging around them. They had sailed through the strait of Gibraltar. The sight of North Africa to the south and the Iberian Peninsula to the north was certainly impressive. They heard the ship's engines quieten and start to slow down. Joan's stomach lurched at the sudden change of pace. At first, she assumed it meant they were on their final approach to port, but a steward appeared and told them that unusually heavy shipping traffic meant they were not going to be able to go ashore at Gibraltar. The news that they were to stay on the ship when they had all been so looking forward to spending a few hours on dry land was met with disappointment.

"Oh well I guess we won't get to see those monkeys, then," said Mickey.

"Apes," replied Dickie flatly, everyone turned to look at him. "They are called Barbary apes, so they are not monkeys."

"Whatever they are, I was looking forward to seeing them," Brenda said with a small amount of irritation in her voice. Dickie had earned himself a bit of a reputation of being a 'know it all'. He didn't mean to, but he was always ready with a new fact or to correct someone when they weren't quite right.

At that moment, a drone of aircraft engines made them all looked upwards to see six bombers heading towards Gibraltar. Moments later they heard a dull thud that came from the direction of Gibraltar itself. There was a second thud, then a third and it was clear that the heavy shipping traffic claim wasn't true. Plumes of smoke were beginning to rise up high enough for everyone on deck to see that Gibraltar was under attack. The steward who had told them they couldn't go ashore was still with them. They all turned and looked at him.

He looked at the floor and said quietly; "Apparently it's the French; retaliating because of what we did to them at Oran. The news said that we killed about 1,500 of their sailors, so the Vichy lot are hitting back."

"Are we at risk?" asked Joan, but the steward shook his head.

"I doubt it. From what I heard, I think we pretty much destroyed their fleet at Oran. They've not got much firepower in the Med now. We'd be a lot more cautious about being this close otherwise. They've just got a few old bombers stationed in Morocco and Algeria. Nothing much to worry about."

With the ship at a safe distance, Joan, Brenda, Mickey and Dickie were part of small group of nurses and naval engineers that sat on deck and watched the attack with mixed feelings of fear, horror and complete awe. Pride filled Joan's chest at the sight of HMS ARK Royal and Valiant. The ships were magnificent. The mere sight of them was enough to give you the shivers. From their vantage point it was a sight to be seen. They all sat and watched the battle unfold before their eyes. Joan was shocked, her stomach knotted in horror at how easily an entire harbour could be destroyed in a matter of minutes. For the first time since setting sail she had a deep sense of foreboding about what might lie ahead.

"Do you think we will be needed?" Brenda had said, wondering how many casualties there might be given such a sustained onslaught. Joan thought it was likely that there would be enough medical staff already there, but with the attack continuing for a number of hours, she grew less certain.

"I think that looks worse than it is," Dickie said. "It looks like they are only targeting the harbour, and there aren't actually that many ships there for them to hit."

Joan turned to Mickey, "Tell me truthfully. How protected do you think we'll be in Hong Kong?"

"In all honesty, I don't think Hong Kong is on anyone's radar, but from what I have heard, the Island would be in real trouble if anyone did decide to attack with the defences as they are. We can only hope to keep our heads down and pray that it all passes us by."

Joan wished she hadn't asked, her friend's words hadn't provided the comfort she sought. They went below deck after watching the battle and ate their evening meal in near silence to the muted sounds of it still raging. Regardless of what the steward had said, it didn't sound as though the Vichy French had little firepower.

Joan spent the night staring at the ceiling of her cabin, listening to the muffled sounds of war that, even from this safe distance, were still far too close for comfort. Strangely, the dull thuds of the attack on Gibraltar harbour had taken on an almost rhythmic quality that lulled her to sleep. She was still tired when she and Brenda got up for their duties the next morning, but was soon wide awake when Matron Hargreaves called them all together to tell that they had been given the all clear to go ashore after all. Joan was instantly wary, but Brenda had let out a little squeal of delight that had the other nurses laughing. Even Matron allowed herself a slight smile at Brenda's inability to contain her excitement.

The Viceroy of India moored up just after noon in the harbour that, 12 hours earlier, had been under attack from French warplanes. Standing on deck, the devastation Joan expected was minimal. Brenda, Mickey, and Dickie agreed they had expected to see more damage. All four of them were surprised at how, despite the fury of the night before, all seemed strangely calm. But as soon as they disembarked, Joan could not wait to get back on board.

Some buildings had been hit and the smell of dust and fires that had been extinguished meant she saw Gibraltar as a battered reminder of the reality of war. She wanted to be back in the comfort and luxury of the ship and the safety that it offered. *Get a grip of yourself, Joan,* she had said to herself, but loud enough for Dickie to look in her direction. She shook her head as if to say it was nothing, thinking that if she was going to a potential war zone, she knew that she may have to get used to scenes far worse than this.

As the day wore on she fervently wished that she had joined Daphne and the other nurses rather than have to bear witness to Brenda and Mickey's outrageous flirting. In Joan's dark mood she did not enjoy feeling like a spare wheel and being forced to make polite conversation with Dickie, whom she was finding more irritating as the day wore on. When he ran out of engineering anecdotes, he moved onto bad jokes and constant attempts to make her 'crack a smile'. She gave up humouring him and decided that the only way forward was to be downright rude. It didn't seem to have any effect. Dickie, when he wasn't feeling awkward in female company, was just one of those eternally cheerful chaps who let little faze him.

"But they look like monkeys," Mickey said.

"Apes," said Dickie for the third time in as many minutes. "They are called Barbary *apes*, which means that they are not bloody monkeys!"

"Does it really matter?" Joan said, a little more angrily than she had meant. Her three companions realised it was time to head back to the ship. Mickey and Brenda had taken to holding hands. Dickie was pretending to be hurt after her little outburst but Joan was past the point of caring. She was just glad to be heading back to the safety of the ship.

With the Viceroy of India refuelled and restocked and having dropped off some passengers and picked up a few others, she set sail for the Atlantic once more. Her destination was the Cape Verde islands which, Joan had been told by Dickie, were a Portuguese protectorate and therefore neutral, even though the Portuguese government was fascist. They didn't agree with the Germans, apparently.

After a few uneventful days of sailing, Joan woke to a wide awake and overly excited Brenda.

"What on earth are you doing?" Joan asked sleepily, as she leant over to check the time on her watch.

"Oh, you know, I just couldn't sleep last night. I'm so excited about going ashore; Cape Verde's out there – take a look. Oh, and there's a deck dance tonight. Can you imagine, Joan? It will be marvellous, but I've no idea what I'm going to wear."

Joan rubbed her eyes and watched as Brenda chattered away; throwing the few outfits she had with her all over the place deciding which one was suitable.

"How can we have a dance on deck with no lights?" Joan asked.

All ships went into blackout as soon as darkness fell, to avoid the risk of attack from German ships or submarines.

"Cape Verde is neutral, silly, so we are having the most colourful deck lights and music and dancing. We're all invited, and it's going to be marvellous." Brenda was almost dancing around the tiny cabin, and then stopped for a moment, her finger tapping her lips. "Now what have I done with my little blue dress?"

Joan, despite the rude awakening, was excited at the prospect of exploring Cape Verde and indeed for the dance later which would be a welcome distraction from the constant talk of war and politics. She had overheard two senior officers talking in the lounge bar. The conversation confirmed what Mickey had been saying about the Hong Kong colony being off radar, which was putting it mildly from the sound of things.

Today was going to be different. Today, she was going to put all her worries about Hong Kong out of her mind. She got dressed, and she and Brenda headed off for their briefing with Matron before going out for a day of sightseeing in the sun, leaving their worries about the war on the deck of the ship

Joan, Brenda, Gwen Colthorpe, and Daphne set off in the sweltering heat and all had the loveliest day exploring the tiny villages and small, quaint little parishes on islands seemingly so removed from the rest of the world. Joan hung back in one of the churches and sat for a while lost in her own thoughts. She tried to absorb the feeling of calmness within its walls knowing that out there in the wider world, it was anything but calm. She always gained so much comfort from God and an instant tranquillity whenever she was in one of His churches.

She thought about her family and what they might be doing. She prayed that they would be safe. She was missing them and the familiarity of home terribly, even with the restrictions on 'normal life' that they were living under. She knew that Alice would stay close to home and look after Mother. She also knew that Bill was off on his own adventure. She hoped that she would hear from him soon. She bowed her head and silently prayed that her family would be kept safe and that Bill would come back from his latest tour of duty unscathed. It was a tall order she knew.

She could not think of her family without feeling helpless and, for the first time, guilty about leaving them in bleakest Britain when here she was in the baking sunshine, in one of the most stunningly beautiful places she had seen in her life while having the most wonderful time. It was probably raining in Manchester. Cold too, even though it was summer. She sighed and reluctantly got up to go and meet the others. It was so strange, but as soon as she stepped outside the church the feeling of peace left her and her orderly thoughts now seemed once again, all confused. It made her feel more anxious than she had since leaving Liverpool. She forced herself not to think of it and painted on the smile for her friends. She was determined to make the most of her day out. When would she next get the opportunity to visit such an incredible place?

They got back on board, completely exhausted from sightseeing and shopping. They had each bought themselves some lovely embroidered doilies to brighten up the Nurses' Quarters when they got to Hong Kong, along with some other bits and bobs that were simply too exquisite to leave behind. It was so good to be able to spend real money without feeling guilty after constantly counting coupons back at home.

Back on board, preparations for the evening ahead were already in full swing and there was a definite holiday atmosphere as the band was practising on deck. Everyone was in high spirits.

Joan had brought along a couple of civilian summer dresses and chose to wear the one her brother Bill said made her look 'almost grown up and very elegant'. She smiled to herself and could almost feel his nod of approval as she took the dress from the wardrobe. It was plain white on top with puffed short sleeves and what her mother would call a 'sensible collar'. The skirt was full, with tiny blue, red and yellow flowers running through it. It flattered her figure without looking too obvious or too overdressed for the occasion. Joan did not tend to wear any makeup but, at Brenda's insistence, put on a dark red lipstick.

Brenda took full advantage of the opportunity to dress to impress. She wore a mid-length red polka dot dress that was pulled in so tightly at the waist that she could not sit down for fear of passing out. She borrowed Joan's lipstick and pulled out of her bag the daintiest pair of red pumps. Joan almost gasped at the impracticality of bringing them on this trip but held her tongue. Her friend did look truly lovely. Mickey could not fail to be impressed. Brenda had fluffed out her curls and pinned a pretty red flower behind her ear that they had picked earlier in the day. She looked nervous and a little uncomfortable in such a girly outfit but the end result was stunning. Joan felt a little frumpy in comparison in her sensible white, go-with-anything pumps and her hair in the same tidy style that she always wore. Brenda must have read her mind because at that moment she stopped preening in front of her tiny mirror and turned to Joan.

"Come on then, let me look at you," Brenda looked her friend up and down and spun her around. "You look lovely, Joan dear. Very lovely. You just need a few finishing touches." Without another word, she whipped out a blue patent leather belt and pulled it around Joan's waist so tightly that she could barely breathe.

"Where on earth did you get this?" Joan asked as she was being twirled and pulled in all directions.

"Oh, don't you worry, it was my sister's. She'll never miss it, she has hundreds! And I don't see why you should be able to breath when I can't!" she smiled and moved on to her friend's hairstyle. "Hmmm, let me see what we can do with this."

Within minutes Joan's hair had been sprayed, teased and pinned to within an inch of its life. She thought that when she looked in the mirror she was going to look ridiculous and was about to protest, but when she finally saw her reflection she was pleasantly surprised. Brenda had managed to achieve a look that Joan would never even attempt. She allowed herself to think that she looked like one of the Hollywood actresses on the cover of Vogue. Her tidy curls had been pulled into more of a wave and her fringe had been swept up and back which, along with the lipstick, made her look very grown up, and dare she say it, glamorous!

"Ah, tres bonne!" said Brenda in a terrible French accent, kissing her fingers like a Parisian waiter.

"Merci, c'est magnifique!" replied Joan suddenly loving the fuss and fun of getting dressed up for a change.

A few tweaks and twists later and the two young nurses were ready. They examined each other one final time and, with an approving nod and a linking of arms, headed out of the cabin making their way to the 'deck for dancing' as it was now nicknamed. There was already quite a crowd forming, mainly officers, all looking extremely handsome in their uniforms. The rule of 'hide everything that says Army' had been relaxed as most of the civilian passengers had already disembarked and so it was mainly servicemen and women that were left.

The men were gathered together in little packs and all heads turned as soon as anyone new entered the bar area. Brenda and Joan got lots of looks of approval and Joan started to relax. She could almost hear her brother Bill say she looked a million dollars, as he often would when she made a bit of an effort back home. But Brenda, super confident, vivacious, and giddy, was now on pins and looking everywhere, clearly for any sign of Mickey. He had obviously been looking out for her too and was by her side in seconds.

"Well, well, look at you two, don't you just scrub up well!" Mickey said as he exaggeratedly looked them both over admiringly. He turned and stuck out his elbows, inviting both Brenda and Joan to link arms with him.

"Now what can I get you two lovely ladies to drink?" He asked as he led them to a table near the bar.

"Water for me, thank you" said Joan.

Mickey looked at her in surprise but did not say anything. He turned his attention to Brenda who whispered, "She's having you on – she'll have a gin fizz same as always, and so will I." Mickey returned with the drinks, Brenda silencing her friend's mock outrage.

79

Brenda continued to talk to Mickey, so Joan turned to speak to the small group of nurses that had gathered. Freda and Daphne were already there and shortly after Joan had joined the group, Gwen also arrived looking extremely glamorous in a bright red dress with a high neckline and tied at the back with an oversized black bow. She was tall and slim so it suited her perfectly. If anything, she had upstaged even Brenda and looked utterly gorgeous, but Joan couldn't help thinking that she would regret that high neck as the warm evening wore on.

Joan had tried, but could not help but dislike to Freda, not that she could put her finger on why she found her so irritating. She was pleasant enough, but that voice! It was like fingernails down a chalkboard. They had been joined by a group of officers who had all taken a shine to Daphne. Predictably, she was thoroughly enjoying the attention. Petite and pretty, Daphne was from Merioneth in North Wales and spoke with a soft Welsh accent which was obviously endearing to the officers gathered around her.

Joan watched the little group engage easily in flirtatious conversation. She had never been that comfortable with men and had never had anything that resembled a relationship.

"A penny for your thoughts." Joan turned to see a slightly older naval officer that had come over to join them.

"I beg your pardon," she said politely, seeing his rank as Captain.

"I was just saying, you look like you're deep in thought," he smiled and held out his hand, "Archie, Archie Smetherick."

Joan smiled and shook his hand in reply, "Joan, very pleased to meet you Archie Smetherick."

"Is it just Joan or does Joan have a surname?"

"Just Joan is fine," came the reply, probably a little too curtly. *Blimey Joan Whiteley,* she thought, *what is wrong with you?* She almost shook herself and decided that she was going to try to relax into the evening.

The band had started to play and the deck was getting more crowded. Joan turned to her new companion: "So, Captain Archie Smetherick, where are you headed?"

"Archie, please. And in answer to your question; Hong Kong. A return journey for me. I have been stationed there for the last three years, and you Just Joan? Where is your final destination?"

Joan ignored the emphasis on her name.

"Well, I certainly hope that it won't be my final destination!" she said, a little surprised by the alarm in her own voice, "but I am also heading for Hong Kong. There are five of us going to Bowen Road Hospital. I'm not sure what to expect. What is it like?"

"Hot!" replied the captain, laughing, "It's damned hot, especially for a Yorkshire lad like me."

Joan was surprised, "You don't sound like a Yorkshireman. Has the Navy beaten that out of you?" She said with a laugh.

"No, my father did that years before," Smetherick was still smiling, "he was also a Navy rat so was determined that no boy of his was going to join the service speaking anything but the King's very best English."

"Quite right too," said Joan, putting on a royal accent, "I agree entirely." Smetherick chuckled and they both fell into a comfortable silence. She fell serious for a moment and looked up at his kind face, wondering whether to ask a question that burned in her as soon as she had heard him utter the words 'Hong Kong'. Smetherick beat her to it.

"You want to know how safe the Colony is, don't you?"

"I've heard so many rumours," she said. "Is it really as defenceless as people are saying?"

The Captain looked out across the deck towards the lights on Cape Verde. There was a breeze getting up. Joan absurdly thought Gwen might have had the right idea after all.

"You shouldn't pay too much attention to the rumour mill, my dear. The stories change day by day. The truth is that the colony is completely blinkered to the fact that there is a war raging around them."

Smetherick looked back at Joan, then at his empty glass as if his next words would be found at the bottom of it. "To be honest, Just Joan, it's pure bloody British Imperial arrogance at its absolute bloody worst. The general thought within the colony is that the war won't impact Hong Kong at all."

"And what do you think, Archie?" Joan asked leaning forward, aware that she was almost holding her breath waiting for his answer.

"I think that we shouldn't underestimate the Japs. Sly little buggers they are. They are causing all sorts of mayhem across China. But we will be ready for them should they decide to attack. Since I left six months ago, there has been work going on to strengthen our defence lines, whether it will be enough, I just don't know." His drink finished, Smetherick took out a pipe from his jacket pocket and begin to fill it with tobacco. "Anyway, my dear, I think that's enough talk of the war for one evening. There is a party going on and drinks to be had. What can I get you?"

He moved to the bar not waiting for her answer. Joan noticed that she had drained her drink already. Brenda was all of a sudden at her side, looking excited and a little out of breath.

"Come on you," she said grabbing Joan's arm to pull her towards the dancefloor. "I know he's a handsome devil, but stop hobnobbing with the top brass when there's dancing to be done!"

Joan laughed and let herself be led. Smetherick watched her go and raised his pipe to her as she mouthed 'sorry' in his direction. Brenda, vivacious and bubbly as ever, had pulled her out of her morbid thoughts in an instant, as she always seemed to do. She would digest what the Captain had said tomorrow. He was right, the war was tiresome, and there was indeed a party in full swing around them.

Joan had never experienced anything like it before. The band had upped the tempo and everyone was now dancing, all thoughts of war had been put firmly to the back of everyone's minds for at least one night. The lights made the ship, so often in sombre darkness, come alive with colour and as the sun went down over Cape Verde, it made it the perfect backdrop for the party. Joan still had to pinch herself that she was here. *How lucky I am* she thought as she was spun around the dancefloor by an unknown serviceman. She could see Matron from the corner of her eye stood in deep conversation with Major Cartland. Joan was in no doubt that she was keeping a close eye on her girls and she, for one, would not be misbehaving.

She looked over her dance partner's shoulder and saw Brenda doing a slow dance with Mickey whilst people were jitterbugging and jiving all around them. Joan smiled and was happy for her friend. She just hoped she didn't get into any trouble.

Lights, dancing partners, gin fizzes: the rest of the night was a bit of a blur, and Joan couldn't remember when she had ever had such a fabulous time. As the band packed up, finishing on the usual slower numbers, she had enjoyed a pleasant little waltz with a well-behaved Dickie. He pecked her cheek as the last notes hung in the cooling Atlantic air, but was gracious when Joan declined his offer to walk her back to her cabin. She was wondering whether she had misjudged him a little as she made her way through the corridors – he was annoying, but when it came to it, he seemed a decent fellow. Joan descended a flight of stairs then rounded another corner and almost walked straight into Captain Smetherick. The ship was on the move again and Brenda had disappeared hours earlier. She hadn't minded at all as she was having such a wonderful time, but she now had no idea what time it was, her feet were agony and her head was a little bit spinny from the gin fizzes.

"Ah, Just Joan," Smetherick said jovially, "how has your evening been? From what I saw, your little feet must be complaining after all that dancing. May I escort you to your cabin my dear?" He smiled and held out his arm. Joan looked at him suspiciously, and Smetherick held up his hands.

"No funny business I promise," He wiggled his wedding finger which sported a wide gold band, "I'm far too frightened of Mrs Captain Smetherick for that!"

He held out his arm again which Joan gladly took. He could at least walk in a straight line, which she was finding increasingly difficult.

Chapter 6

After an easy couple of weeks at sea, the now-good friends had settled into a happy routine of swimming, sunbathing and playing tennis during the day and drinking up on the deck at night. Even Matron had joined them on occasion, although Joan suspected that this was more to keep an eye on them than anything else. Joan could not remember ever feeling so relaxed. She had never been on holiday outside of England before and so this was nothing like she had ever experienced.

It was 11th August and they were on their way to Cape Town. Brenda was particularly excited as her mother had arranged for her to meet up with some relatives whilst she was there. She had never met her cousin and her family but they were to pick them up at the dock and take them to Table Mountain. They were sunbathing on deck when Matron Hughes appeared, looking extremely business-like.

"Can I see all of you in the briefing room in 15 minutes please," she said without even stopping to look at them, "in uniform!" she barked over her shoulder before marching towards the next group of nurses sunbathing further along the deck.

"Blimey! I wonder what all that's about?" said Freda, jumping up and gathering up her belongings.

"I have no idea, we probably looked far too relaxed for her

liking and she's going to have us do some bandaging practice." Groaned Brenda as she slung her towel over her shoulder and started to hurry towards their cabin. Joan laughed and followed suit.

Within 15 minutes all nurses were gathered in the drawing room looking flushed and out of breath but all standing to attention when Matron Hughes swept into the room joined by Captain Smetherick. Joan raised her eyebrows in surprise. *What on earth is going on?* she thought.

"Right ladies, take a seat," instructed Matron. "No need to panic but we are taking a slight detour. We have had news that a ship heading to Cape Town has been hit during the night by a passing ship - not an enemy ship thankfully. As far as we are aware, there are no casualties, but we cannot confirm anything further at this stage." She paused and looked around the room. The young nurses were all holding their breath waiting for further instruction.

"We have arranged for the ballroom to be cleared so we can check them all over and make them comfortable. As far as we are aware, the majority of the passengers of the SS Ceramic are Canadian women and children. That means you, officers, will be expected to give up your cabins for them until we reach Cape Town." The nurses all looked at each other, obviously dismayed at having to give up their lovely comfortable cabins.

"Any questions?" asked Matron. All the nurses shook their

heads. "We will inform you of where you will be sleeping in due course. You are to split into two groups. Joan, can you please report to Captain Smetherick on deck with Annette and Freda? Can the rest of you please go straight to the Ballroom to get the supplies ready and assist with setting up the room? That is all."

The young nurses filed out in silence until they were out of earshot.

"Well," said Daphne. "I was planning on working on my tan this afternoon but I suppose a change is as good as a rest, so my mother says." Joan and Brenda rolled their eyes at each other. Joan didn't think she had ever met anyone quite so vain, but Daphne did make her laugh. She certainly wasn't as irritating as Freda who was already bossing poor Annette about before turning her attention to Joan;

"Come along Joan, let's hurry and see what we can do up on deck, it's actually all quite exciting don't you think?"

Joan had to admit that it was. She obviously hoped that there were not any injuries but it was nice to be able to do something useful after a couple of weeks of lazing about.

When she reached the deck, the scene before her was a rescue in full flow. Men were shouting orders and there were ship stewards running backwards and forwards with blankets and huge flasks of steaming hot tea. Once up on deck, Joan learned that the ship was the SS Ceramic and had been hit by a ship named The Testbank which had more damage than the Ceramic but was not carrying any passengers. This was, apparently, a common occurrence with the lights out rule.

As Matron had said, the Ceramic had been carrying hundreds of Canadian women and children, who, as Joan looked out to sea, were being ferried over to the Viceroy on life boats. It was quite a sight. Despite the disaster, everything seemed relatively calm and under control. Brenda appeared at Joan's side with her camera. Joan opened her mouth to ask what on earth she was doing when Brenda shushed her. "Don't worry Joan, I have had permission from your friend the Captain, he suggested that we get some photographs of the rescue. Not sure old Hughes was too impressed but she let me come up on deck anyway."

"I wasn't going to say anything!" Joan protested.

"No of course you weren't my dear," teased Brenda, "wow! Would you look at that?" She exclaimed, pointing her camera out to sea, "now that is not a sight that you see every day, is it?"

They both turned to look at the activity going on around them. There were two lifeboats nearing the ship, each with about 30 women and children all huddled together. Joan and Brenda set to work finding blankets to wrap around the weary evacuees. They soon had an efficient system in place where the women and children were helped on board by the naval officers and handed over to the QA's to check over and get them settled. In no time at all, the women and children were safely on board and gathered in the ballroom. Everywhere she looked Joan could see women huddled together with whatever belongings they could carry and frightened children clinging to them. The ship echoed with sounds of whimpering children and mothers soothing voices trying to calm them. Thankfully, there were no serious casualties, so tea and sympathy was all that was required. They had had a real fright, but were all so grateful to have been rescued. The fact that there had been a couple of British ships nearby to help the damaged vessel was a miracle, and they were obviously painfully aware of how things could have gone had they not been found.

Joan chuckled to herself at one point, as she looked around. You would never have known that there had been a party in this room the night before, or that there would have been more than a few sore heads among the nurses and soldiers that had sprung into action as soon as was necessary. The whole thing seemed surreal, but Joan was proud. The grand Ballroom was now a makeshift hospital ward with lines of women and their children all huddled around whatever belongings they had been able to carry.

Joan was so engrossed in her work that she had completely forgotten about Brenda and her camera. She looked around to find Brenda sitting on the floor with a little boy who could have been no older than two on her knee. The little boy's mother was obviously completely exhausted and was curled up fast asleep on a pile of blankets next to them. Joan went over to see if everything was ok. Brenda nodded and whispered, "This is Bobby, I found him wandering about. He was a bit upset but we've found his mammy and we're just sitting down here quietly until she wakes up. Aren't we Bobby?" Brenda looked down at the little boy who was snuggled to her, earnestly sucking his thumb. He turned his tear-streaked face to Joan and nodded slowly.

Joan turned to look at his mother and realised that she had a little baby in her arms. They were both fast asleep. Joan felt the young mother's forehead and realised she was very hot and seemed feverish. She called over Annette who was nearby and asked her whether the mother had been given anything for the fever. Annette nodded. "Yes," she whispered. "I checked over the baby too and she's fine. Mum here is just getting some well-earned rest, isn't she Bobby?" Little Bobby nodded again. Joan smiled and thanked Annette who hurried off to get some more hot water for tea. Joan smiled and looked down to see that he was clutching a small blue teddy.

"And who's this?" she asked kindly.

"Blue Ted," Bobby said quietly, "he hurt his leg." He held the small blue teddy bear out to Joan and showed her a dirty oil mark on its leg, probably from the lifeboat.

"Oh no!" said Joan, "shall I have a little look at him? I am a nurse." Bobby nodded and handed Blue Ted over. Joan rested the teddy against Brenda's outstretched leg and pretended to examine him for broken bones. She looked back at Bobby and said, "Well I'm pleased to say it's nothing serious but I do think that he needs a bandage on that leg, what you think?"

Bobby nodded, smiling and enjoying the game. Joan set about putting a small bandage over the oil mark and handed Blue Ted back to the little boy. Bobby grinned and hugged the bear.

"Why don't you try and get some sleep like your mum and baby sister? Brenda here will make sure Blue Ted is safe." Bobby nodded again and snuggled further into Brenda's arms. Brenda gave him an affectionate squeeze and started to stroke his hair and quietly hum a lullaby, rocking him slowly back and forth. He was asleep within minutes. Brenda sighed with relief when he was finally asleep.

"Thank you," she said. "He was getting himself all upset. Think he frightened himself when he lost sight of his mum. Poor little man has had a hell of a day." She paused and looked around. "Any chance of a cup of tea? It looks like I'm going to be here some time." She smiled cheekily at Joan who shook her head at the cheek but went off to find them both a well-earned cup of tea.

The rest of the day was uneventful. The nurses all worked hard to make sure their new guests were looked after and at the end of the day the girls and other officers gladly gave up their cabins. Brenda had insisted that she settle Bobby and his mum, whose name was Rose, and baby sister in their cabins as they were adjoining, hopefully Rose would be able to get some proper rest in a bed of her own.

The nurses all happily bunked down on the ballroom floor, completely exhausted. Despite herself, Joan could not stop smiling. She was bone-weary, sleeping on a hard, cold floor but at that moment she knew that she had done the right thing by joining up. This was what she had become a QA for. The reality of war had again reminded them all why they were there. She started to settle into a contented sleep when Brenda came over and nudged her.

"Come on sleepy head," she whispered, "we're all going up on deck." She nodded over towards the door where Freda, Gwen, and Daphne were all sneaking out of the ballroom, wrapped in blankets. Joan was about to protest when Brenda opened her coat to reveal a bottle of whisky. Joan laughed and rolled her eyes, "Oh for goodness sake, do I have a choice?" she said getting up and throwing a blanket around her shoulders. Brenda grinned and said, "Of course not!"

They got up onto the deck and a small group had gathered. They were all huddled together in a sheltered corner of the 'deck for drinking'. A friendly steward had brought them a little paraffin heater and some glasses. As the girls approached the group she could hear Dickie talking passionately about the Ceramic and its history. The girls looked at each other and rolled their eyes playfully before sitting down. Joan noticed that Brenda went straight for the seat next to Mickey, which he pulled closer to him as she sat down. No one spoke, they just settled in together in a comfortable silence listening to Dickie as he educated them all on the SS Ceramic.

"She's a triple-screw steamer," he was saying, "same as the Titanic…"

"Yes, and look what good it did them!" interrupted Daphne, the group all giggled. Dickie shot her a look and continued, "she's really a feet of modern engineering, practically unsinkable which is why there is not much damage. The cargo steamer practically crumpled on impact but the Ceramic is all double and triple riveted and has 12 transverse watertight bulkheads, they go much higher up the ship so make the flotation more sturdy, even in an emergency. For such a big ship, it's really quite remarkable!" He paused for breath and took a sip of his whisky. His captive audience all breathed a sigh of relief that he was done.

"And it has electromagnetic switches which control all the doors to the boiler and engine rooms," he continued, "the Captain can literally flick a switch and close all the doors - practically unsinkable! Really incredible engineering…" Brenda touched Dickie on the knee and laughed,

"All completely fascinating Dickie my dear, as usual we are all riveted."

"Is that double or triple riveted?!" smirked Daphne, giggling at her own joke. Dickie couldn't help but laugh and joined in. The group were still giddy when Matron arrived, also wrapped in a blanket. She had been checking on the nurses in the ballroom and had noticed that a few were missing. She had no doubt where she would find them. The nurses all turned in fright when they saw her approach.

"We're in for it now." Joan said under her breath.

"Ok gentlemen I think it's time for you to retire for the evening don't you?" she said, without looking at either of the two men. They both got up and disappeared without question. The girls all held their breath and looked expectantly at their leader, wondering what on earth she was going to say about them being out after lights out. They had to be disciplined and take their roles seriously. Catherine Hughes had known that she would find it hard to strike a balance between instilling some firm discipline in her nurses and allowing them to enjoy the luxury and freedom of the ship. Some of them, she knew, where heading towards an awful lot of hard work and sights that they could now not even contemplate. She had lost many good friends already and had seen some soldiers so badly mutilated and wounded, she often wondered whether she would ever be able to close her eyes again without seeing their stricken faces. She cleared her throat, "I am sure that I do not have to remind you that you are not here at the generosity and good grace of the Army, you are here as ambassadors of the Army Nurses and I expect you to behave as such."

"Yes Matron," muttered a couple of the nurses.

"That said," she paused and took a deep breath, "I did want to say how proud I was of you today. You all worked hard and were a credit to the QA's."

The young women looked at each other opened mouthed. They had not expected that. "But it is late and I do think it's time you all got some sleep. Good night ladies." She bowed her head and walked back towards the ballroom.

Gwen sniggered and said, "That woman never ceases to amaze me, I never know what she's going to come out with next."

"I agree," said Brenda, "I think we better head back before she changes her mind about reprimanding us."

They all agreed and hurried back to their makeshift beds on the Ballroom floor. Joan fell asleep smiling.

Chapter 7

After days at sea, the 5th of September snuck up quickly. They would arrive in Hong Kong soon. Joan and Brenda decided to write letters home, telling their families about their journey so far, before they landed and real work began. What was beginning to feel like an endless journey was now coming to an end.

The girls had chosen the drawing room to sit and write their letters in peace and quiet. Joan liked the calmness of the room, it was less fussy than some of the others, but you could still easily believe that you were in a grand palace somewhere. There were ornate writing desks and chairs, all equipped with embossed writing paper and pens. Joan loved the smell of the room. It reminded her of her grandparents' house, which was full of old books and oversized armchairs.

Joan took some paper and sat a desk facing the fireplace. A steward appeared with a tray of tea and sandwiches and set it down on the table. Without a word he started to pour into the delicate little china cups.

Joan smiled and said to Brenda, "How will we ever get used to looking after ourselves again? We have been so spoilt on this trip." She nodded her thanks to the steward who gave a shy smile and a nod as he turned and left the room. Joan handed Brenda her steaming cup of tea and settled back into her chair.

"Where on earth do I start?" she said, half to herself, half to Brenda-looking at the blank sheet of paper in front on her.

Brenda chuckled. "How about the pool party in Port Reitz with half of the British Navy? Or what about causing unholy chaos in Bombay by insulting their sacred beast? Or what about the cocktails in Columbo? I'm not sure there is enough paper!" Joan shot her a look of disdain and sighed. They really had had the most wonderful time.

"Hmmm, I think I might just focus on the picnic we had on Table Mountain with your cousins and the snake charmers in Mombasa rather than the pool party, I don't want to give dear mother a heart attack. I doubt that she even knows what a pool party is! *'Most unbecoming of a young girl to be frolicking around half dressed in front of complete strangers!'* she mimicked her mother and laughed. "Will you have photographs I can send them of the picnic, if they've turned out ok? I wonder whether we will be able to get them developed in Hong Kong?"

Brenda had been busy taking photographs throughout the whole trip on a new Kodak camera—a gift from her father. They had both promised to send as many pictures back home as they could and had already gone through two of the rolls of film that Brenda had brought with her. Joan couldn't wait to see the pictures. Now that she sat and looked back on their trip so far, she felt quite exhausted. The routine of hospital life in Leeds already seemed like a lifetime ago, and although the trip had surpassed anything that she could have imagined, she could not wait to get back onto dry land and into a proper routine. It did feel a little bit like they were on an extended holiday. She wondered what the hospital would be like and how different, or the same, it would be from home. She was looking forward to getting settled into the Nurses' Quarters, and exploring Hong Kong. Brenda had ignored her question about the photographs but eventually asked, "How far have you got Whiteley?"

Joan looked up and pulled a face. Brenda threw her head back and laughed. "You're going to have to get used to it Joan dear, it seems to be the norm in the Army. Even for the nurses." Joan ignored her and cleared her throat,

"Pay attention *Morgan* and listen…" she lifted up the paper in front her and started to read just as the door burst open. It was Mickey, who was obviously out of breath.

"I've been looking for you everywhere," Mickey panted, trying to catch his breath," come on Brenda grab your camera; we've got dolphins *and* whales following us. It's an incredible sight, come on!" he said with urgency. The girls gathered up their things and quickly following him. Letter writing quickly forgotten

The next day was a sad day for Joan. They had arrived in Singapore, and the nurses who were to be stationed there were getting

101

ready to go. They had all become such good friends on the voyage, it seemed so sad that it was now coming to an end. They decided to have a final girl's night out at Raffles Hotel. Joan and Brenda set about getting themselves ready. They were to meet Daphne, Gwen and Freda in the bar at the hotel. Joan was both nervous and excited at going ashore without any chaperone. They had decided not to tell Matron that they were going, it would be more than frowned upon if they were found out. Joan had never heard of the famous Raffles Hotel before setting sail but soon realised that she was the only one who hadn't. Brenda had been talking about it since she realised that they were heading to Singapore and there were lots of officers and servicemen that had already been. They had told wonderful tales of how glamorous both the hotel and its clientele were. The girls were so excited. They had decided to go in their whites, they had both got a bit of colour from their travels and their tanned skin set off the bright white of their uniforms nicely. They were both aware of making heads turn as they made their way from their rooms and could not help smiling at each other as they stepped off the ship into the heavy humidity of Singapore.

"So much for doing my hair," groaned Brenda," this humidity is going to have it back to its usual frizz before we even get to the hotel!"

Joan smiled, "Well that will make two of us then." she said, linking her arm and heading in the direction of the hotel.

The rest of the nurses were already settled in the Long Bar when they arrived. They were chatting away with some Naval Officers who were talking them through the cocktail menu. Joan looked around her and whistled, "Blimey Brenda, would you look at this?!" She had never seen anything quite like it.

The mahogany wooden bar seemed to go on forever with several couples sat on the high bar stools deep in their own conversations, sipping their cocktails. To the left of the bar there were clusters of rattan tables with glass tops and vases of brightly coloured flowers that Joan had seen nothing like before. They were surrounded by huge, high-backed rattan chairs with colourful cushions. The whole colonial scene was finished off by the huge palm trees that were dotted about and the whirring fans overhead. It could not have been more exotic. Joan looked over to one end of the room where there was an impressive mahogany wood spiral staircase, snaking its way up to the floor above. It was all simply spectacular, and she couldn't take it all in.

Gwen spotted them and jumped up immediately to greet her friends.

"Hey, you made it," she said, pulling more chairs around the table to allow them to sit, "please meet our new friends James and Manley." She gestured towards the two handsome Naval Officers sat at the table.

"Manley?" said Joan, "really?" The group all looked at her, slightly amused by the fact she had obviously been caught off guard by the unusual name, Joan realised her obvious rudeness and clapped her hand to her mouth. "Oh, my goodness, I'm so sorry. How rude of me!" She flushed and sat down quickly.

Manley grinned, "Don't worry, I get that a lot. I blame my mother," he said with a wink, "now what can we get you ladies to drink?" He got up to make his way to the bar. Brenda gave Joan a dig in the ribs and giggled at her tactlessness. It was usually her getting them into trouble! Joan glared back at her with a look that clearly said, *not another word!* Brenda laughed and grabbed the menu. She looked at James.

"So, what would you recommend?"

James pointed to the menu and said, "Well, for the ladies, when at Raffles, one should at least try the famous Singapore Sling," He pointed to it on the menu. Brenda read out the ingredients.

"Gin, cherry brandy, pineapple, lime, Cointreau, Dom Benedictine and grenadine," she looked up at James and handed him the menu. "I have no idea what half of those are, but we'll have two!"

She grinned excitedly as the two men made their way to the bar. Brenda turned to Freda and giggled "Well you lot don't waste any time, do you? Where did you find them??" she said.

Freda smiled and said, "Well, they were wandering around

looking a bit lost, we took pity on them and said they could join us."
Gwen pushed Freda's shoulder and said

"What?! You practically tripped poor James up so he'd notice you!" She turned to Joan and said, "And I'll think you'll find that it was us wandering around looking a bit lost. They kindly offered to escort us here. We couldn't exactly just send them on their way now could we??" The girls were all laughing as the boys brought back the drinks and sat down.

"So, we understand that you ladies have had quite the adventure so far?" said Manley. "What have been the highlights?"

Daphne and Gwen started to tell them about the rescue of the Ceramic and of their various day trips.

The group spent an easy two hours laughing and swapping stories. They found out that the officers were stationed in Singapore and had been there for about 6 months. They were clearly having a ball and had already offered to be the girl's guides around the Island and show them the sights.

"So, Brenda, what has been your favourite country that so far?" asked James.

"Oh, I think India. I thought it was just wonderful. I had no idea what to expect but I wasn't expecting it to be as busy and so completely chaotic!" said Brenda, "it was amazing. The smells, the colours, the people...the food!" With that she looked at Joan and they both laughed.

"We went to a restaurant that had been recommended to us. It was a bit more off the beaten track. When we got there and had no idea what anything on the menu was. The waiter was lovely and said that he would bring us a selection of not too spicy dishes 'for our English bellies'." Joan interrupted her and said, laughing,

"They brought all these dishes and laid them out in front of us. I still had no idea what any of them were, despite them explaining them to us. I just couldn't identify anything. I asked them to point out the mildest, which one of them did, but good grief, I have never tasted anything like it! I really thought my mouth was on fire! It was so unbelievably hot, it took my breath away!"

Brenda said, "I have never seen anyone change colour so quickly, she went bright red! Then, a bit green, then back to red! I think you must have gulped down at least two pints of water, which apparently didn't help in the slightest!" Joan was shaking her head and laughing.

"I think that the waiter did it on purpose! They were all laughing nearly as much as Brenda! It was terrible! But once I could feel my gums and lips again, we had a really nice meal! I would not say that Indian food was my favourite. I've tried it - and they can keep it. Give me one of my mother's roast dinners any day!" she declared.

"Yes," replied Brenda, "you can take the girl out of Manchester..." without drawing breath Brenda went on, "I don't know what was funnier, the restaurant or the cow??"

Joan nearly choked on her drink, "Oh no don't! That was just awful! I nearly caused a riot!" James and Manley both raised a quizzical eyebrow, clearly amused by the two northern nurses.

Brenda chuckled and told how they had been trying to get through a crowd of people on a fairly narrow street.

"We were in such a hurry as we had no idea how far away from the ship we were and had to get back. Anyway, in the middle of all of these people there was a cow that just seemed quite happy to be standing there, holding everybody up. Everybody seemed perfectly happy waiting for the beast to move along but Joan here had got fed up with waiting, marched right up to it and gave it a good slap on its backside to get it moving! It certainly did that, and got the people moving too! They were suddenly all shouting and waving their arms about, pointing at Joan and then the cow. It was complete pandemonium! We just had to turn and run to get away from the madness." Brenda was doubled over and could hardly get the words out. The small group all broke into hysterical laughter. Joan was wiping her eyes.

"How was I supposed to know that they were sacred animals?! It was terrible! We barely got out alive!"

The group were by now a few cocktails in and were falling about with laughter. They continued to tell their tales until they were politely

107

shooed out of the Long Bar and onto the long veranda, which wrapped around the hotel with more tables and the huge rattan chairs. On each of the tables there was a bowl of water with a flower and a candle floating in it. The mood was calm and a slight breeze brought some welcome fresh air after the stifling humidity earlier in the day. Joan took a deep breath of the warm, sweet smelling air. Happy and relaxed, Joan made a mental note that she must come back and visit Singapore; it sounded the most intriguing of places.

The change of scenery broke the mood slightly, and the group became more serious. The girls realised that they would now have to say goodbye, not knowing whether they would see each other again. All of a sudden nobody wanted to drink any more. The girls turned to each other and made their promises to stay in touch. They all had each other's addresses at home and vowed to get together once this dreadful war business was over. None of them dared to acknowledge the reality of what may lie ahead. The Singapore nurses reluctantly turned away from the hotel and walked towards the city centre with their new chaperones. Gwen, Freda and Daphne had decided to join them for 'one more for the road'. Joan and Brenda stood and waved until they were out of sight. Brenda sighed and gave Joan a big hug.

"Come on old girl; let's get ourselves back on board before we get ourselves into trouble." Joan nodded and they turned to head arm in arm back towards the harbour.

As they were walking, two Chinese boys on rickshaws appeared at their sides, honking their horns and sounding their bells. They were beckoning for the girls to get on. Both girls knew that they had probably had one too many cocktails and so were suddenly very grateful for the opportunity to not to have to walk the whole way. The journey back went by in a blur. The boys were obviously used to racing each other and both set off at a pace, laughing as they went. The girls squealed with delight as they were thrown around the busy streets in their unwieldy little vehicles honking and ringing their bells. By the time they got back to the ship they were exhausted from laughing. They thanked their young chauffeurs and gave them enough money to feed their families for a week!

They collapsed into their beds still giggling to themselves and thinking again how lucky they were. Who would have thought they would get to sip cocktails at the Raffles Hotel?! Joan's last thought as she drifted off to sleep was how much her life had changed in such a short period of time. All of a sudden it was full of colour and laughter. She tried not to let her mind wander to home and her family. It only made her feel sad and homesick. They would never have been able to even imagine some of the things that she had seen in the last few weeks. And this was only the beginning.

The last leg of the journey was a straight run to Hong Kong. By this time Brenda and Mickey were inseparable and busy making plans to explore Hong Kong Island together. Joan was pleased for her friend. She had not had much luck with men in the past; she always seemed to choose drifters or 'plodders' as her father called them. Mickey seemed nice. They were good fun to be around and made each other and everyone else laugh with their stories and the pranks that they constantly played on each other. In Brenda's own words, *they were simply perfect together.*

Joan had no desire to get romantically involved with anyone. She was happy enjoying the company of the soldiers and officers on board and was certain that she had made some friends for life. Captain Smetherick in particular had become a close friend and she had spent many evenings listening to his stories of Hong Kong life. It all sounded so glamorous, she wondered how anyone ever managed to get any work done in between parties, the beach, playing tennis and fancy dinners. She was comfortable with the Captain, probably because there was no ulterior motive for his attention and friendship. He talked about his wife constantly and she was looking forward to meeting her once they finally arrived in Hong Kong.

Joan had arranged to meet Captain Smetherick on the evening of 8th September. They had been sailing non-stop since leaving Singapore and there was a growing sense of excitement on board at the prospect of reaching their final destination in just a matter of days.

Joan had got to the Lounge Bar first. It was the main meeting place in the evenings and was always busy. She found a table and settled with a book whilst waiting for the Captain to arrive. She spotted him arrive with another Navy Captain that they had been travelling with. It irritated Joan that she could never remember his name. They both looked in deep conversation when Archie spotted Joan; he waved and indicated that he would be over in 1 minute. Joan waved back and smiled. She continued to watch them and it was obvious that they were troubled by something. *I wonder whether something has happened?* She thought of England and her family. She had heard that the air raids and bombing had increased since they had left. When she listened to the officers discussing what was going on in Europe it always made her blood run cold. Thankfully, there still didn't seem to be any real concern about where they were heading, which was a relief, but it did not alleviate her worry for her family back home.

Archie finally arrived at the table holding a gin and tonic for each of them. He handed the drink to Joan and sat heavily in his chair.

"Oh dear," said Joan, "do I want to know what's troubling you?"

Archie sighed then smiled. "We've just had our de-brief with Commodore Bates," he took a sip of his drink and settled into his chair, "it would seem that our friend Adolf has ramped up the air attack on Britain significantly over the last few days. Yesterday, London took a real hit. A right old mess by all accounts - something like 300 German bombers & 600 fighters - it seems that the buggers have unlimited resources! They seem to be targeting the factories and assembly lines as well as the airfields. So, rationing has been reduced again. I must say it was a grim picture that was being painted. They can't gain control via the channel as we clearly have naval superiority," he gave a cheeky wink. "So, they're going for air control," he tried a smile but sighed again and looked at Joan's concerned face. "It sounds like Manchester and Leeds have got off lightly though in comparison to Liverpool and London. We just have to hope that they've been frugal with their ration books so far." He put a comforting hand on Joan's. "The family will be fine. They are well out of it."

For the moment Joan thought to herself. She chose to try to change the subject slightly.

"So, the Jerries are obviously busy, what about the Japs? Any news there?"

"It's all speculation at this stage. It seems to me that Japan is at a bit of a stalemate, despite their best efforts, they are still not in control of China & the Chinese can't get rid of them from the areas that they have invaded. I don't know which way it will go but I have the feeling that the Japs will kick back at western interventions. We are apparently imposing all sorts of sanctions. The main one being oil. I can't see that one ending well. They are not very good at having their toys taken away. I think that puts us more in the firing line in Hong Kong." He looked at Joan who was listening intently, taking in every word, "but that's just me speculating Just Joan. What do I know?"

"Well it makes sense I suppose. Will Hong Kong be ready?" This was still a huge concern for her based on what she had heard so far. Archie just shrugged as his eye was caught by Matron Hughes who had just walked into the bar. He waved her over. Joan wanted to kick him under the table but remembered his rank. *What on earth has he called her over for?!* She straightened up and smiled politely as she walked over to join them. For once Matron looked relaxed and was smiling as she took a seat at the table.

"Good evening Archie," she said and turned to Joan, "good evening Sister Whiteley. This all looks very serious."

Archie laughed, "Oh you know how this war can be, most tiresome, now may I get you a drink my dear?" he said getting up.

"You know what, you may," said Matron cheerfully, "I'll have a G&T."

Joan nearly choked on her drink! *Blimey* she thought, *I've only seen her with water or tea for the whole trip.* She looked over at Catherine Hughes and wondered what she was really like. Apparently, she had seen active duty already but she didn't know where. As Joan sat in uncomfortable silence, she spotted Brenda and Freda walking into the bar. They both spotted Joan sat with Matron and immediately turned on their heels, giggling and almost tripping over themselves to get out of the bar before being asked to join the small table. Joan narrowed her eyes at them with a look that said *thanks a lot*! But smiled to herself, she probably would have done the same. Thankfully Archie appeared with the drinks and took charge of the conversation.

"I was just been updating Joan here on the latest goings on back home," he said.

"Ah," acknowledged Matron, "now I understand why so serious."

"I'd say we were far better off where we are going by the sound of it," ventured Joan.

"It would seem so," replied Matron Hughes.

"This will be a holiday camp for you in comparison to France surely?" said Archie.

"Gosh, I should hope so," said Hughes. "I can't imagine this being anything like being on the front."

"Gosh!" exclaimed Joan. "You were at the Western Front?"

"I was indeed. A very unpleasant experience that I would not want to repeat. Thankfully, nursing has moved on a bit since then," she took a sip of her drink, "it seems like an awful long time ago now."

"We studied it during my nursing training," said Joan, "I just can't imagine what it must have been like."

"Well, it was loud and bloody. It was less mopping fevered brows and more holding crushed or injured limbs whilst the doctors lopped them off," she said with little emotion, "not a great place for a young nurse but it was an experience and it definitely toughened me up a bit."

Joan looked horrified. She knew from her training that this is what is would have been like but to hear someone who had lived through it made it seem all the more dreadful. Archie smiled, he had obviously heard some of the stories before.

"We don't need to bore young Joan with those tales of blood, guts and war at its worst now do we? Drink up old bean; we are heading towards a veritable paradise!"

Joan sighed with relief and smiled as the unlikely threesome raised a glass to Hong Kong.

Chapter 8

They pulled into Hong Kong's bustling harbour on the11th of September 1940. Joan was immediately struck by the contrast of what she had left behind. Home was tired, grey, and war-weary, looking ahead of her at a scene that was breath-taking and almost peaceful; it was hard to believe it was the same world. The lush green mountains in the distance dropped down into golden, sandy bays, and impressive looking buildings rising at the foot of the mountains. Butterflies danced in Joan's stomach, and she wasn't sure if they were due to excitement or nerves. She couldn't wait to explore the island. From where she was standing, it was hard to imagine that there was a war going on; it certainly wasn't going on here.

Joan felt almost sad to be leaving the comfort and security of ship they had called home for the last six weeks. The fear of the unknown was returning but looking around her, it seemed that everyone was feeling the same. The five remaining Nursing Sisters were nervously huddled together, trying to avoid being trampled by the flow of people all disembarking. They were all gaping at the scenery in complete awe.

"Well, I think this will do us, don't you?" Said Freda cheerfully, gently nudging Gwen forwards with her kit bag, "come on, there's

Matron."

The five women all looked at each other, unable to keep the smiles from their faces. Archie was right, Joan thought, a veritable paradise indeed.

As they stepped off the ship and onto dry land for the first time in days, there were people everywhere. Joan felt quite dizzy, and the humidity was almost suffocating. The curls at the nape of her neck were already wet with perspiration. They all set down their kit bags. "Oh my, I don't think I will cope well with this heat." She said, wiping the back of her neck with her handkerchief.

"Oh, don't worry," said a familiar voice coming up behind them, "its cyclone season. That'll soon cool things down." They all turned as Dickie joined them. His kit bag thrown over his shoulder and another huge bag in his hand.

"Cyclone? Really?" questioned Daphne, "don't you mean typhoon?" Dickie gave an exaggerated sigh as he threw his heavy bag to the ground.

"Do you know," he said, "just once I would like someone to say 'oh really? That's interesting Dickie' or 'how do you know these things Dickie?' Instead, I get questioned or ridiculed when all I am trying to do is educate you young ladies."

Joan smiled as she listened. Daphne rolled her eyes, "Oh for goodness sake, don't be so testy," she grabbed his cheeks like a baby and said, "nobody likes a peevish Dickie."

He started to protest "I am a Naval Officer, it is my job to know about weather!" Mickey appeared behind him, also laden down with kit. "You are a Naval Engineer old chap, it is your job to know about engineering." He gave Daphne a wink and leant over to kiss Brenda on the cheek, "Come on before we get Court Martialled for being late to the barracks," he turned to Brenda, "will we see you later?" Brenda was beaming,

"You will indeed."

The girls laughed as Mickey pushed Dickie along who was muttering to himself about 'not even getting any credit from his mates'.

"I think I'll miss seeing those two every day," said Daphne watching them go.

"Oh, I don't think we'll be getting rid of them any time soon," said Joan, grinning at Brenda.

She turned to look around and tried to make sense of the scene before her. There were Chinese harbour coolies running up and down with rickshaws taking people here and there. There seemed to be hundreds if not thousands of servicemen and women arriving, leaving, and going about their daily business. There must have been another ship arrive with them to generate this much human traffic! And everyone seemed to be shouting! Shouting orders, shouting to catch the eyes of people they were there to meet, shouting to get help with mooring up their sampan boats, shouting to buy and sell food or wares. The noise was deafening after the relative peace and quiet of the last week at sea.

Joan could not imagine how she would ever get used to this strange new world. It was simply spectacular. Everywhere was so colourful. There were bright red and blue fishing boats bobbing about in between the huge ships and the sampans that looked like whole families lived on them. Everyone looked tanned and healthy and servicemen in their tropical uniforms were certainly a sight to see. Joan felt a huge pang of sadness when she thought of her family. Their lives were almost in black and white in comparison.

"Joan! What on earth are you doing just standing there? You're going to get trampled!" Brenda was nudging Joan with her kit bag to get her to move forward. "Can you believe this place?!" Brenda was looking around in as much wonder as Joan. "I have no idea where we're to go, do you?" The girls all shook their heads.

"Come on girls, chop chop," Matron Hughes suddenly appeared next to them and steered them towards a military building at the end far end of the harbour.

As they walked, Joan noticed that everyone was smiling. The Chinese all smiled and bowed their heads in greeting as they passed.

"Do any of these people even know that there is a war on??" she whispered, "I have never seen people so happy and cheerful." Brenda nodded in agreement as she struggled with her overfilled kit bag.

They were 'processed' at the harbour military building and were soon at their new home. Bowen Road British Military Hospital. The building was splendid. It was set on a hill with some amazing views of the harbour. Joan could not have been more excited. She just wanted to get settled and get to work. In one of their lectures on board they'd learned that the main problem at the hospital was malaria. Many of the soldiers had not had sufficient immunisations before they were posted, and most of the wards were filled with soldiers suffering as a result. Joan was, admittedly, a little relieved that she they wouldn't be dealing with injured soldiers. She wasn't sure how she would deal with the severed limbs and broken bodies that Matron had described. She looked around her again and smiled a satisfied smile to herself.

Chapter 9

The girls had not even finished unpacking when Mickey and Dickie appeared in full uniform looking very excited.

"Come on ladies, we are going to paint this little old town red tonight," said Mickey with a wink.

Joan snorted and replied, "You can all please yourselves, I'm not going anywhere! We've been up since 4.30 a.m. and we're expected on duty tomorrow!" She shooed a smiling Mickey out of her way as she tried to find homes for her few belongings.

"Come on Whiteley, where's your sense of adventure?" Dickie teased. "We've been invited to a bit of a gathering at The Repulse Bay Hotel. We can't say no! It's our first night! We need to get our bearings as quickly as possible."

Joan rolled her eyes at Brenda who was already getting ready to go. Brenda just shrugged and did not attempt to convince Joan, she knew that the boys would wear her down eventually.

Joan was still protesting, adamant that she was getting some sleep before her first shift the following morning, when there was a knock on the door. A small, pretty, orderly nurse popped her head round and cheerfully announced that the girls would not be expected on the wards until Friday morning at 7.30. She now had no excuse not to go. Joan groaned and threw herself on the bed. She was soon set upon by Brenda and the boys and knew that resistance was futile. She reluctantly shook out her whites and got herself ready to see more of this strange new paradise that she had found herself in.

The other nurses had decided to stay behind and get settled in properly. Joan wished that she was doing the same but instead dutifully followed Brenda.

They made their way out of the hospital grounds and headed down the hill via Bowen Road. They walked in comfortable silence for most of the way, each of them taking in their new surroundings. It was all so green and lush, even the air smelt sweet in the early evening as the sun was starting to go down. Brenda remarked at how clean and fresh everything seemed in comparison to home. They all agreed. It was just paradise.

The boys had arranged to meet up with some of their Navy buddies who had been in Hong Kong for a while at The Repulse Bay Hotel, which was apparently one of the main hot spots.

When they reached the hotel, it was an impressive looking white building with a grand staircase leading up to the entrance. As they walked in they all gasped at the magnificence of it all. Joan felt instantly uncomfortable as she always did in places as grand as this.

"Are you sure they'll let us in?" she whispered to Brenda who just smiled.

When they got to the lounge bar, Joan looked around and thought immediately that she would struggle with most of these people. Her initial observation was that there seemed to be a strange, unspoken segregation in the room. Officers in uniform clustered together and well dressed, official looking gents with their equally well-dressed wives, girlfriends, or mistresses sat around the tables dotted around the bar. The room was filled with the sound of high pitched laughter from the women who seemed to be gliding from table to table, talking excitedly about who knows what.

The small group made their way to an empty table near to the bar. The girls sat down and looked around them. Mickey had recognised one of his troop and was heading in his direction. Joan looked at Brenda and rolled her eyes. Brenda leaned in to Joan. "Just your sort of place hey Joan? You might have to try harder to hide your disapproval my dear!"

Joan sighed, "My goodness, is this what it will all be like? Just look at them, I bet they have never done a day's work in their lives."

"I think you have to feel sorry for them in a way, just look at the pompous, stuffed shirts that they are married to. I think that's too high a price to pay for nice dresses and membership to fancy clubs." Joan had to agree.

"Very true, I can't imagine ever getting married for anything other than love."

Brenda looked at her friend in surprise. "Well well! There is a romantic bone in that body after all!"

Brenda laughed and grabbed her reluctant friends' arm, pulling her towards the group of men now greeting Mickey and Dickie.

"Come on Whiteley, at least pretend that you might have a good time!" she said.

Joan laughed and allowed Brenda to lead her over to meet a group of officers. Despite herself, she began to relax and enjoy her evening. She thoroughly enjoyed listening to the stories and anecdotes and banter among the group. The conversation, inevitably, focused on the war and everyone seemed to be of the same opinion that the Japs would not dare invade the pride of the Empire. Joan noted that many of the officers had an extremely low opinion of the Japanese soldiers and their ability to pull off any kind of invasion.

"They are causing complete havoc in China though," said one Officer, who was slightly older than the rest of the group, "I wouldn't underestimate the sly little bastards. We can't be arrogant enough to think that they wouldn't dare try to attack Hong Kong. If you ask me, I'd say it was inevitable and not a question of if, but when."

"Well, aren't you a ray of sunshine," laughed Dickie. "You'll have us all racing for the next boat out of here with talk like that."

Mickey shot him a look that said, 'don't start'.

The officer, whose name was Lt Butlin, just smiled and shrugged his shoulders,

"If we continue to bury our heads in the sand and pretend that the war is just going to pass us by, we really are for it. Especially with the latest attacks in China and what is going on in Europe. All I'm saying is that we need to be prepared. Did you not see what they did in Nanking? And their armies have doubled, if not tripled, since then. I think that we would do well not to underestimate them. That's all."

"Well, I'm not sure that we should fear much in terms of military intelligence and expertise from a race of people who think that their Emperor is a God in human form." Snorted Dickie.

"My my," replied Joan, "I didn't have you down as an Imperialist Dickie. They are surely just following orders in the same way that we are?"

"We cannot compare ourselves to them in any way." he said, "Yes, I am proud to fight for my country and I will fight for this colony. That doesn't make me an Imperialist. There can be no pride taken from what they did in Nanking. They see each kill as a badge of honour. How is that superior to us? They are nothing but unintelligent mutts bullying their way across China picking on women and children, all in the name of their Emperor!" He looked around as though to gauge the reaction of his audience. "And they look down on us like we are the animals! We'll see what happens when they come up against a real army."

The group all looked at Dickie in stunned silence. Dickie realised that he may well have gone a step too far and shifted uncomfortably from one foot to the other before saying, "In the meantime, let's enjoy all of what Hong Kong has to offer. Who wants another drink?" He drained his glass and headed for the bar, clearly not wanting to continue the conversation.

"Don't mind him," said Mickey, "he knows full well there is a storm coming."

"Why would you say that?" asked Joan. "I thought you said that we weren't on anyone's radar?"

"Well now that we're here it is clear that we must be, seeing as though all of the women and children were shipped off to Australia a couple of months ago. The pill boxes along the Gin Drinkers' Line are all being reinforced and there are food stores popping up all over the place being filled with essential supplies. Someone must think that something is heading our way." Mickey looked at Lt Butlin for confirmation.

"Yes, all of that is true, defences are being tightened, although it doesn't seem as though any reinforcements are coming our way. I think Churchill has got his hands full at the moment and lots of our troops are being sent to South Africa to defend the Suez. I'm thinking that he must have his fingers crossed that the Japs do stay in China and not cross the border. I'm not sure what we could throw at an attack."

"I heard today that the RAF only has five planes, all over 10 years old?" asked Mickey. "Let's hope that the Japs are as unsophisticated as we think they are or we don't stand a chance."

Lieutenant Butlin just smiled, "We will put up a good fight, don't you worry but I do think that an army who would rather die than surrender, is a very dangerous army indeed."

"Goodness me!" cried Brenda. "You boys are not instilling much confidence. Surely, should the time come, our boys will be ready for action?"

"I think some of them are more than ready for action, looking at the state of some them, the only action they have seen recently has been in a bar or a brothel!" laughed Mickey. The group laughed but they all knew it was true. The troops who had been stationed in Hong Kong for some time had certainly indulged in all that Hong Kong and its champagne lifestyle had to offer. They had been told that along with malaria a huge problem for the hospitals was gonorrhoea.

Joan looked around the room and was puzzled,

"If all the women and children have been forced to evacuate," she asked, "why are there still so many around?" she nodded towards the tables of men and the glamorous looking women.

"That, my dear, is an excellent question." said a familiar voice. Joan turned to see that Captain Smetherick had joined them. She smiled and thought just how pleased she was to see him, although a little surprised he was here, as he had been so desperate to see his wife. He shook hands with all the men and accepted a drink from Dickie, who had returned from the bar, closely followed by a Chinese waiter carrying a tray full of tumblers of whisky and was handing them out.

"As soon as the notice came out that all 'pure' British women had to leave the colony, a large number who did not want to leave their husbands and clearly don't think there is a war on, suddenly became patriotic and put their hands up for official positions or volunteered for the VAD's. That's where the Mrs is tonight, driving an ambulance around no less." He went on, "cheers lads and lasses!" and he raised his glass.

"Cheers!" they all said in unison.

"What do you mean by pure?" Joan asked.

"Anyone with a British only passport." Mickey added.

"That's right," nodded Captain Smetherick, "anyone with a sniff of anything foreign weren't allowed into Australia, so everyone was claiming half Irish fathers, Scottish mothers, etc. and the Eurasians didn't stand a chance"

"Eurasian?" asked Brenda.

Archie laughed and said, "Has no one explained the colony class

130

system to you yet my dear? Give it a week and you'll soon see what I mean."

Brenda and Joan looked at each other, slightly puzzled, but decided not to question further. Thankfully Dickie, who was still determined to change the subject after his outburst started to ask the Captain about the better clubs that they should join.

After that, the conversation was light, and the group became more jovial. They began making plans to explore the colony. There was so much to see and do, Joan was itching to see more of the Island, and the more she heard about it the more excited she was. They had such fabulous things in store - sailing and visiting the New Territories and Lantau Island for starters. It all sounded so incredible. Before they left the hotel, they made plans to meet up at the beach that weekend. There were, apparently, countless secluded bays where you could swim and dive.

Repulse Bay itself seemed to be the most popular. They planned to take a picnic and make a day of it. Joan could not wait.

Chapter 10

Fri 13th Sept 1940 - On duty 7.30 - lots of malaria patients, in at deep end!

Joan woke up early the next day. She hadn't been able to sleep for thinking about her first shift at the hospital. Up and dressed, she decided to go for a walk to try to get her bearings before reporting for duty at 7.30am. Steaming cup of coffee in hand, Joan made her way to the veranda of the Nurses' Quarters to take in the view. The scene took her breath away. Just past the harbour, mountains, still shrouded with early morning mist echoed with exotic sounds of the island waking up. It was magnificent.

The Nurses' Quarters were on a higher level than the hospital itself so she was able to get a good view of the building's layout. The hospital was built with two wings three stories high, connected by a central block. Beyond the hospital, she could see Magazine Gap, where the roads passed from one side of the Island to the other. Joan loved the wide shady verandas and noted that all the windows had heavy wooden shutters, she assumed for use during typhoon season. It was all so colonial. She breathed in the warm, lightly fragrant air and let out a contented sigh. *I could definitely get used to this*, she thought to herself.

She wandered along the veranda and down to the hospital level. She came across the male staff quarters and a recreation block; she was surprised to find a tennis court and smiled as she remembered her interview. She was looking forward to putting those tennis skills to good use. She turned and looked back at the buildings behind her. It was impressive, but as she stood taking in her surroundings, she realised just how exposed the hospital was if the Japanese did decide to attack from the harbour. She hoped that the fact that the hospital was still fully operational, and the staff and patients had not been relocated to one of the smaller hospitals further inland, was a good sign. They were obviously not expecting the hospital to be a target. She shuddered at the thought and decided to head to the ward to start work early. She was itching to get started.

She got to the ward to find Brenda already there. They both laughed.

"Couldn't sleep either?"

"No, not a wink. I've just been for a walk about and decided to come and get started."

"Well aren't you two keen?" said a young VAD nurse, "Matron isn't on the ward yet, she usually gets here about 7. Would you like me to show you around?"

Joan and Brenda both nodded and followed the nurse, a young

Chinese volunteer nurse named Renate. They both liked her immediately. She was no older than 18 or 19 but chattered away happily introducing the two Sisters to the patients. As Joan had suspected, the majority were suffering from malaria and gonorrhoea, as was discussed the previous evening, and a few suffering from cholera and dysentery. Not a crushed limb in sight thought Joan with relief. Renate was obviously popular with the patients. She knew them all by name and laughed and joked with them all as they made their rounds.

There was no time to 'settle in'. As soon as the Matron appeared on the ward it was all hands on deck and Joan was soon well into the swing of things. She was relieved that the hospital wasn't hugely different to what she was used to. She hadn't known what to expect but instantly felt right at home and able to get stuck in. She quickly learned that the majority of the nursing staff were volunteers, and as Captain Smetherick had said most of them wives and girlfriends of officers who had volunteered to avoid being evacuated. Most of them had never had to work before, and the difference in work ethic was immediately obvious. Joan sighed to herself; she knew that she was going to find this infuriating. It was not the case for all of the VAD's, the likes of Renate, but she did notice on several occasions throughout the day that the same small group of VAD's would gather together in corners whispering and giggling. She had no time or patience for the silliness that they seemed happy to fill their day with, especially when there was work to be done, and there was plenty of that. They were introduced to two other QA's, Miriam Godsell and Molly Gordon. They had been stationed at the hospital for a few months already and were busy changing beds on Ward 9.

"Welcome," Miriam said with a wave, "enjoy your first day. We'll probably catch up with you in the Mess later on. We can introduce you to the others then." Joan smiled and waved back, relieved that at least the other QA's were friendly.

There was no time for chit chat, the two nurses obviously had a lot of work to do and so Renate hurried along with her tour, leaving them to it.

Joan had never come across malaria before, and soon realised that the patients needed round the clock care just to keep their fever under control. It seemed like it was a bit of a race against time before the disease completely took hold. Renate told them that since the Japanese had embarked on its attack across Asia, it had become increasingly difficult to get hold of the much-needed quinine, an anti-parasitic medicine, which was the only treatment for the deadly disease. They had to make do with keeping the fever down with cool flannels as best they could before administering some of the much needed drug.

Renate introduced them to the 'Gin Drinkers' Ward' where most of the patients were being treated for the consequences of indulging in the less glamorous side of Hong Kong. None of them seemed in the least bit ashamed about their condition and most of them seemed to be enjoying the camaraderie and being waited on hand and foot.

"Why do you call it the Gin Drinkers' Ward?" Brenda asked Renate.

"Well, that's what we call the borderline where all the brothels are. That's where they will have enjoyed most of their time. There is not much for the soldiers here to do at moment apart from drink and get themselves into trouble."

Brenda and Joan looked at each other in surprise but did not say anything. There was obviously another side to Hong Kong, which seemed to go completely against the calmness and serenity that they had experienced so far. Joan couldn't help feeling a little disappointed in the soldiers, hardly shining examples of the Great British Army.

God help us if we have to rely on this sorry lot, she thought to herself.

At 1pm Gwen and Freda joined them for the afternoon shift; Daphne had drawn the short straw with the first run of night duty. Joan was a little bit relieved, as she still found that she struggled with Daphne on occasion and had, so far, found her to be an expert in just about everything. She hoped that they would find a way of working together without rubbing each other up the wrong way too much as she was quite sure the feeling was mutual. Luckily, Gwen was much easier to be around, full of infectiously contagious energy. The afternoon flew by and, before they knew it, they were handing in their shift reports and hanging up their nurses' caps for the evening.

They headed straight back to the Nurses' Mess for a much-needed iced water on the veranda. It was still so hot and humid, there never seemed to be any respite from the relentless heat. Both agreed that they had thoroughly enjoyed getting back into the swing of work after such a long break from real nursing during their voyage.

"So, what did you make of the lovely Mrs. Heywood then?" asked Brenda, mischievously eying her friend over her glass as she took a sip. Mrs Heywood was a government officials' wife who had volunteered as a VAD and had managed to get on the wrong side of Joan already.

"Oh, for goodness sake, do not get me started!" Joan sat up in her seat, "it is completely ludicrous that those women were allowed to stay, on the pretence of wanting to 'help the cause'. That woman has never had to work in her life. Did you see her nails? Perfectly manicured."

Brenda sniggered and allowed her friend to continue.

"I doubt that her husband is even that important, to hear her talk, you would think he was the Commander in Chief! How dare she hand me the laundry like I was one of her servant girls! I could barely speak I was so shocked. She didn't even utter a word; she just nodded me in the direction of the laundry room. Well, it won't happen a second time

I can assure you…" Joan's rant was interrupted by the appearance of Mickey.

"Good evening ladies, how are we?" He looked over at Brenda with a raised eyebrow and nodded in Joan's direction. "Is it safe to enter?"

Brenda laughed and got up to greet him. "Oh, don't mind her. She's just had her feathers ruffled by one of the VAD's today who clearly thought that doing the laundry was beneath her."

Joan realised Brenda had been teasing her and laughed as she too got up to greet Mickey. "Yes, don't mind me my dear, but her card is marked I can tell you," she winked.

Mickey laughed and said, "Well, we have our day at the beach tomorrow to take your mind off it all. My friend John has managed to get hold of a boat so we can go for a sail. Now, are you ready Brenda?"

"Oh yes!" She took Mickey's arm and followed him towards the steps leading down to the tennis courts, "I can't wait to see the beach! And a sail around the bay sounds more than fine."

"Yes of course, sounds wonderful." Said Joan as she cleared away the glasses. "I'm going for a nice long soak in the bath. I will see you two later." She waved them off as they headed for a walk around the grounds and was glad for some time to herself after her busy day.

She was very much looking forward to heading to the beach tomorrow. What a lovely way to spend a weekend. A Saturday back home would usually involve working or heading to the local market with mother and Alice to shop for meat and veg for the week. The afternoon would then be spent preparing meals and doing chores. She could only imagine her mother's reaction to a frivolous day of swimming and sailing at the beach. Oh how different life was!

The next day, they set out early. Joan could not believe the hive of activity that swarmed Repulse Bay. It seemed that plenty of other servicemen and women had had the same idea. Brenda looked over at her and said just what Joan was thinking, "Does nobody actually work here? Where have all these people come from?" Joan just laughed. Brenda looked decidedly miffed as they made their way down the rocky path towards the bay. The beach was littered with little groups all setting out their picnics or bathing in the crystal clear water. Mickey had arranged to John, who they had met on The Viceroy on their journey over to Hong Kong. He was bringing his friends' little boat Diana around from the harbour. The plan was that they were going to sail on to the next bay later in the evening, where there was a beach café with food and dancing. It sounded perfect, and it was.

They met up with Freda and Gwen and soon bumped into Molly, who they had met the day before, and two other QA's, Edith Butlin, who turned out to be the wife of the Officer that Dickie had got into a spat with the night before, and Margaret North. They all seemed very happy and settled into the colonial way of life. The group quickly settled into an afternoon of swimming and sunbathing.

"This is the life, hey Brenda?" said Joan as John expertly sailed the boat back around the bay towards the Repulse Bay Hotel.

"My word, isn't it just. Today has been heavenly. Who'd have thought it? Us two northern lasses living the life of Riley! Mrs Heywood might even by slightly jealous!" Joan's face clouded over for a moment at the mention of the name but then laughed. They smiled at each other and raised their glasses.

The following weeks were a whirlwind of work, parties, swimming at the beach, and more work. Joan had never been so exhausted or so exhilarated and happy. She had not had time to feel homesick or think about the life and friends that she had left behind. Every so often, she would feel a pang of guilt and resolve to write to mother. There just never seemed to be the time. But she needed to let her know that things were going well.

As the weekend drew nearer, it was clear that they were going to have to put off their plans for another time, as Brenda came down with malaria and was admitted to the women's ward at the hospital. Joan chose to work back-to-back shifts to make sure that she was there to check on her. There seemed to be a sudden influx of more malaria patients following a couple of thunderstorms that had hit the island the week before.

"Whips up the mozzies into a frenzy." Renate had said.

Thankfully, Brenda had recognised the symptoms straight away so, despite being poorly for a few days, she was in no danger. Joan thought that she was now actually quite enjoying being the patient for a change. It did make Joan realise how much she missed her friend whilst she was in the hospital and that they should be making the most of their off duty together. She sat down and wrote a list of the things that she wanted to see and do with the intention of ticking them off as she went. At the bottom of this list she made a note.

October 1940 - Brenda rather ill - many malaria patients

She wanted to remember as much as she possibly could and was all of a sudden aware of how quickly time was flying.

A week later she wrote;

15th October 1940 - off night duty - on days, called to matron's office, instructed to give course of lectures to the orderlies - shaking in my shoes!

Brenda, who was now out of hospital and on bed rest, laughed out loud when Joan told her about being summoned to the Matron's office earlier that day.

"Well, that will teach you to keep your thoughts to yourself on how the orderlies need more training in future," she laughed again, "what on earth are you going to write the lectures on? How to make up a bed properly?"

"I have absolutely no idea!" She had been completely taken by surprise by Matron, but had to admit that she had probably brought it on herself by complaining about the lack of basic training the VAD's had been given. Through no fault of their own, they seemed to have been given a uniform and left to get on with it.

"I might do an ABC guide to nursing," she said, "I may also enlist the help of Daphne and the other Sisters to help me pull the lectures together and make them a bit more interesting. What do you think?"

"Good idea, if you can get them off the tennis courts or the beach on their days off. I doubt you'll have them banging down the door to help. I would just do the basics and hope that Matron forgets about it soon."

Hmmm some hope, she thought as she started to mark on the calendar the number of days to the first lecture.

"Six days!" she said, "I've got six days to pull together what we learned in three years!"

"I don't think that Matron expects that level of detail my dear, just a few basic pointers would suffice I would have thought."

Joan looked unconvinced as she busied herself with her books and notes that she had brought with her. She was determined to be well prepared.

21st October 1940 - 1st lecture! About to start - S.M (Matron) announced all lectures cancelled for duration of war - relief!

The next few weeks, turned into months, Joan didn't feel like their feet had touched the ground. They were working hard, but there always seemed to be plenty of time for entertainment. Joan still smiled to herself when she was heading to the tennis club. She would now be able to tell the Army Matron, with confidence, that she was an accomplished player and took every opportunity to improve her game. Everyone played and she had thrown herself into the colonial lifestyle with great gusto. There was just so much to do. She was either playing tennis, swimming, or playing Bridge. The rest of the time was spent exploring, shopping, or going to dinner or dances with the odd trip to the cinema thrown in. Life was good.

"Do you know, Brenda," Joan said as she was getting ready for her night shift. "I'm going to have to start a diary so I can remember all of the things we have done and places we have been."

"Good idea," said Brenda as she stood looking in the mirror and putting on her nurses' cap. "I'd be hopeless at keeping a diary. I would always forget to write in it."

Joan smiled. "Well, I'm going to get us both one in the morning." she said, putting on her shoes, "we'll just have to try and remember what we've been doing for the past week!"

True to her word, the next day she arrived back with two pocket diaries. She threw one over to Brenda.

"Be a dear and put the kettle on, will you?" she said. "I'm parched and quite fancy sitting on the veranda, taking tea and filling in one's diary." Brenda laughed at Joan's exaggerated English accent.

"Of course my dear, what a jolly nice idea!"

Brenda brought out the tea and looked over Joan's shoulder at what she was writing.

"Goodness me, Joan!" she laughed "I don't think 'War & Peace' has got anything to worry about."

"What do you mean?" said Joan with mock hurt in her voice.

"Well, let's see," Brenda grabbed the diary and started to read

Weds 1st Jan 1941 - Had party at Mrs Butlins - quite good fun.

Thurs 2nd Jan - Tennis at H.S.R.C. with Poppy. Major Boyce & Capt. Head. Fri 3rd Jan - received cable from home."

She looked up at Joan who was smiling despite herself. She leant over to try and grab the diary back. Brenda snatched it away and continued, "no wait! It starts to get good...

Sun 5th Jan - went to tea at Punjab mess. Mon 6th Jan - Had dinner at the

Peninsular with Capt Head. Tues 7th Jan - Morning off. Had eyes tested. Thurs 9th

Jan - Out walking with Captain Head. Dinner at night."

Brenda looked over the table at Joan who was now rolling her
eyes.

"It might not convey much in terms of emotion and inner most
thoughts...but it does highlight how much time you are spending with a
certain Punjab Captain?? Anything you want to tell me?" She laughed as
she teased her friend.

"Don't be so absurd," said Joan, rather too quickly, "of course
there is nothing going on. We are just friends." She stood up and grabbed
the diary, "which is more than we will be if you continue to be so
ridiculous!"

She stalked into the dorm and put the diary in her drawer. She
had indeed been spending a lot of time with Captain Head but there was
no romance, although she did sometimes wonder whether he was as clear
about that as she was. He did seem rather keen to see her. He had been
out to camp for 4 days and had insisted on taking her to dinner as soon as
he arrived back. She would have to speak to him to make sure there was

no misunderstanding. That would never do. She was due to see him for dinner at the Peninsular Hotel later that week so she would speak with him then.

"You need a diary to just keep up with all of your social engagements!" Brenda called from outside. "Aren't you due to go to dinner with the lovely Mr Cockell this evening? It's actually becoming quite difficult to keep up with you." Joan knew that Brenda was teasing. Things were going so well with her and Mickey. It was nice to see her friend so happy. She had been worried that she would be left home alone most evenings but as it turned out, Joan was out most evenings having a right old time.

She made a mental note to get a try to get a day off together and tick off some of the things on her list, which seemed to be getting longer by the day.

Chapter 11

Finally, a rare day when both Joan and Brenda were not working came around. They were exhausted, not so much from the work, which they were both thoroughly enjoying, but from cramming as much as they could into each day. They had been promised that they would get more off duty once the rest of the nurses arrived. It felt like they had been working back-to-back shifts since they had landed. They now had a well-earned weekend off and they were going to make the most of it. They had planned to take the tram to The Peak and explore the mountains. Joan could not get over how much there was to see on this tiny island.

Joan was looking forward to going to The Peak, she loved seeing the fine-looking houses of the rich and elite of the colony and going from the hustle and bustle of the Queens Road, to the peace and calm of The Peak which looked over the colony with its own sense of superiority.

Yet again, war seemed a long way away. Joan almost dreaded seeing the soldiers on the streets as they were a reminder of why they were here. Even in the hospital, they were still only treating malaria and soldiers with their 'social' diseases. Joan was becoming less shocked at some of the life they had discovered in Hong Kong. She had initially been saddened at how people could make such a beautiful place feel so dirty. Hong Kong featured multitudes of sleazy women, corrupt officials, and

149

spies that were apparently dotted about all over the place, passing information to who knows where and who knows who.

The socialites, who seemed to have made a career out of organising Bridge Games and gossip and charity dinners, irritated her the most. They seemed completely oblivious to any war or any kind of suffering going on just across the border. They were most definitely not concerned about any impending attack, filling their days with nonsense and giving themselves an air of self-importance that made Joan cringe. What was the point? To have a feeling of purpose in this god-awful war?? Joan doubted it.

It was every man and woman for themselves and the war did not seem to have dampened the social climbing within the colony. She did not understand this side of human nature and she struggled to bring herself to try. She had her purpose and that was all she needed. Brenda was much more accepting of the grubbier side of Hong Kong. She loved coming home and telling stories of the Chinese baker who was apparently selling secrets to the Japanese. The tailor who was selling secrets to the British Intelligence…the list went on.

"Honestly Joan," she would say, "you could write a book on all of the dodgy dealings going on out there!"

"Who would want to read a book like that?" Joan asked. "There is enough reminder of the war and the dark side of humanity as it is. All you need to do is listen to the news."

"Blimey! You need to cheer up!" Brenda replied, picking up her bathing suit. "Come on, we are meeting everyone at the beach."

Joan never tired of Brenda's ability to shrug off the war and make light of all that was dark. Joan smiled and followed her. They were meeting friends in their favourite spot. The others were already there and the gimlets were already flowing. Joan said a quick hello before throwing down her towel and heading straight for the water. She was so hot. She was always so hot! She just could not get used to the humidity of the climate and despaired at how frizzy it made her hair, and at how all of her clothes clung to her as soon as she put them on. The coolness of the water was her only relief. She loved it here.

She climbed up onto the diving platform and dived in. She held her breath and stayed under the water for as long as she could. When she came up for air, she took a deep breath and looked out across the bay. She would never get tired of it. Something about the contrast of the mountains as the backdrop to the bay, always made her feel calm. She planned to paint it one day. Not that she could ever imagine having any spare time to paint.

She turned to look towards the beach and scanned all of the clusters of people for Brenda. When she spotted her, she noticed that their little group had been joined by some people that she did not recognise. She sighed as she started to swim back; she was not in the mood for meeting new people. Since she had been in Hong Kong, she had found herself more suspicious of people and definitely less tolerant. She couldn't help thinking that everyone was just out for themselves and getting what they could out of their fortunate situation in unfortunate circumstances. She found the whole thing quite exhausting. Thankfully, Brenda was always there as her wingman to do the chitter-chatter for her.

She swam towards the beach and headed towards the group. She squinted in the sun and noticed one of the new group was slightly older than the others. She recognised him from The Repulse Bay Hotel. He was stood in a crisp white shirt and tailored shorts. His had his hands in his pockets and was laughing at something that John was saying. Joan caught her breath and walked slowly towards the group. He was very dapper in his casuals. He was obviously an officer of some kind, an authoritative air hung about him. As she got closer, she caught Brenda's eye and nodded towards their new friend as though to say, 'who is this?'

Brenda immediately leapt on Joan and dragged her over, chattering excitedly in her ear. Joan heard nothing that Brenda was saying. She felt herself hold her hand out to shake hands and was vaguely aware of her introducing herself. She was more aware of what a fright she must look. She desperately tried to smooth down her unruly hair and tried to get herself dried off as elegantly as she could, not something that she was finding easy.

Joan heard nothing of the conversation, just the baritone of the stranger's laughter. His right cheek dimpled as he listened to Mickey's story about a monkey and some sort of talking bird, but Joan could hardly concentrate. Her mind was spinning in circles, and the air had been sucked out of her lungs. Realising she was staring at the new guy, she quickly busied herself with laying out the towel and settling herself down to sunbathe. She put on her sunglasses and tried to study his face. She had completely missed his name. All that she knew was that he was one of John's friends, so presumably in the Navy, and that he was Scottish. She listened to him talking and loved his accent. His blonde/brown hair was slicked back and his blue eyes had a sparkly glint of mischief about them. She tried to guess how old he was. Older than her. Nearly 30 maybe? She would need to ask Brenda later.

John appeared at her side and handed her a drink, and she gratefully accepted. John was obviously greatly amused by how uncomfortable she was looking.

"So, Forbes?" he asked, turning to the dapper officer with the twinkly eyes. Joan held her breath, *what on earth was he going to say? Please don't embarrass me*, she thought to herself, please, please. John continued, "where would you recommend for sightseeing on this old Island then? You've been here for a while now, you must be well in with the local establishments too I suppose?"

Forbes turned and smiled. *Oh blimey*, thought Joan, *he really does have the most perfect smile, and the most twinkly eyes...and that voice, I don't think that I would never tire of it.* She smiled to herself and started to relax. The gimlet was beginning to take effect and she began to feel more at ease. She looked over at some of the other girls and wondered how they managed to look so gorgeous and glamorous on the beach. She tried to arrange herself on her towel, lying on her back, propping herself up on her elbows. She looked over at Daphne who was doing the same whilst playing with the sand with her foot. Joan began to do the same. She tipped her head back and closed her eyes, taking in the sun and tried to lengthen her body to look as elegant as possible. She was not convinced that she was pulling it off but no-one seemed to care.

Forbes was in full flow about The Peak and Kowloon and some wonderful sounding places he had discovered since arriving in Hong Kong. She cleared her throat and asked, "So, how long have you been here then Forbes? You obviously love it." There she had said it and she didn't think that she sounded too much of a fool either. Forbes turned his full attention to her. *Oh Lordy!*

"It is truly amazing," he said. "I still feel like I have only scratched the surface of the place. I got here in Nov 1938. Dropped lucky I suppose, although I'm not sure what use an accountant would be on the

Frontline so they thought they'd stick me in an office over here for me to try to make sense of the banking system," his eyes were smiling as he spoke, "I still haven't figured it out so I suppose they're letting me stay on until I do!"

Much to Joan's dismay their conversation was now centre stage. Brenda threw herself down next to Joan, shuffling herself onto her towel to get off the hot sand.

"So, where would you take a couple of nurses in need of a night out on the tiles? Somewhere fun, not with the usual stuffed shirts and Matron glaring at us from a corner somewhere!" Brenda asked, her eyes dancing with mischief. Again, Joan held her breath praying that Brenda would not.... well, be Brenda!

Forbes laughed, "Oh there are plenty of places," he said. "The Jockey Club is always worth a visit..." Joan groaned and rolled her eyes. Brenda immediately jumped in to answer Forbes and his quizzically raised eyebrow.

"Joan can be a terrible bore and will not just smile sweetly and enjoy herself," she said quickly, "she finds most of the wives and 'friends' most infuriating and terribly irritating."

She was laughing now doing her best impression of Joan. Forbes laughed and thankfully looked impressed.

"Well, that my dear, is something that we already have in

common." He bowed his head and raised his glass to Joan; she thought that she might faint. *Get a grip Whiteley!*

Chapter 12

After meeting Forbes at the beach, Joan had a long and busy day at the hospital. She was helping to look after the new orderlies and so had volunteered to do extra shifts. Her meeting with Forbes had greatly unsettled her but, despite feeling that she had probably made a complete fool of herself, she could not get him out of her mind.

At the end of their shift, Joan and Brenda were sitting on the veranda with a cup of tea when he appeared, looking suave and relaxed in his shirt and shorts. He beamed at them as he approached. Again, Joan was horrified at what a fright she must have looked! He didn't to seem to mind. He went and helped himself to tea and sat down alongside her like it was something they did every day. Brenda made her excuses and left them to it giving Joan a knowing look as she made a great show of being tired and needing to get some sleep.

Joan's stomach was in knots as she desperately tried to think of something sensible to say.

"Hope you don't mind me just dropping in on you like this?" he said as he looked out at the view. "I bumped into Daphne and she told me what time you were clocking off. I enjoyed meeting you at the beach yesterday. I hope I'm not being too bold?"

Well Daphne could have warned me! "Of course not, it's a very pleasant surprise. You'll just have to excuse the appearance."

"You look quite lovely my dear, don't worry about that."

Freda and Gwen then arrived at the Mess to get their evening meal. Both raised their eyebrows and gave an approving nod as they walked past. Forbes smiled. "Well, it'll give them something to talk about over dinner at least."

Joan laughed. *It will indeed* she thought, surprising herself at how relaxed she felt. Normally, the thought of being the centre of any gossip would get her into a bit of a lather. But she didn't care. She was very happy that he was here.

They talked for hours about home, family, work, Hong Kong, the locals and their struggle with the Japanese. Forbes seemed to be extremely well informed and had been in Hong Kong long enough to have worked out what made the colony tick. She loved that he listened to her and answered her questions without making her feel foolish. Something that she had found rare in the men she had met so far.

She was relieved to learn that he shared her opinion of the blatantly obvious, but seemingly accepted class segregation within the colony. Everyone had a label and their place in society. He told her about the Chinese *coolies* who worked so hard as servants and tradesmen, all hopeful of a better life for their families. The *Taipans*, Eurasian merchants, who had firmly integrated themselves within civilised society as influential businessmen, were seemingly desperate to be considered in the same class as the British businessmen and government officials. It seemed that they were constantly trying to climb the social ladder and be accepted amongst the 'Peakites' and top tier of Hong Kong society. Joan had observed this during her many visits to the Hong Kong Hotel, a place which she did not enjoy but found completely fascinating.

The *Taipans* or *Big shots* as Forbes called them would seem to congregate there for business meetings and social gatherings. They were always surrounded by elegant Eurasian women who hung on their every word, knowing that any moment they could be discarded for another younger, more attractive, version of themselves. Joan found it all completely superficial and sad to watch. They talked on and on and the fatigue of the day disappeared as they spent a very easy evening together.

The following day, she was on duty with Daphne who wasted no time in trying to get the gossip.

"So Joan, have you seen the dashing Mr MacLeod again since the beach?" She asked as they made up beds for the latest influx of patients, knowing full well that he had called on her the day before. Joan decided to play it cool, she didn't want to appear to have gone silly over someone after meeting them for the first time and she certainly didn't want Daphne gossiping about it.

"Oh Forbes? Yes, he's quite a dear. He called on me yesterday." She busied herself with fussing over invisible creases in the sheets, well aware that she was blushing.

"Well I'm glad. He's quite the catch. Some of the girls are really quite envious. He seemed very taken with you," Daphne threw over a pile of folded sheets and continued, "be careful though, you know what these older men are like. Always have a few skeletons in their closets."

"Well, I'm not sure that you can class him as an older man. He can't be more than 27!" Joan immediately felt flustered by Daphne's comment.

"Well, I'm just saying. He's been here a couple of years and is not attached and has never been associated with anyone in particular." Daphne looked at Joan pointedly. "I'm just saying be careful my dear." She gathered up the dirty laundry and turned on her heels towards the laundry room.

How does she manage to do that every time? thought Joan, agitated by the comments. *Did she do that on purpose? Did she know something? There may be something in what she had said?* As irritated as she was by the comments, she could not get it out of her mind for the rest of the day.

She told Brenda of the conversation over dinner that evening. Brenda waved her hand dismissively.

"Oh just ignore her Joan, she's like a smiling assassin. She just said it to torment you. I'd say it is probably her that is 'quite envious'. Don't give it another thought. She'll be proved wrong soon enough."

Joan smiled. *Thank God for you.*

Over the next couple of weeks, Joan did her level best to make sure she was too busy to take Forbes up on one of his many invites. She was determined to not appear to be too keen.

"Well you're most definitely doing that Joan!" Brenda had said to her after Joan had turned down yet another invite to dinner. "I don't understand you at all. He's a thoroughly decent chap and you enjoy his company. I don't know why you are running away from him and instead accepting every other invite that comes your way. I thought you liked him?"

"I do." Joan protested, "It's just I don't want him to think that I'm like the other girls, falling all over him."

Brenda laughed, "Well, no chance of that my dear! If I were him, I would have given up long ago. I hope you are not still thinking about what Daphne said?"

"Well, I can't pretend it hasn't crossed my mind."

"Look," Brenda paused while folding a sheet and looked at her pointedly, "we are all going to a party at The Hermitage on Wednesday. Forbes will be there. Why don't you come along? At least then it's not a date and you can then make your mind up as to whether he is a dreadful, philandering, heart breaker."

Maybe she had been a little bit excessive in her attempt to be cool and aloof? She was already looking forward to seeing him and hoped that he hadn't given up on her just yet.

The Hermitage was a private hotel not far from Bowen Road. Joan liked it because it was less pretentious than the Hong Kong Hotel or The Jockey Club. She was always far more relaxed and loved the view of the hillside and magnificent mountains beyond from the main bar. She arrived after the rest of the group and had made a determined effort to look like she'd made no effort at all. She wore a plain white dress, nipped in at her tiny waist by a navy blue belt. She wore flat navy pumps and had swept her hair back off her face. She looked healthy and relaxed and turned more than a few heads as she walked through the bar. She saw Forbes immediately. He was in deep conversation with Mickey and did not see her as she walked in. She went over to Brenda who was stood with Molly Gordon and Freda.

"Here she is!" Brenda exclaimed. "I thought you'd decided to stand us up. Let's get you a drink." She led Joan over to a table laid out with glasses of champagne. "It's not real champagne, but it's close enough." Joan took a glass, feeling surprisingly nervous. "Don't look so worried, nobody is going to bite."

No sooner as they had returned to the group, Forbes appeared at her side.

"So? Found a window in your busy schedule then?" He winked and smiled at her and she instantly relaxed.

"Well, yes," she smiled back. "Things have been a bit hectic but have hopefully settled down now."

"Glad to hear it." Forbes replied. "So you'll be free for a drive around the island on Saturday then?" Joan could feel Brenda's eyes burning into the side of her head.

"Yes, that sounds lovely." She replied, shooting a triumphant look over at Brenda who laughed and shook her head. She had been completely flummoxed by Joan's reaction to attention from Forbes. She could only think that it was because she did really like him. The pair did not leave each other's side for the rest of the evening. As soon as Forbes left to go to the bar, Brenda was by Joan's side. "So? How's it going? Has the great wall you had built around you started to crumble yet?"

Joan laughed. "Pleased with yourself?"

"Of course! I think I'm allowed a little smug moment don't you?" Brenda lowered her voice and said. "So, is he a terrible philanderer then? Or maybe he's a spy? That must be it! He's a Secret Service spy and so has never been able to get involved with a woman for fear of her getting caught up in his web of lies and deceit!"

"Now you're being absurd, of course he's not a spy! And I know

I have been a bit ridiculous so I promise I will try to relax and just go with it from now on."

"Amen to that." Brenda said, chinking her glass against Joan's just as Forbes arrived back to the group.

"So, what are you two whispering about then? Should my ears be burning?"

"Absolutely!" Brenda was about to go on until Joan gave her a gentle dig in the ribs.

"Absolutely not!" Said Joan, giving Brenda a silencing look. "We were just saying how much we prefer it here to the pretentious Jockey Club."

"I agree ladies," Forbes looked at Joan, "you will have to let me take you to The Peninsula one evening. You would love it there."

"That sounds lovely, thank you."

Brenda gave Joan a knowing wink before disappearing off to try find Gwen and Freda who were supposed to be arranging a tennis game for the following day. Joan watched her disappear and smiled. She knew she was in for a whole lot of 'I told you so's.

As promised, Forbes arrived on Saturday with a light picnic and full itinerary of places they were going to visit. Joan was immediately aware that there was nothing that she could do to stop herself from falling for the man who stood in front of her, opening the car door motioning for her to get in. She decided there and then to stop trying and just enjoy. Who knew where this god-awful war was going to lead them so she had succumbed to the fact that she should make every effort to just enjoy every minute.

After that, they spent all days off and available hours together. He took her on his own tour of Hong Kong and Kowloon. They went to Lantau Village and the Ping Yang Floating Docks. He took her to his favourite restaurants, introduced her to his friends, and took her to Navy dinner dances. Their feet didn't seem to touch the ground and they quickly became an established couple.

As a group of friends, they spent the most perfect days at a waterfall and lagoon at Silvermine Bay. He made her feel safe in the still alien surroundings. Joan felt like she was in a dream.

They had had the most wonderful couple of weeks and it was as though she had known him forever. She sometimes had to pinch herself to remind herself that this was all real. Daphne's words had long since been forgotten.

Chapter 13

Brenda and Joan had managed to get another day off together and had planned to have a girlie day shopping to add some home comforts to their dorm. Joan noticed that Brenda seemed far less enthusiastic about their day than she had the night before.

"Are you not feeling well Brenda?" She asked. "You're not at all your usual self."

"No, I'm fine, don't worry. I think I'm just tired. A day of shopping is just what I need." She gave a slight smile. Joan wasn't convinced but said nothing as they got themselves ready. It was another ridiculously hot and humid day so it was a relief to not have to put on their nurses' uniform and put on their civvies. They headed off arm in arm down towards the Queens Road. More and more used to the hustle and bustle of the city, they were far more confident in haggling with locals. There was always a better price to be had and it was expected that you had to negotiate and put up a bit of a fight before agreeing to hand over any precious Hong Kong dollars. It was something that the girls usually enjoyed and had become quite competitive at who was able to get the best price. Today, Brenda most definitely seemed distracted and was very quickly becoming bored and irritable in the unrelenting heat.

"Joan, let's go and get some lemonade and have a sit down." She said, already sounding weary.

"Good grief woman, we've only just got here!" Joan laughed, "What's the matter with you today? Late night last night?" Joan nudged her playfully but Brenda was in an unusually grumpy mood.

"Oh dear," said Joan in mock exasperation, "I think it's going to take more than lemonade to put a smile on that face!"

The girls bought their lemonade from a toothless, but very smiley, Chinese shopkeeper and went to find a bench to sit on further down the road.

"Let me tell you about my wonderful day yesterday. Forbes and I took a picnic over to the hills. Did you know that there are tunnels that run all the way through the hillside? You can actually walk, or crawl, through from one side to the other if you fancied!" Joan said excitedly.

They found a bench and sat down. Joan was talking nonstop about Forbes. Brenda didn't seem to be listening.

"Oh for goodness sake Brenda," Joan said, beginning to get exasperated with her friend. "I thought you'd be pleased for me? I've had to listen to you prattle on about Mickey for the past six months..."

"It's Forbes, Joan. He's engaged." Brenda said, flatly. Cutting Joan off mid-sentence. "I'm so sorry, but he's engaged. Mickey told me last night. It seems that he has a little redheaded sweetheart back home in Glasgow." Brenda sighed and shook her head. "I am so cross with Mickey for not telling me sooner but, sadly, he is not the most observant and had assumed that you knew. I don't know what Forbes' game is, but I'll be giving him a piece of my mind when I see him! I feel just terrible for pushing you together like I did, especially after what Daphne had said."

For the second time since meeting Forbes, the air was sucked from her lungs. Of course he was bloody engaged! Why wouldn't he be?! He was certainly old enough and what reason did he have to tell her?? She barely knew him! What a complete fool she was for getting so excited. He was obviously quite the charmer after all. Why had he NOT told her he was engaged and not available? That was surely a little misleading after the time that they had spent together and the many conversations they had been having about home and their families. Not once did he mention a sweetheart.

Joan frowned and said, "He hasn't said anything about her at all. Why would he not mention her to any of us?" Tears were stinging her eyes. "Well, that's that then." she said, her voice catching in her throat.

"Oh Joan I'm so sorry. I know that you liked him. I've never seen you like that before," Brenda smiled, "it was actually quite nice to see you smitten and ridiculous for a change." She took Joan's hand. "I know you're disappointed but I had to tell you."

"Well, I did think it was all too good to be true. What a complete cad. Why did he not just tell me?? I feel such a fool!" Joan shook her head. She put her hand on her forehead and closed her eyes, cringing at how she had behaved and how she had let herself believe that they might be more than friends. How would she feel if she was the fiancée at home and her man was off sightseeing and out for dinner with another girl? She would not be happy, that is for certain!

"Oh Brenda, what an idiot I am."

"No you're not. Far from it. He's the fool if you ask me." Joan straightened her back and took a deep breath.

"Yes, he most certainly is! And you know what the worst of it is?" She looked over at Brenda, "Bloody Daphne was right!"

Despite themselves they laughed but Joan's stomach was in knots. What on earth was she going to do now? They clearly couldn't see each other again. He had made her feel so special and had hinted at spending more time alone. He hadn't come across as being a cad at all. He had been the perfect gentleman. *Just shows what I know* she thought, *I should have gone with my gut instinct and ran a mile.*

They sat in silence for a moment before Joan jumped up and pulled at Brenda to get up.

"Come on, I'm not going to let it spoil our day. There is shopping to be done and bargains to be had." She forced a smile and the girls spent the next few hours wandering the streets and markets, not looking for anything in particular but mostly marvelling at the strange and exotic sights that were all around them. They could buy anything from pearls to elephant tusks to the most exquisite and intricate wood carvings. They wandered along Queens Road and came across a set of stalls that worked themselves up alongside a flight of steps at Aberdeen Street. Joan thought the buildings were just beautiful with their ornate roofs and bright colours. The air was filled with the sweet and enticing aroma coming from the sugar cane and hot doughnut stalls.

Like most of the other street vendors, the sugar cane vendor was elderly and Chinese with a big toothless grin. The girls stood back and watched him, fascinated by the theatre involved in selling his wares.

"One buy, one look!" he would shout at confused passers-by. Most would stop though, captivated by the sweet smell. Once the negotiating was done, and a sale had been agreed, he would take a knife and expertly strip the sugar cane of its tough outer skin and drop it into a bucket of boiling water to soften the cane enough to chew. The smell was amazing, and combined with the smell of the soap stall next to him; it was difficult to pass without being drawn in like bees to honey.

The girls graciously declined his fervent offers of 'one buy, one look' and spent a lazy couple of hours window shopping before they decided to head back to the Nurses' Mess at the hospital. As they were walking back, they came across a stall that they had probably passed every day and never noticed. Joan's eye was immediately drawn to a beautifully carved camphor wood chest. She ran her fingers over the expertly carved top. She looked over to the stall owner who was watching her with interest.

"Did you carve this?" she asked.

The man shook his head and pointed over to a young Chinese boy who was sat on the floor behind the stall busily chipping away at a large block of wood. The boy looked up and nodded proudly. He could not have been more than 13 or 14. Joan and Brenda looked at each other in surprise.

"It really is very beautiful," Joan said to the boy, "you are very clever."

The boy smiled and said with a cheeky grin, "You like it? You buy it." He looked away quickly and returned his attention to his carving, still smiling.

The elderly stall owner laughed and walked over to Joan and Brenda.

"You want to buy?" He asked. "Good price, good price I do for you."

Joan knelt and took a closer look at the traditional Chinese images of cherry blossom, Chinese figures, temples, and junks carved into the chest. She took a deep breath and took in the scent of the wood. It had an almost medicinal smell. It reminded her of home and the chest rubs that her mother would put on them all when they were unwell as children.

"What is a good price?" she asked him. The Chinese boy looked up from his work expectantly.

The stall owner was now clearly very excited at the prospect of a sale and was babbling at Joan in rapid Chinese. He lifted the shiny brass lock and opened the chest, motioning for her to look inside. He was making gestures to indicate storing blankets inside or clothes. Joan looked over his shoulder at Brenda who was rolling her eyes and beckoning her to walk away. She laughed and turned back to the Chinese man.

"So? How much is a good price?"

"50 dollar I do for you." He said, still waving his arms and pulling her to look at other side of the chest.

Joan looked at him with mock horror.

"50? No, no I'm sorry" she shook her head and started to walk away. The boy jumped up from his stool and ran over to Joan.

"Please Miss, you buy...I bring." He was pointing up the hill towards the hospital nodding at her in earnest.

"Oh for goodness sake, what have you got us into here?" Brenda said impatiently, walking over to Joan and taking her arm to pull her away. As she started to pull Joan's arm all three of them shouted, "No no no!" at Brenda. She let go and held her hands up in surrender.

173

"Ok ok! Good grief!" She laughed and looked at Joan. "Well, go on then, hurry up and do your deal you crazy fool, then we can get going! I am so hot, I think I might actually melt!" She said, fanning herself with her hand.

Joan was determined to buy the wooden chest. She had already justified the cost in her head, she definitely needed storage space in their tiny dorm but it was the smell of home had sealed the deal for her. After a few more minutes of negotiating she had bought the chest and the little Chinese boy was going to deliver it to their quarters later that day.

She walked back over to Brenda, full of smiles.

"Well, that was a very successful little shopping trip my dear!" She said, putting her arm through Brenda's as they walked back to the hospital.

"At least it took your mind off old whatshisname," Brenda said.

Joan's face clouded over for a moment.

"Can we please not mention old whatshisname?" she said in an especially haughty voice, "I wouldn't want to ruin a perfectly lovely day!"

They both laughed, although both were well aware that the news of Forbes' engagement had bothered Joan more than she would care to admit.

Weds 30th April

174

Wrote home I couldn't help putting a little of my fedupness into the letter

Always feel such a cad at complaining

May 1941

Thurs 1st May *

Had afternoon shopping & rummaging expedition. Strange what a tonic effect this has on me. I felt in the depths of depression when I set out but after buying 2 worthless articles I felt much better! I wrote a more cheerful letter home

Fri 2nd May

Went to see "Mrs Dot"-by Somerset Maughan. Given by the Y.M.C.A extremely well done. Went on to the 'Gripps' afterwards - hate the place.

Sat 3rd May

Feeling absolutely frightful in fact could scream.

Into town to try on dresses.

Sun 4th May

Sailing!

Joan had discovered a love of sailing and was eternally grateful to the boys and their friend Bill for having acquired their little yacht, Diana, and she took them up on every opportunity that she could to go off around the bay and the islands. Her favourite time of day was coming back into Victoria Harbour at sunset when the sky and the water turned the most stunning shades of orange and crimson. The lights from the bobbing fishing boats made it feel almost magical. Joan was always at her most relaxed when out on the water and had taken to try to sketch the many incredible views and landscapes. She could get completely immersed in her drawings and any thoughts of Forbes were forced from her mind.

Chapter 14

It was a few weeks before Joan saw Forbes again. She had made sure she was busy working, playing tennis or anything where she already had plans whenever he asked to see her. She had thought long and hard about what she would say to him, but when the moment came she was completely lost for words. He had bounded up the steps to the nurses dorm. Full of smiles and laden down with picnic paraphernalia. He had a picnic hamper and blanket under one arm, a bottle of wine in the other.

"I thought that you couldn't possibly be able to brush me off again, so I have come prepared!"

He walked over to Joan to plant a kiss on her cheek. Joan was taking clothes from the clothes line and turned away to busy herself with folding her uniform, leaving his kiss hanging in the air.

"Come on Joan, I know you are cross with me, although I'm not sure why?" Forbes asked, setting down the basket. "It seems an age since I last saw you. Thought we could make a day of it?" He was already sounding less certain, clearly reading Joan's body language.

"I'm sorry Forbes," said Joan, "but I can't come with you today. I'm very busy and don't think that it is altogether appropriate."

"Appropriate??" laughed Forbes. "What on earth do you mean by that?"

177

He sat himself down on one of the wicker chairs on the veranda outside the dorm and looked at Joan quizzically.

"Have I done something wrong?" he said, trying to catch her eye.

Joan just wished that this moment was over and that he would just go. Whilst she had not seen him she had managed to stay indignant and cross about the fact that he had not told her about his fiancée, who she now knew was called Mary.

She had set Brenda the task of finding out as much as she could about the fiancée waiting patiently at home (not that she had needed much encouragement). What she had found out was quite shocking. Forbes and Mary had obviously been sweethearts for many years. Mary had had a huge falling out with her parents and had moved in with Forbes and his family. The only way that this could be acceptable was for them to be engaged to be married. Forbes' parents had insisted on it before taking her in. She had apparently lived in the family home in Bishop Briggs in Glasgow for a couple of years before Forbes took the posting to Hong Kong. The plan was for him to get settled and she would follow. He had been in Hong Kong now for 2 years, with no visits home and no plans to bring Mary over. Joan had found this very strange yet was secretly pleased, but she still had to find out exactly what the situation was and whether she had indeed made a huge fool of herself. She turned to him and said,

"Tell me about Mary." She had tried to sound matter of fact but knew she had not quite managed it.

"Ah," Forbes said, standing up. He stuffed his hands in his pockets and couldn't have looked more uncomfortable. He looked at the floor and began kicking at some moss that was growing in the cracks of the veranda with the toe of his shoe. "I'm very sorry Joan; I suppose I do owe you an explanation."

Fury bubbled in her chest.

"No Forbes, you do not owe me anything. You clearly feel that it is nothing to do with me, and that I shouldn't concern myself with the fact that you have a fiancée back at home. I do find it rude and a little absurd that you had not mentioned it to me in all of the time that we have spent together. You have made me look and feel like a complete fool." She was trying hard to keep her voice level and not let it crack with the tears that she could already feel building up.

"I really am sorry Joan," he said walking over to her, "the last thing that I would want to do would be make you look or feel like a fool." He stood in front of her and looked at her intently. "I never meant to deceive you or to mislead you in any way. It's complicated but I think that I do indeed owe you an explanation." He was suddenly cheerful again and walked over to the picnic basket and picked it up.

"Come on," he said holding out his hand, "let's go to the beach and at least not waste the picnic. I will tell you everything you want to know."

"No," said Joan firmly, "I don't think that is a good idea. I think it is better that you just go." She turned her back to him and carried on busying herself with hanging out the washing. Her heart felt like it was going to beat out of her chest!

The door of the dorm opened and Brenda appeared. She had been listening to the exchange from inside and whilst she was proud of her friend for standing her ground, she also knew that Joan would regret it if she didn't hear him out. Mickey had stopped her from interfering and giving Forbes a piece of her mind, instead she had stood back and watched Joan put a brave face on it but on hearing the exchange between the two she had to save her stubborn friend from herself.

"For goodness sake Joan, just go and listen to what he has to say." She was picking up Joan's beach bag, putting it in Joan's hand and practically pushing her towards Forbes. Joan turned and looked at her in surprise. Brenda ignored the look, "worst case scenario is that you just don't have to cook for yourself today. You never know you might actually enjoy yourself!" She turned to Forbes with a scowl, "That said - you had better have a bloody good explanation Mr MacLeod."

With an extra push from her best friend, Joan found herself walking down the steps reluctantly following Forbes towards the beach.

They walked to the beach in silence. Joan had no idea what to say, and Forbes was clearly busy cooking up his story. When they eventually got to the beach, they automatically walked to their favourite spot and again, without saying a word, started laying out the picnic. Joan couldn't help smiling to herself at the effort that he had obviously put into it.

The bread stick was still warm. He had managed to get hold of real butter and some delicious looking cooked ham. There were different cheeses (one of them smoked - *where did you even get smoked cheese from in wartime Hong Kong??* she wondered) and enough fruit to feed a small army. Forbes was pleased that she was at least a little bit impressed by the efforts he had made and started to relax a little. He pulled two glasses out of the hamper followed by a chilled bottle of white wine. Joan did not really like wine but did not want to seem unsophisticated or ungrateful. He had obviously gone to a lot of trouble. Clearly a sign of guilt, she thought to herself crossly.

Forbes poured the wine and handed her a glass. She took a sip and tried hard not to pull a face. It was so sweet and syrupy. Not at all appropriate for an afternoon on the beach she thought, but who was she to talk about what was sophisticated and what wasn't? She had never even tasted wine before coming out to Hong Kong. Forbes laughed and said,

"You don't need to drink it if you don't like it, my dear. I have brought some lemonade just in case." Joan breathed a sigh of relief and filled the rest of the glass with the lemonade.

"There you go," she giggled, "white wine cocktail!"

Forbes smiled back at her before taking a deep breath.

"Look," he said, "I know you are upset with me and I completely understand why. I don't know why I didn't mention Mary to you. I just didn't want to spoil the lovely time that we were having. I can see now how selfish that must appear."

Joan bristled at the mention of her name. Forbes cleared his throat and quickly went on to tell Joan the story.

Mary came from a much poorer family in Glasgow. She had tried hard to break away from them and was putting herself through university to do her accountancy exams. That was where they had met. She was a fiery red head and he had been charmed and impressed with her spirit and determination. They had quickly become good friends. They started to study together and Mary began to spend more and more time at his parents' house. She got on well with his parents and they became very fond of her. He was also fond of her and found it difficult to hear of the stories she would tell of her father beating her and her brother taking any little money that she earned from sewing and doing alterations, for drink and who knows what else. After one night when Mary had turned up at the house black and blue from the latest beating, he told her she was never going back. That was how they became engaged.

His parents were not so much traditionalists but his mother was an active member of the church and he knew what was expected in terms of respectability. He did not love Mary in the way that he should, but he was fond of her and felt very protective towards her. Until now that was enough for him.

Joan became aware that he had stopped talking and was looking at her, searching her face for some kind of reaction.

"What do you mean until now?" she asked. She was almost embarrassed to ask, but every inch of her body was tense in anticipation of his answer.

"What do you think I mean, Joan?" He looked uncomfortable and was picking up sand and letting it fall through his fingers into a pile in front of him.

"Well, I'm sure I don't know," said Joan, suddenly all flustered and ready to just pick up and leave. It was only the thought of having to face the expectant Brenda when she returned to the dorm that she stopped herself. "Why don't you tell me?" she said, all of a sudden brave. "Why don't you tell me and whilst you're at it, why don't you tell me why you thought that it was ok not to mention this to me before?" She tried to steady her voice. Forbes turned to her and looked her straight in the face.

"Never for one moment did I think that I would meet someone and fall in love with them," he went on without letting the stunned Joan get a word in. "I thought that if I told you, you would immediately insist on a chaperone or worse still, refuse to see me." He looked at the floor and said quietly. "I really did not mean to be deceitful, or to mislead you in any way. I just wanted to spend time with you and the more I did, the more I realised how wrong I was about just settling for what Mary and I had, when I was beginning to have feelings for you." Joan opened her mouth to speak. He put his finger to her lips and said, "Just let me finish..."

Joan sat back down and realised that it was all that she could do to just breathe. There was no chance of her making anything resembling a graceful exit so she resigned herself to just sit there and listen.

"I had promised myself that I would look after Mary and, if I'm completely honest with myself, taking the post to Hong Kong was a way of avoiding the situation. I have never really admitted this to myself or anyone else but I was hoping that by the time I went home I would be able to do the right thing and get married and make everyone happy." He sighed and shook his head slowly. "I have made every excuse in the book to avoid going home or for Mary to join me here." He looked at Joan and took her hand. "I didn't know why until I met you."

"Well that's ridiculous." she said, not making eye contact. "You hardly know me." She looked out to sea and frantically tried to gather her thoughts.

"Of course I know you," he said. His voice was soft and he sounded almost vulnerable. "I feel like I have known you forever and I have always known deep down, that I didn't feel the way I should for Mary. I think that she would say that she felt the same. We worked for a time because we needed to. She needed to get away from her family and I could not stand by and let her go home to the same abuse night after night. I thought that would be enough. Like I said, until I met you." He sat up and tried to catch Joan's eye. "I did not expect to have any feelings for you. I did not expect to have any feelings for anyone. All I do know is that I cannot stop thinking about you and all I want to do is get to know you more and spend more time with you." He let out a deep breath. "I think we have the makings of something great here. Who knows what will happen over the next few weeks or months but I do know that I would regret spending every available moment that I have left with you."

Joan heart was racing. This was not what she had been expecting at all. She looked at him and said,

"I just don't know what to say."

"Good," he said, leaning over, "then don't say anything." He looked at her and kissed her gently on the lips. Joan pulled away.

"Muriel Joan Whiteley," he said with amusement, "I promise not to do anything to dishonour you in any way. I will write to Mary and tell her everything."

Joan pulled herself together.

"Well, Forbes MacLeod, you had better." Her eyes were smiling but her tone gave away the fact that he had to stand by his word. He cleared his throat and said,

"I give you my word Muriel Joan, that I will sort this out at my earliest convenience."

"You'd better," she laughed, "and if you call me Muriel again, there will be hell to pay!"

Forbes leaned over and kissed her again. This time she responded and let herself relax. She knew in her heart that he was telling her the truth and trusted that he would stand by his word.

The next day Forbes wrote to Mary and to his mother to tell them of his feelings for Joan. Whilst waiting for a response, Joan and Forbes spent a blissful few weeks exploring Kowloon and New Territories. There was no doubt in either Forbes' or Joan's mind that they were meant to be together, but until they heard back from Mary, neither of them could move forward. Until then, they had to hold back and just enjoy being in one another's company. Time was flying by so fast that Joan barely had time to write in her diary and when she did, there seemed so much to write. She hoped that writing brief notes to herself would be enough to remember the wonderful time that she was having.

She was sat on her bed reading through the entries that she had made about her trip to Landau. They had had the most amazing time, despite some shocking weather. She couldn't wait to go again.

July 1941

Tues 1st July

Set off at 6pm having been on duty until 5pm. Typhoon signal came down about 3pm

Sailed away - spent first night Junk Bay. Bought eggs here.

Weds 2nd July

Port Shelter. Bought ice.

Simply marvellous weather. Having a grand time.

Thur 3rd July

Clear Water Bay

Fri 4th July

Started away for Junk Bay. Swarmed with flies so decided to go back home. Arrived mess 10pm. Typhoon signal up.

Sat 5th July

Weather very bad. Set off 10am for 11am ferry to Lantau. Waited about all day. Met Bill Nicholl. Eventually got away at 4.15am. Silver Mine at 6pm. Got up to mess 8.30pm stiff climb. Very happy and very wet.

Sun 6th Jul

Mist mist & more mist

Had service in mess. Swam afterwards. Country danced at night.

Mon 7th Jul

Went walk both heels off shoes.

Thurs 10th July

Went walk. Waited for Bill Reame on trail.

Fri 11th Jul

Hike to perfect pool. What a day! What a place - simply marvellous.
Set out at 10.30am and back 6.30pm

She sat reading the notes back to herself, satisfied that they were enough to bring back the memories of a fabulous summer. It was now October and she was still in short sleeves and sandals. Joan thought of the grey and grim Octobers back home and smiled to herself. *I wonder if I will ever get used to this crazy place and its crazy climate?*

This particular week, there had been great excitement amongst the nurses. Miriam and Teddy had announced their engagement. Joan smiled again as she wrote in her diary. Things happened so much more quickly here. It would certainly have been frowned upon in normal circumstances, but it was a welcome distraction and there was lots of excitement about the impending wedding.

Sat 4th Oct

2-5 off

Learn that Miriam Godsell & Teddy Beman are engaged - great excitement. I do believe every one of us is envious!

Sun 5th Oct

½ day

Spent afternoon with MacLeod. Had a walk & dinner at Southcliffe. Lovely time. Met Miriam & Teddy Beman at Lido. Toasted their good health & happiness.

Mon 6th Oct

Off 5-8

Went to dinner Forbes MacLeod.

The arrival of Major Edith Dyson had caused quite a stir amongst the QA's. She brought with her a formidable reputation of being very strict and forthright. Joan was surprised when they met the tall, striking woman. She seemed far more personable than they had been led to believe but her first shift at the hospital soon confirmed how she had reached the position of Major at such a young age.

"How old do you think she is?" Brenda asked after her first shift with the Major.

"No more than 30 I would have thought." Said Joan, "She is certainly whipping us all into shape that's for sure. The poor VAD's don't know what has hit them!" Brenda laughed.

"Freda is arranging a welcome party for her tomorrow night, are you going to go?" Joan rolled her eyes. "Well, can you imagine how it would look if we didn't go?"

"Exactly," said Brenda, "I'm going just to avoid the grief I would get from Freda if I didn't!"

"Goodness me! Can you imagine?!" Joan laughed, "I'm sure it will be fun."

They arrived at the party when it was in full swing. Major Dyson looked happy and relaxed and Freda was in her element as hostess.

"Where have you two been?" She hissed at them as they walked in, "your absence has already been noted."

"I'm quite sure it hasn't my dear," said Brenda giving the flustered hostess a peck on the cheek. "We wouldn't have missed it for the world." She gave her best smile. Freda gave her a playful nudge, "Oh just go and get a drink, and don't forget to actually speak to the guest of honour!" She turned and disappeared into the crowd.

"Does she think we are children?" said Joan, already irritated by Freda.

"Oh Joan, she doesn't mean anything by it. I find her quite amusing. Come on let's get a drink and enjoy the evening." She linked Joan's arm and led her towards the bar.

They joined the group surrounding Major Dyson in time for them to hear that the stern Matron was engaged to be married and was currently waiting for news about her fiancé who was stationed in Burma. She hadn't heard from him in weeks and was clearly concerned in a very British 'stiff upper lip' way. Joan couldn't imagine how it must feel not to know where Forbes was and whether he was alive or dead. It was just unthinkable. The thought completely unsettled her. She looked at the matron and was in awe of how composed and together she was. She couldn't help thinking that if the worst happened, they were in good hands.

Tues 7th Oct

Took an appendix in theatre - not too good.

Weds 8th Oct

Had my 2nd violin lesson. Very keen but oh my - will I ever manage it

Have to practice 2 hours daily!

Took an appendix! (2nd)

Feel terribly tired.

Thurs 9th Oct

5-8 off

Out with Forbes

Fri 10th Oct

Day off. Can't make up my mind what to do!!

Spent wonderful day out with Forbes! Swam in the morning. Lunch at Fanling.

Walked. Dinner at Peninsular - finished off at The Ritz!!

Sat 11th Oct

Out to the films. Way Down Rio!

Sun 12th October

¹/₂ day

Spent pottering here & there - catching up on washing and such like.

Chapter 15

Joan loved the time that she and Forbes spent together. She loved how they talked for hours about anything and everything. She loved how well he knew the Island and how much he wanted to share it with her. She even loved to listen to him talking about politics and his views on the war. He seemed to know a great deal. So much so, it sometimes worried her that he was more involved than he let on. He assured her that wasn't the case. He had just made lots of friends in high places who loved to talk. And he listened. Joan thought that she needed to stop listening to Brenda and her conspiracy theories about spies and dodgy dealings.

They had decided to go to The Peninsular for lunch before Joan started her night shift that evening. Joan had now become more accustomed to the lavish lifestyle that she was leading. At one point, she would have seen lunch at The Peninsular as an unnecessary extravagance, now she just took it in her stride and thoroughly enjoyed being treated to such wonderful experiences. They had finished lunch and were having coffee. Forbes had been in an unusually sombre mood, clearly distracted by something. Joan hadn't pushed the issue and had hoped that he would relax over lunch.

"You seem more relaxed than earlier," she said, "is everything ok?"

Forbes flashed her one of his smiles and replied, "My dear, an hour in your company would cheer any man alive."

"Oh stop it," she laughed. "I'm being serious, it's not like you. Is everything ok at work?"

"Yes," he sighed and reached for his cigarettes. "We're just in trying times that's all. I find it frustrating that we are just expected to sit and wait for attack and then just do the best we can with what we have." Joan said nothing and let him continue. This wasn't like him at all.

"Last month Churchill obviously had a moment of clarity and finally acknowledged the position that we are in, and agreed to send more troops to fortify the defence lines and at least give us a fighting chance. I heard this morning that those plans have now been cancelled and even the tanks that were on their way to us have now been diverted."

"But I thought that now we were on high alert that defences were being strengthened. They were down at the beach yesterday putting more barbed wire down there. It makes it look so ugly and sinister."

"I know. We're doing what we can, but our troops add up to no more than 14,000. From what I have heard, the Japs have more than double that with far more resources at their disposal." He took a long drag on his cigarette, "Everyone is still pointing all our defences at the sea. If the buggers come at us with an air raid attack or from the mainland, we're sitting ducks I'm afraid. I don't know how long we could hold out."

He looked at Joan who was now looking decidedly worried. Talk like this always made her blood run cold. "But let's not worry ourselves about it all today; let the powers that be worry about it." He grabbed Joan's hand and gave it a reassuring squeeze. "Shall we take our coffee outside my dear?"

Joan smiled, "That would be lovely. I have just spotted Betty and Freddie. I will just go and say a quick hello. I will meet you out there." She took a deep breath as she walked over to her friends, glad of the break in conversation. Forbes was normally the one to reassure her but he was clearly worried.

Forbes made his way outside and scanned the tables for a spare seat, when he heard a familiar voice call out.

"Forbes old chap, over here!" He looked over to see Archie Smetherick and his wife sat at a shaded table. Archie was an old friend and Forbes was immensely pleased to see him.

"Come and join us old man, what a pleasant surprise!" Archie turned and waved to one of the waiters standing by. Without a word two chairs were brought to the table and it was immediately laid with coffee cups and a steaming jug of freshly brewed coffee. The two men greeted each other with affection and Mrs Smetherick stood to give him a warm hug.

"Sit down, sit down." Archie said gesturing for Forbes to take a seat.

"If you're sure we're not intruding?" Forbes asked.

"Not at all, not at all. Who are you here with?" Archie asked just as Joan appeared in the doorway looking for Forbes. He caught her eye and waved her over. Joan's initial look of confusion turned into recognition and a wide beaming smile as she weaved her way between the tables towards them.

"Well well," Chuckled Archie, standing to greet her with his arms outstretched. "Just Joan! How the devil are you?" Mrs Smetherick also stood and gave Joan an affectionate hug.

"Captain Smetherick! It's so lovely to see you." Joan gave him an affectionate squeeze and took her seat. "I thought that they'd shipped you off again as I haven't seen or heard from you."

"No such luck I'm afraid," He chuckled. "It must be months since we've seen each other my dear," he said turning back to her. "I feel quite the rat for not getting in touch, there is obviously much to catch up on!" He said jovially winking over towards Forbes.

"Well quite right too, I have been sat waiting for my invitation to Casa Smetherick for some time, I had almost given up!" She teased.

"Well, it's this blasted war thing. Keeps a man quite busy these days!" Archie replied. "Even Martha has been caught up in it all now that she's got herself an official position as a driver for the Red Cross. We hardly see each other. She's busier than me!"

"Ah so that's why I haven't seen you on the golf course recently then?" Forbes asked. "I thought it was because you were tired of being humiliated." He smiled.

"I will choose to ignore that remark. So, you two are an item then I see?" He asked. "How wonderful! I couldn't have put two more suited people together. I don't know why I hadn't thought of it myself. Although…" He stopped himself short of asking about Mary to avoid putting his foot in it.

"Don't worry, Captain. There is nothing dishonourable going on here. I have written to Mary and broken off our engagement."

Archie laughed with relief. "Thank goodness for that, I thought I was going to have to fight for the lovely Joan's honour for a moment."

"So? How do you two know each other?" Joan asked.

"Oh we go way back. I knew Forbes when he first joined up in Glasgow. I was stationed there for a while. It was me who recommended him for the post out here, which I think has suited him quite well."

Forbes nodded and smiled "It was indeed, so you have him to blame Joan."

"Oh I don't know that blame is the right word." Joan replied shyly.

"Well you must both come to dinner then!" said Martha. "You would be most welcome. We haven't done any entertaining for an age. It would be nice to dust off the silverware. What do you think Archie?"

"Absolutely! We've both been so busy; I just don't know where the time has gone. We should do it soon too before this bloody war is upon us."

"I take it you know about our boys being sent to Singapore instead of here then?" Forbes asked.

"Yes, I know." replied Archie, more serious all of a sudden. "I think Churchill must feel like he's just moving pieces around on a games board at the moment. I'm not sure I envy the job of trying to second guess the Japs and Hitler at the same time. I do know that the Canadians have volunteered some of their men so they will be a most welcome addition to our troops and swell our numbers."

"Really?" said Forbes, "well that is good news."

"Indeed," nodded Archie, "on their way as we speak apparently, so should be here in a matter of weeks and not before time too."

Forbes raised his eyebrow, "Do you know something I don't Captain?"

"No no, not at all," said Archie shifting slightly in his seat. "The Canadians arriving will be a huge boost to the colony - those of us that know there is a war going on that is!" He looked around him and gestured towards the smiling couples and groups of friends sat around them. "Anyway, enough of boring these lovely ladies with the war. Why don't we meet up for a game of golf and you can humiliate me once again!"

Forbes laughed and said, "That, old man, is a date."

Chapter 16

Fri 17th Oct 1941 - Dinner with Brenda, Mick, and Forbes

Joan had not seen Forbes for a few days when he turned up at the Nurses' Quarters dressed in full uniform. Joan gasped at the sight of him. He looked so handsome with his tanned skin and sparkly blue eyes.

"Come on my dear, I'm taking you to dinner." he said offering him her arm.

"But I'm not dressed for dinner," Joan replied, her hands going straight to her head to try to tame her unruly curls. Forbes laughed, "You obviously look lovely as you are but yes, I think that a change of outfit might be in order."

Brenda appeared from behind her, holding out a very elegant looking silk dress, smiling like the Cheshire Cat.

"Try this on for size," she said handing Joan the dress. Joan gasped; it really was the most beautiful dress she had ever seen. Cut in traditional Chinese style with a Mandarin collar and 3 silk covered buttons at the shoulder. It was oyster coloured with a stunning print of butterflies and birds, almost flying upwards from the hemline. It was clearly cut to skim the silhouette; Joan had a fleeting fear that it may not fit her. She reached out and touched the silk.

"Oh my," she said," I absolutely love it!" Where on earth did

203

you get it?" She turned to Forbes who was also grinning from ear to ear.

"I had a tailor friend of mine make it. His wife picked out the fabric and Brenda stole one of your dresses for sizing and kindly picked it up for me today. I'm rather pleased with it. Now, go and try it on for size."

Joan leaned over and kissed his cheek as she took the dress from Brenda and rushed inside to try it on. Brenda followed. On Joan's bed Brenda had laid out shoes, bag and hosiery and a sparkling jewelled hair grip. Joan looked at her and laughed.

"I should be cross at you for conspiring against me! But just look at this," she smoothed down the fabric of the dress and did a twirl. It fitted perfectly.

"I love it. It's so unusual. Nothing like anything that I would ever normally choose." She looked down at the intricate design, admiring the colours and the work that had gone into it. It came to just below the knee and looked perfect with the silk pumps that Brenda had picked out for her. She looked at her friend who was now fixing the hairgrip into place.

"I am lucky to have such a wonderful friend. Thank you so much."

"I agree," smiled Brenda, "I searched high and low for those blasted pumps!"

The girls laughed and hugged. Brenda broke away first and said gleefully, "you're not so lucky that you think you are getting the night to yourselves though! We're coming with you!" She laughed and linked her friends arm, leading her outside where Mickey was stood smoking with Forbes. He let out a long whistle as the girls made it out onto the veranda.

"Wowzers, aren't you two a sight for sore eyes." He scooped Brenda up and kissed her. In all the excitement, Joan hadn't even noticed that Brenda was already all dolled up. She took Forbes' arm and the four friends headed down the hill.

Joan took a deep breath as they rounded a bend that opened up the view of the sparkling sea with the fishing boats bobbing around in the harbour.

"Now that is a view that I just never get tired of." She said. The others nodded in agreement.

"We are so lucky, I sometimes have to pinch myself that I am here - who else gets to see sights like this each night?" Joan cast her eyes to the ground as she thought of home. What were they seeing right now? Certainly, nothing as spectacular as this. She missed them terribly and decided that she would write to them the next day.

"Come on birthday girl," Forbes laughed and pulled her along, "we have dinner reservations!"

"But it's not my birthday until next week!" Joan exclaimed.

"Well, we're celebrating early. Who knows what will happen between now and then! We're seizing the moment!" Brenda said as she linked Joan's other arm.

The four friends chatted away until they reached the restaurant on Murray Street. It was a traditional Chinese restaurant that Joan knew was usually frequented by businessmen and government officials. She frowned as they walked through the door, wondered why on earth Forbes had chosen here?

As they walked in, there was a full party in swing. Forbes was immediately greeted by a short, middle aged Chinese man and his wife.

"Welcome, welcome." said the man waving them inside. He shook Forbes' hand and bowed to the ladies. He ushered them through the crowded restaurant talking in an animated fashion to Forbes. As far as Joan could make out, it was his daughter's birthday and they were throwing her a party. The restaurant was decorated with pink and white cherry blossom. Joan spotted a petite, shy looking Chinese girl who she guessed was the birthday girl, surrounded by friends and family. She bowed her head as they passed her. Brenda whispered to Joan,

"Don't look so worried Joan, it's a party!"

"Oh I'm so confused! I have no idea what is going on!" she held on tightly to Forbes' hand as they were led through the restaurant and out onto a stunning terrace. It looked magical with hundreds of tiny lights and cherry blossom trees, overlooking the mountains on the other side of the harbour. It seemed so peaceful and the sunset glowed in shades of orange and pink. Joan closed her eyes, thinking that she wanted to remember this moment forever. They were shown to a table at the edge of the terrace. Forbes introduced Niu and his wife Mingzhu. Mingzhu was as graceful and elegant as only the Chinese can be. She was tiny, so petite and dainty that Joan felt like a clumsy giant in her presence. Forbes started to explain that Niu was also the tailor that had made Joan's dress and that Mingzhu had carefully selected the fabric. Joan nodded her thanks.

"Niu invited us to her daughter's birthday party, and of course I could not refuse such a kind offer." He bowed his head in gratitude to Niu.

"So, how do you gentlemen know each other," Mickey asked as they took their seats.

"Niu is the best tailor in town!" exclaimed Forbes, "and this is the best Chinese restaurant in town." Niu laughed and clapped Forbes on the back.

"And this gentleman is the best accountant in town," he said in perfect English and winked at Joan. Joan smiled and looked over at Brenda who was giving her a knowing look. Joan frowned and wondered what on earth she was doing - then she remembered Brenda's comments about the corrupt tailor selling information to the British Intelligence.

Joan laughed at her friend and shook her head; she was the most intolerable gossip. She decided to ignore Brenda's more fervent nods and gestures and instead turned to Mingzhu and said,

"Thank you so much for your part in my fabulous new dress. The fabric is wonderful, I don't think that I could have chosen better myself."

"It is my pleasure madam; I am so pleased that you like it." With that she gestured for Joan to take a seat before giving a tiny bow and disappearing back to the party.

The foursome took their seats and proceeded to be presented with enough food to feed a small army. Forbes leant over to Joan and said,

"It's a traditional Chinese banquet, there are 12 courses; something that swam, something that flew and something that crawled, followed by Shark Fin soup."

"Wow!" said Brenda who had been listening intently, "what a wonderful tradition! I can't wait."

Joan could not believe the amount of food and the number of expensive delicacies that were included. It almost felt wrong to be indulging like this during wartime. There were dishes of pork, pigeon, beef, fish and poultry with a huge bowl of fried rice in the middle.

"Goodness! I have never seen so much food!" exclaimed Joan,

"Isn't all of this awfully expensive?" she whispered.

"Don't you worry my dear," he leant over and whispered, "I helped my friend there straighten out his accounts so this is his way of saying thank you," Joan nodded and smiled again at Brenda's over active imagination. Forbes sat back up in his seat and said, "And we are celebrating, so dig in!" The two men winked at each other just as Niu appeared with a tray of champagne flutes. Joan had not tasted real champagne since Bill's 21st birthday. What a treat! What on earth were they celebrating?

There did not seem much to celebrate at the moment. The colony was still on high alert of an attack and there was an 8.30 curfew in place at the hospital. The tension could be felt across the colony. But as they sat here in such a magical and opulent setting, it was hard to imagine that the war could come to them. Joan was determined to enjoy every minute and not think of the infernal war.

Forbes was now handing out the glasses of champagne to everyone and stood up to make a toast. He cleared his throat and looked at Joan,

"Well, I never expected to come to Hong Kong and meet such a wonderful girl. There I was, happily minding my own business and you come along and turn my world upside down." He smiled and Joan rolled her eyes. "And I'm very glad that you did. I want to cherish every moment that we have and celebrate all our special times together with our good friends."

He turned and nodded to Brenda and Mickey, "So tonight I thought it fitting to celebrate some news that we have been waiting for, for some time." He paused for dramatic effect and took a sip from his glass. Joan rolled her eyes again, "Oh do get on with it, the suspense is killing me!" She had an idea that it would be to do with Mary but she was not expecting what came next.

"Ok," Forbes said, clearing his throat, "I had a letter from Mary yesterday. She sends us her best wishes and shared the news that she is engaged!" He raised his glass in congratulations,

"To Mary!"

"To Mary!" They all chorused. Joan clapped her hands together in excitement and pulled Forbes down to his seat.

"So, she is ok and all is fine?" She asked nervously.

"Yes, his name is Frank and seems like a good chap. He apparently proposed as soon as they got my letter." He cleared his throat again and took another nervous gulp of his champagne whilst reaching into his jacket pocket. "I wanted to mark the occasion with something special. I hope you like it." He placed a small brown leather box in front of her. She looked at him, eyes wide with surprise and pushed the small button on the front of the box to open the lid. She gasped as it opened.

Brenda strained to get a better look whilst being pulled back by an amused Mickey, shaking his head at her obvious intrusion into their moment. Inside the box was the most exquisite pearl ring. Joan had never seen anything like it before, it was just perfect. It was a simple gold setting with three perfectly egg-shaped pearls set on a diagonal. Joan lifted it out of the box and put it on to the ring finger on her right hand and held it up to admire it in the light.

"Oh my goodness Forbes, it's gorgeous. I love it." She leant over to kiss him on the cheek. "I can't believe it. What a perfect evening." She was beaming from ear to ear.

It was now Mickey's turn to stand and clear his throat to make a toast.

"Congratulations, to you both. I'm so pleased that things are coming together for you after a bit of a shaky start." Forbes nodded his thanks and raised his glass.

"We are so pleased to be here with you both this evening and thought that it would be a good time to share some news of our own. This wonderful and clearly foolish young woman has agreed to be my wife. We are engaged and plan to marry in the New Year!"

Beaming down at Brenda he continued, "We are going to celebrate in style at the flat next month, but in the meantime, wanted to share our good news with you." He raised his glass and they toasted their good health.

"Congratulations to all of us and more happy times to come," said Brenda.

"Congratulations!"

A shout of 'yum shing', meaning 'drink it all' came from the party in the restaurant. The foursome looked at each other and laughed. "Yum Shing!" They all shouted.

Joan could not have been more thrilled, it was simply the best evening. Brenda and Mickey's news was wonderful but the fact that Forbes was now free of his responsibility to Mary and the fact that they themselves could now start to make plans for the future was just too wonderful for words.

As the 8.30 curfew loomed, the two couples took their own paths back to the hospital. Joan felt like she might burst with happiness, she had never been so spoilt in her life and she was enjoying every minute of it. As they walked Joan asked about the letter from Mary.

"To be honest she sounded relieved," said Forbes, "she has already moved out of my parents' house and moved in with him. I'm pleased for her." He stopped in the middle of the street and turned her towards him.

"I'm happier for us," he said "we can finally move on and I can finally do what I have wanted to do since the first moment I laid eyes on you." He lifted her chin towards him and kissed her, slowly and intently. Joan thought she might faint but let him scoop her into a tight embrace. The world around them had slowed and it was only the two of them standing in the busy street.

He eventually let her go and looked deep into her eyes. Without another word, he took her hand and led her with purpose back to the dorm; she followed in silence, her heart ready to pound out of her chest. They got inside and he locked the door behind them. He looked at her and smiled. He pulled her towards him, held her close and began kissing her softly, planting delicate butterfly-like kisses on her cheeks, her forehead, and finally her nose before kissing her on the mouth. It was the kind of fairy-tale kiss that all girls dream about.

Joan could barely breathe, her stomach was flipping somersaults and her legs felt like they would give way any minute. She pulled away from him and put her hands on his chest, looking up at him but did not say a word. He smiled again, his eyes conveying the longing that he felt. He reached and tucked a bit of stray hair behind her ear.

"You are so very beautiful Joan Whiteley. I will never get tired of looking into those lovely eyes. They truly are the windows to a beautiful soul. I am the luckiest man alive." he said softly, almost in a whisper. Joan stopped herself from telling him not to be so ridiculous and instead reached up and took his face in her hands and kissed him slowly.

"And I am the luckiest girl in the world." She replied, shyly reaching out to turn out the light. Later that evening, she wrote in her diary;

'And the trumpets were sounded

And the walls of Jericho crumbled and fell'

And I fell like a stone in a pond for a certain Mr MacLeod

Chapter 17

Sun 26th Oct - Day off. Had a lovely day. Betty Chart Fry & Bill. Michael came out at night & I had a birthday party. Forbes gave me pearls.

It was Joan's birthday and they had arranged to go to her favourite restaurant at Southcliff hotel. She had been working double shifts and was relieved to have a day off to relax. Brenda had arranged to meet the boys at the restaurant and for the girls to have a drink at the Sisters' Mess before they went.

Gwen and Daphne were the first to arrive, bringing the champagne glasses from their room with them, closely followed by Freda and Miriam who had managed to get hold of a bottle of sparkling wine. As the drinks were poured, Brenda proudly presented Joan with a carefully wrapped present.

"This is from all of us, Joan. Happy Birthday my lovely!"

They all watched as Joan tore open the paper and pulled out a black leather-bound photo album.

"We know you have been busy snapping away since we've been here." said Miriam, "so we thought you'd like it."

"I love it! Thank you all so much!" She ran her fingers over the embossed cover, tracing the traditional Chinese image of a temple and cherry blossom trees and a Chinese junk boat. "I can't wait to fill it. What a lovely idea!" Joan was thrilled and grateful for the thoughtful gift from her friends. She had been feeling homesick all day and this had cheered her up no end. They finished their drinks quickly and headed towards the restaurant where there was a little party waiting for her.

When they arrived, Forbes greeted her straight away and before she had even sat down had presented her with a flat, square black box.

"Happy birthday my dear." He said kissing her on the cheek.

"Oh Forbes, you shouldn't have after giving me my beautiful ring." She just couldn't believe how spoilt she had been. She sat down and opened the box. Inside was a lustrous set of pearls with a diamond clasp. She looked at Forbes and gasped. "Oh my goodness! They are stunning Forbes, thank you so much." She said as she lifted them from the box.

"They are to match the ring. I hope you like them."

"How could I not? They are simply gorgeous." She took them out of the box and handed them to Forbes to fasten them around her neck.

"My my," whistled Daphne, appearing at their side. "Would you look at them? What a lucky girl you are, Joan."

The girls all gathered around and fussed around her new necklace. Joan looked around, she couldn't ask for a better group of friends. She had never felt so happy. She would write home tomorrow to tell mother all about her amazing birthday.

Tues 28th Oct - Dinner in the mess as farewell party for Miriam. Spent lunch time with Forbes buying a wedding present

Weds 29th Oct - Wedding Miriam & Teddy. Very nice.

Despite the excitement of the wedding, there had been more talk of the Japs getting closer and there was a now a constant air of tension. Military activity had been stepped up and the boys were busy carrying out their exercises to make sure they were ready for an attack. Everywhere you looked there were soldiers with their guns, mainly guarding the government buildings but their constant presence altered the mood of the colony considerably. A wedding was a welcome distraction and the QA's loved the excuse for them all to get together. It was just lovely that Miriam was now married, Brenda engaged, Joan happily settled with Forbes. How things had changed for so many of them since arriving.

Joan had promised herself that she would write home and on her next full day off. So, put off tennis by the unusually wet weather, decided to sit down and fill the family in on all of her news.

"So, what do you think of this?" Joan said to Brenda who was sat opposite, waving the delicate notepaper in the air to dry the ink.

Brenda stopped scribbling her own letter to listen.

Hong Kong 12.11.41

My dear mum and dad, Alice, Harold and Janet, Edith, Les, David,
Mary and Bill (wherever he is) Auntie Emily,

Christmas greetings to you! May you be happy and a Happy New Year to
all. After much pondering, I decided that a combined letter would be better than many
cards after the disappointing effort last year when all my home going mail was lost. I
have received Christmas cards from several people already. I have also received a very
beautiful book. You certainly know my failing for books and the choice is excellent.
Thank you all very much.

Brenda and I are off together this afternoon she is sitting on one side of the
table writing and I am on the other, she bids me thank you very much for the card it
was a very pleasant surprise.

I hope you had my recent letters telling you the collapse of the Whiteley front,
in other words Forbes. How would you like a Scotch son-in-law?

This weekend brings many new faces to swell the numbers here I wondered if
I might see one familiar one from Canada but there seems very little hope. I wonder why
he has gone there?

Don't you think this is jolly note paper?

Tonight is a black out and will be the first night for a month that I haven't been out. Don't worry I don't have a late night every night, invariably just a walk, you see no home to go to sit comfortably chat makes such a difference, we have to either sit in the hotel, go to pictures or walk, so as I said, we walk. I'm now trying to save up to get things made and so on, so you see how I feel about the whole thing.

There has been a big change in the weather this last day or two, terribly cold, my good old tan has seen the light of day again-a real good stand by!

I went to an amateur theatrical show last weekend, it was excellent, the week before to a chamber music concert, gone all high brow! Not really because I didn't enjoy it terribly – only went because it was in aid of China Medical Relief and of course Forbes took me!

Last Sunday F and I went to Chapel, it being Armistice Sunday. On Tuesday the 11th he had a day off and I had a half day so we sallied forth into the new territories, he has an old standard car which rattles and bangs its way round. I as a great concession am allowed to drive it - I haven't got a driving license.

Do you remember me telling you I had bought a camphor wood box? Well, I sent it back last week with a very sticky note, the camphor wood lining had warped, so next wednesday I am delving deep into the Chinese quarters to a factory where I hope to procure another one. I must do that or buy a tin trunk as the wet weather is almost upon us and things begin to go mouldy.

Our staff here is being increased quite considerably but I can't tell you more of that until later.

All goods are becoming very expensive, I am apt to look on a dollar as being

1/1- whereas it is really 1/3. I had to pay 25 dollars for a very plain hat for the wedding, the difficulty is of course we can't get goods from either UK or USA at least once every blue moon.

I had a very nice letter from Miss Young last week which I haven't yet replied to. I was sorry to hear Mother dear that your eyes had gone off, are they any better?

Ok, what a wonderful day here, letters and a cable! Imagine that. A letter from Bill and a snap. Three from mum, two from Auntie Emily, one from Dad, and one from Edith. Tonight F and I went a walk and on my return, I found a cable to say you have received a parcel. I am thrilled about that and most anxious to hear about the contents - if they were in good order - I hope so. I'm glad everybody seems to be fairly well. Bill sent me a lovely letter and a gem of a snap. I'm anxiously waiting to see where his next move will be. He looks a tough old lumberjack in the snap.

I must close this to-night ready to mail in the morning and I want to find a snap or two if possible to enclose.

Once again I wish you all the happiness you deserve, enjoy to the full what circumstances will allow.

Good bye for now,

All my love

Joan xxx

kisses for Janet

kisses for David

Joan looked up. 'Do you think I've been a bit too cryptic in parts? I don't want them to think that I have completely lost my head over Forbes but to know that I'm serious about him. What do you think?"

"I don't think it's cryptic at all. Who has gone to Canada though? Bill?"

"Yes, I think that's where he has gone anyway, maybe I'll take that out - I'm not sure that mother even knows that he might be headed to Canada. It might worry her. Have you told them about the engagement?" She asked, turning her attention to Brenda's letter.

"Yes, I'm struggling to know what else to say though." Brenda sighed. "Everything else sounds so forced, I'm not sure I'm being very reassuring. Maybe I should do this another day?"

"Reassuring about what? The war?"

"Yes, the boys were talking at the flat last night and were all excited about the Canadians arriving. They were saying that it's just to show the Japs that they would have a hell of a fight if they chose to attack. I'm just not convinced. Surely drafting in more soldiers means that someone knows there is something going on? I mean, we have cut off their oil, and tin, and steel, I believe. If I were the Japs I'd certainly be thinking about fighting back against the West. How are they to survive otherwise?"

It wasn't often that Brenda was so serious about the war but she was clearly worried. She decided not to tell her of the conversation that she had been having the night before. Forbes was saying that the Japanese may well have cottoned on to the fact that now that the railway route was cut after the fall of Canton, Hong Kong harbour was being used to smuggle munitions, and whatever else they could, into China via the junks. If the Japs took Hong Kong, and control of the harbour, then China would likely to be put into a helpless position and agree to terms of surrender. This made complete sense to Joan; of course they would want to take control of Hong Kong and its borders. It would strengthen their position against China and start a fight with Britain to negotiate getting their trade deals reinstated. The more she thought about it, Archie was right. It wasn't a case of if, but when.

"Well regardless of why they are here, I think we should be thankful that they are. It can only be a good thing surely, whether we get attacked or not." Joan said finally. "I agree it is difficult to be cheery all the time. Maybe just tell them about the engagement and the Tin Hat Ball and of our scary new Matron?"

"I suppose you're right, but aren't you worried? I'm terrified of Mickey going to fight. He is itching to see some action though, of course, but I am afraid for our boys. It would certainly seem that our fun in paradise is about to come to an end."

"Oh my goodness Brenda!" exclaimed Joan, "this isn't like you at all! Snap out of it and we'll go and see who is in the Sisters' Mess for a game of cards. I don't feel like doing much else in this weather." She pulled on a cardigan from her wardrobe and looked out of the window of their dorm. It was dark and gloomy outside and the temperature had dropped. "It certainly looks like our sailing trips might be done for the year."

"Oh, I forgot to tell you. The boys have had to sell the boat. Something about settling some debts. What a shame though. Maybe we should think about buying one of our own?"

Joan could not believe that the little boat Diana had been sold. Now she really did need cheering up!

Chapter 18

The day that the Canadians arrived in Hong Kong there was a Carnival like atmosphere. People had lined the streets to welcome the soldiers as they marched triumphantly, proudly holding the Canadian flags.

Joan, Brenda and Molly had gone to Nathan Street to see them arrive.

"My goodness," said Molly, "look at how young some of them are! Just babies!" Joan had to agree, some of them looked like they'd just left school. They couldn't have had much military experience.

"Well they are here, at least, and they look fresh and ready for whatever the Japs might throw at them." She said.

"Let's hope so Joan, let's hope so." said Brenda, almost to herself. The mood in the colony had most certainly lifted and the recent air of tension seemed to subside. Even the Chinese coolies were looking on with interest at the troops making their way through the streets, bringing with them hope and a renewed confidence.

The Canadians themselves looked like they had hit the jackpot and landed in paradise. Grinning from ear to ear and walking like they were 10 feet tall.

There was much to celebrate that week as Brenda and Mickey announced their engagement at Mickey's flat. Joan, Brenda, and Daphne had spent the afternoon shopping for new dresses and food for the party.

"I'm just so jealous." Daphne had said, "First Miriam, then you, next it will be Joan. Why do I keep meeting the wrong ones?" She threw her head back in mock anguish. "I'm destined to be an old maid, left high on the shelf whilst you gals are busy having babies!" Joan and Brenda shot each other a look.

"Well, Daphne darling, if you didn't get bored of the poor boys after five minutes, you might have more chance of getting a ring on your finger." Brenda said, giving her a friendly nudge.

"That is very true," agreed Daphne, "there are just so many to choose from and now the Canadians have arrived, I will need more hours in my day!" The girls laughed, knowing she was only half joking. There was nothing Daphne would have wanted more than for someone to sweep her off her feet. As it was, she kept her dance card full and didn't give any poor chap a chance.

The engagement party was a great success. Everyone had made a real effort. The boys in full uniform, the girls in their finery. All thoughts of war disappeared for the evening. Mickey had saved some sparkling wine and made a toast.

"I'd like to thank you all for coming. I know it's been a busy few weeks for everyone all told, so my fiancée and I would like to thank you for taking the time to join us for our little celebration!" At the mention of the word 'fiancée' the room erupted into cheers. Mickey motioned for Brenda to come and join him and put a protective arm around her.

"I truly am the luckiest man alive." He continued, "Never in my wildest dreams did I think that I would meet my best friend and soul mate on this tour of duty. I can honestly say that my time here in Hong Kong has been the best time of my life. I have met the love of my life and some of the best friends a chap could hope for. I will cherish these memories and look back on this time that we have had with great fondness."

"Bloody hell mate, you're not doing a farewell speech. We're supposed to be celebrating!" Shouted Dickie from the back of the room. "Charge your glasses people and 3 cheers for Brenda and the very soppy Mickey! Hip Hip!"

"Hooray!"

"Hip hip!"

"Hooray!"

"Hip hip!"

"Hooray!"

"In all seriousness," Dickie began, "many congratulations to you both. I can't think of a couple better suited." He looked over at Teddy and Miriam. "Well apart from you two obviously!" He laughed. Forbes cleared his throat beside him. "And of course you two…"He looked around the room for help but they all just laughed at his sudden discomfort.

"To Brenda and Mickey!" Forbes shouted raising his glass.

"Brenda and Mickey!" They all chorused.

Chapter 19

The next two weeks went by as normal. The turn in weather had stopped the trips to the beach and most of the outdoor activities. Time passed in a blur of work and it was becoming obvious at how ill equipped the poor Canadians were for their tropical posting, especially in the hospital wards, which rapidly filled with cases of malaria and diphtheria. The nurses soon learned that the troops had not been given any malaria injections, or any kind of training for tropical warfare. One saving grace was the arrival of Nursing Sisters Kay Christie and May Waters. Joan liked them both immediately. They were no nonsense, get stuck in kind of girls. Just what the hospital needed. They had enough VAD's and orderlies who were afraid of getting their hands dirty.

To introduce them to the sights and sounds of Hong Kong, Daphne and Freda invited them to the Peninsular Hotel for drinks. There, they met up with Mickey and the boys and they were soon joined by Forbes and Archie Smetherick who had spent the day on the golf course, despite the cold weather. Joan was pleased to see Forbes; she had been working nights for the past week so had hardly seen him.

He greeted her with a huge bear hug and kiss on the cheek. Whispering in her ear, "Missed you Whiteley."

She smiled shyly at him. Her eyes telling him she felt the same.

The group were in high spirits and the evening was spent swapping stories and filling the Canadian nurses in on all the colony gossip.

"There aren't really spies in the colony are there?" asked Kay. "The Chinese nurses were telling us all about it earlier; it all sounds a bit cloak and dagger." At this point Brenda butted into the conversation.

"Oh my dear, you would not believe the goings on." She said looking over her shoulder dramatically. "You just don't know who to trust. Mickey is convinced that the barber at the Hong Kong Hotel is a Japanese spy." She nodded her head at them all, waiting for them to process before going on, "and I heard that there is a jeweller in Wanchai and I'm quite sure some of the waiters here are far too interested in our conversations."

Joan laughed and rolled her eyes. "Brenda, do you hear yourself? You sound unhinged. You can't suspect everyone of being a spy."

"Oh yes I can," she narrowed her eyes and looked hard at Joan, "come to think of it, where have you been for the last few nights?" She couldn't hold her stern face and the group broke into laughter, "I will definitely say though - you look at that barber next time you are at the Hong Kong Hotel. He looks like he would slit your throat with his razor in a heartbeat."

Kay looked at May in amusement, secretly hoping that this was just banter and that she hadn't just landed in a tropical den of corruption.

There were so many rumours flying around though. It was hard to know what to believe. Depending on whom you spoke to, it was either a matter of time before they were attacked or there was no chance that the Japs were interested or even equipped to take Hong Kong. As far as Kay was concerned, the war was out of her control. She would have to deal with whatever happened, she was just glad to be of service. There had been so little news of the war in Toronto. She had no idea what to expect, and now that she was here, she had no idea what to believe.

Joan broke away from the group of nurses to go and find Forbes who had disappeared. She found him and Archie in deep conversation outside on the patio. She did wonder whether she should interrupt them or leave them to their boy talk. *No, it's a party* she thought, *they have had enough time to analyse the war on the golf course.* She walked over quietly and stood waiting for them to finish before interrupting.

"It's just ludicrous." Archie was saying, clearly animated about something. "Why would the fool think that it's ok to leave Hong Kong to its own devices, the pride of the fucking Empire! Sending troops and essential resource to bloody Malaya!! What is he thinking? Maltby has a battle on his hands before the Japs even show up! The old goat still believes that they are an inferior force and our less than inferior, unfit infantries are more than a match for them. He's out of his mind and too close to the Japs in Tokyo if you ask me! He continues to tell us there is no immediate threat when there clearly is." Archie was getting more and more angry as he spoke, waving his glass of whisky around to emphasis his point. Forbes turned to acknowledge Joan and put a protective arm around her waist.

"But isn't Maltby concentrating all defences on the Gin Drinkers' Line? Won't that hold them off getting to Shing Mun Redoubt? Surely the biggest risk to the civilian defence of the colony is if they take control of that vantage point?" Forbes asked calmly. He knew that Archie had had a difficult few days trying to work with Major Maltby on defences of the Island and being challenged at every turn by Major Charles Boxer and Air Marshal Commander Brookes-Popham.

"My good man, that would be the ideal scenario - we concentrate our forces along the Gin Drinkers' Line and force the bastards back into China or at least protect Kai Tak Airfield and civil defences. They think they can hold it for a week at least. The reality is - my informants tell me that the Japs have had scouts along the line for months and are now fully aware of how weak the line actually is. We would need thousands more men there to defend it properly. A resource that we just don't have, and I am still having the argument that the Japs are an inferior fighting force which could not be further from the truth..."

Joan couldn't help but interrupt, "But what about the Canadian troops, surely they have swelled our numbers?" Archie snorted and Joan realised that he was actually quite drunk.

"My dear, the 1500 men, sorry boys, that they have sent are ill informed, ill equipped and not trained. They have sent those boys on a suicide mission - and for what? To show that they have made a half-arsed gesture to help us defend the colony. It's all nonsense." He was shaking his head clearly in frustration and despair. Joan said nothing. "Do you know," he continued, swaying slightly and pointing the glass towards her. Joan felt Forbes' grip tightening around her waist. "Do you know that we have ten thousand men? Ten thousand! And do you know how many they have??"

Joan shook her head, not really wanting to know the answer.

"Fifty thousand. Fifty thousand of the sly little bastards are going to cross the border and annihilate our troops. And there is nothing we can do about it but sit and wait for it to happen. Two million people in the colony, two million people to defend with ten thousand men. It's a fucking disgrace." Joan looked at Forbes in alarm.

"Ok old boy, let's get you home." Forbes said forcefully, taking the glass from him and linking his arm. "I think we've had enough whisky and war for one night." He turned to Joan, "I'm sorry darling, I will have to get him back before he has the whole hotel in a complete state of panic. I'll come back as soon as I can." He pecked her on the cheek and led Archie away.

Joan stood and watched them leave in stunned silence. If all of that was true, they really were sitting ducks. She felt sick to her stomach. What on earth were they to do? Her thoughts were, thankfully, interrupted by Brenda appearing at her side.

"Blimey Joan, you look like you've seen a ghost. What on earth has happened?" She looked at Joan with concern. Joan looked at her, took a deep breath and smiled.

"Oh, you really don't want to know!" She linked Brenda's arm and headed back inside the hotel to join the others. Brenda eyed her suspiciously. "Don't worry my dear; it's just Archie having one too many whisky's. Forbes has taken him home to sleep it off."

Brenda seemed happy with that and led her back to the party.

Chapter 20

The rumour mill continued and gathered momentum. Suddenly, the whole colony seemed to be on high alert and military operations seemed to be even more constant. The boys were busy doing back-to-back training exercises and defence preparations. The Royal Scots had already been sent to occupy and work on the Gin Drinkers' Line. They had previously been based on the Island and so were unfamiliar with their new position. Working the line in preparation was recommended by Brigadier Wallis, a formidable and ambitious soldier who had apparently seen many battles in the First World War where he had lost his left eye, so was distinctive by the dark patch or monocle that he always wore. Joan had seen him at The Gripps a number of times and had asked Forbes about him.

The troops had a great deal of respect for him and felt the mainland was in good hands under his command. He was not a fan of the champagne lifestyle in Hong Kong. He also shared Archie's view of the Japanese and was known to have little faith in Popham-Brookes and his 'misguided advice' and made no secret of the fact that he thought many of the officials liked to hear and believe in whatever meant that their 'carefree, elegant lifestyles' would not be interfered with. Unfortunately, the battalions' most immediate fight was with malaria. The area was badly

235

infested with mosquitoes and so despite working hard wiring and digging to strengthen the line, they were weakened in numbers by more soldiers being struck down by the illness.

At Bowen Road, despite the rumours, spirits were high. The nurses were thoroughly enjoying working under the command of Matron 'Billie' Dyson, as she was now known. There was a structure and order to the running of the wards that made nursing completely satisfying and they could have a bit of fun along the way.

When Joan was working, she forgot all about the threat of the Japanese attack and so was working every hour that she could. She felt safe and in control in two places; at the hospital, and with Forbes. All other times, her stomach was in knots, anxious over the impending attack.

All the nurses seemed to find reprieve in the hurriedness of working. They had the support and camaraderie of their little sisterhood, making them able to deal with anything that was thrown at them. Outside of the hospital walls, in their moments alone, it was an entirely different story. They felt vulnerable in this strange land with dark clouds of uncertainty hanging over them. The increase in soldiers falling sick with malaria was putting a great strain on the hospital—they were running out of beds.

In charge of the hospital theatres was Theatre Sister, Kathleen Thomson - a New Zealander who had been transferred from Shanghai the previous year. She was always calm and serene, which was just as well, given the strain that was being put on the theatre staff with the constant stream of soldiers in need of surgical attention. Joan knew that her role was becoming increasingly difficult and just trying to find spare beds or even ward space for the constant influx of sickly soldiers was challenge enough.

Early on the morning of 8th December Sister Thomson answered a phone call, anticipating being asked to open theatre for an emergency operation. She was already thinking about the shortage of beds and how she could accommodate the request. The message she was given could not have been more different.

'The CO's compliments Sister, and Great Britain has declared war on Japan.' said the voice of the duty sergeant at the other end of the line.

'Thank you.' replied Sister Thomson. Joan was on duty at the time and looked over at Sister Thomson as she hung up the receiver. Joan frowned as she caught her eye, Sister Thomson simply said, "Heaven help us." Joan's stomach lurched, realising that their worst fears had just become a reality. She looked at the sister in horror. Sister Thomson took a deep breath and smoothed down her uniform. "There is nothing to be done but business as usual. There are patients to be cared for and so we all need to keep our heads." Joan could not speak, she just nodded and

237

followed her back to the ward where Mary Currie, the Home Sister at Bowen Road was speaking with a group of QA's, going through the day's duty rota. She cleared her throat and addressed the nurses.

"It seems, after months of looking over our shoulders, we are indeed now at war with Japan." The Nurses all looked at her open mouthed, despite every warning that this would happen at some point, it still came as a shock. "I have no more information than that and do not know whether we are in any immediate danger. I think at this stage all that we can do is carry on as normal." She turned her attention to Home Sister Currie. "Mary, are the theatres in the basement now fully operational? I would suggest that we only use the basement until we have a better idea of where the Japs are focussing their attack. The last thing we need is for operating theatres to be taken out."

"Yes Sister, we can use them right away. I'll arrange for as much equipment to be moved down there as we can manage" Replied Sister Currie.

"Good, Ok well let's try not to stir up the troops. Good luck ladies." She turned on her heels leaving the young nurses staring after her. Without a word they all looked at each other before springing into action with their daily duties. The only thing they could do was keep busy and keep the hospital running as best they could. Joan's first thought was Forbes. *Where was he? Was he ok? What was happening out there? How bad was it?* So far, in the sanctuary of the hospital, there was no sense of the panic that must be sweeping the colony.

Within hours they got news that Kai Tak Airfield had been completely destroyed. The air attack then focussed its attention on the Island. The sky suddenly seemed filled with planes, swarming in like a plague of locusts. The sound was completely deafening. Joan could not look, but the vibration from the planes and the high-pitched screech from the bombs as they fell, was hard to ignore. Joan's hands were trembling as she poured tea for the less poorly patients. The screeching of bombs seemed to go on forever; Joan held her breath and the first bomb hit the hospital, destroying the kitchens. Joan felt the shake and shudder of the building and thought she might faint with fright. The screaming bombs and subsequent thuds of the shells continued throughout the day. Joan was paralysed with fear and it took all her strength to continue and try to calm the now panic-stricken patients. Her only comfort was the fact that they were all in it together. They had no choice other than to just get on with making life as normal as possible and pray that they got through each day unscathed.

There had been plans to use nearby St Albert's Convent as an auxiliary hospital and potential temporary kitchen facilities. Unfortunately, there had not been time to put these plans into action so they had to work quickly to get the kitchens set up.

Sister Thomson was put in charge of setting up St Albert's and she asked Brenda and Daphne to help her, it was all hands on deck to get equipment over to the hospital and get much needed beds and operating theatres up and running. The three of them worked tirelessly to get everything set up and for the next few days Brenda and Joan barely saw each other. Joan was working back-to-back shifts to keep on top of the sudden influx of patients. The wards and corridors were filled with casualties and soldiers suffering with dysentery and malaria as well as the wounded. Joan was exhausted in a way that she had never been before. Her whole body cried out for her to rest. There was no chance of that. Each day they had to go through the exhausting and near impossible task of moving patients up and down the stairs from the top floors in the hospital to the bottom, depending on where the bombs were falling. Joan was amazed at how quickly everyone just took this in their stride. It had become more of an irritation and an interruption to the nurses' work rather than completely terrifying.

They soon learned that the Japanese had indeed bombed and destroyed the RAF airfield, destroying all but one of the decrepit fighter planes that the British had been left to defend the Island with. They were then free to bomb the Island indiscriminately. There seemed to be no let up at all. Joan had got used to the constant sounds of planes and bombs whistling through the air and the eventual explosion followed by falling rubble, shattering glass and the screaming and shouting that inevitably followed. She had stopped holding her breath waiting for the bombs to land. She now just carried on and hoped that it wouldn't be them that got hit this time. She was now used to the distant sounds of gunfire and shouting. On a rare break from the wards, the nurses would sit in the Nurses' mess and listen to the sounds of gunshots, men shouting orders, the sounds of boots running and women screaming. The sounds seemed to carry up the hill from the mainland miles away. The sounds of war were deafening and terrifying, but they were now just part of life. How did that happen? Joan wondered. How can all of this mayhem and carnage now be so normal in just a short space of time?

Days after the outbreak of the hostilities the Japanese were rapidly advancing towards Kowloon. The nurses were getting snippets of information about what was going on outside of the hospital walls. Brenda and Joan had both finished their shifts and were making their way to their dorm to try and get some much-needed sleep.

"I'm so tired; I can't even remember when I last ate." Said Brenda as she took off her nurses' cap and ran her fingers through her curls. "I dread to think what I must look like."

Joan just nodded. "You look much the same as the rest of us. Completely exhausted and in need of a long hot bath." They continued on in silence along one of the top floor corridors until Brenda grabbed hold of Joan's arm and pointed out of the window towards the harbour. Joan

gasped as she followed Brenda's gaze. They could see what looked like

thousands of tiny little figures, moving about like ants in the harbour

approaches. The girls stood rooted to the spot watching in horror as the

figures got closer and closer. They frantically waved over to Matron

Dyson who was stood in the doorway leading to Ward 9 talking to one of

the VAD's. She walked over, took one look at the scene below and turned

to the girls.

"Go and tell all of the Sisters that with immediate effect, they are

to leave the Nurses' Quarters and come and live within the walls of the

hospital." She looked at them both. "There is a great deal to do."

Joan and Brenda nodded and immediately headed off to make

the necessary arrangements and set up makeshift dorms in the basement

of the hospital. Neither of them mentioned it but both were thinking

about what had happened to the nurses in China. It was a terrifying

thought.

"We should have done this as soon as the buggers attacked,"

said Brenda, throwing a large laundry bag full of bedding onto the floor.

"We need to keep together. No one should be allowed to wander about

on their own. Who knows what will happen when they get to the

hospital." Joan could not even bring herself to respond. She knew that

Brenda was right. She was also very grateful that they would all be sleeping together in the hospital. She didn't feel safe anywhere else. Instead she just sighed and started to shake out the sheets to make the beds. She still hadn't heard anything from Forbes. Thankfully she was so busy that it distracted her thoughts from thinking the worst. *Stay positive Joan, we will get through this!*

On 16th December, after 8 days of fighting, the hospital was flooded with casualties. The more lucid soldiers told the nurses heart stopping stories of how the Japanese were overrunning the British. One young private who had been brought in with wounds to his legs and burns to his arms and face told Joan of how the Japs had located their position at the Gin Drinkers' Line by a line of underwear hanging to dry on the line.

"They told us the enemy was nowhere near." He said, clearly in distress. "They told us there was no immediate danger! And then suddenly there they were, right on top of us, throwing grenades into the tunnels and bayoneting anyone who tried to get out. I had to play dead. I thought I was gonna die in there. There was so much screaming and shouting. It seemed to go on for hours." He burst into tears. Joan just listened as she redressed his wounds. The poor boy couldn't have been more than 19. Her stomach was churning and her mind full of images of the panic in those tunnels, but outwardly she was calm and composed. "Well, you're safe now," she soothed, "and we'll have you patched up in no time. You

243

just need to rest now so get some sleep." Joan walked away thinking about what Forbes and Archie had said about the Gin Drinkers' Line. If the Japs had already taken the line then they were much closer than any of them had realised. It seemed that the whole of the mainland had descended into chaos. Apparently, in an attempt to protect the food and water supply on the Island, the army had forbidden any Chinese to cross the harbour without special permits. The majority of Europeans had already been evacuated from Kowloon but as the Chinese were inhabitants, they were pretty much left to their own devices. As panic continued to rise after word of the setbacks at the front filtered through, a lot of them felt that their only option was to run. Word had got to the hospital that even on the first day of the attack Chinese doctors and orderlies failed to show up at their posts at the makeshift hospital at the Peninsula Hotel. The streets were apparently littered with helmets and armbands of Chinese constables and ambulance drivers. This sudden haemorrhage of ancillary workers put a huge amount of strain on the British troops trying to keep order on the streets. In addition to the panic and chaos one soldier had told her that the 'plain clothed Japanese' were sabotaging the troops at every turn. Barbed wire and telephone lines were cut, soapy water poured into engines and wireless batteries used by the signal corps at British headquarters. "Well, they are certainly resourceful." Joan had said.

"That's not the half of it." The soldier went on to tell her that the '5th column' were causing havoc in the refugee camps 'whipping up the Chinese into a frenzy' he said. "The police are coming under fire from the Chinese as they are looting and trying to get on the ferries. Someone told me that at a camp in Kam Tin, the triads stole all of the rice and beheaded the European Superintendent right in front of them all." Joan shook her head in disbelief, and all of this before the Japs even reach Kowloon she thought. It was all far more shocking than she had ever imagined. *God help us all.*

Joan finished her shift and was looking forward to laying her head for a couple of hours before going back on duty when Brenda came running up to the Nurses' Quarters. She was packing up some of the more non-essential items that they had not yet taken to the temporary dorm.

"Joan, are you free to come and help?" She panted. "I am going back over to St Albert's with Sister Thomson to finish getting things set up over there. We've just had an influx of casualties and I need you to cover here. Is that ok?"

Brenda knew the answer, and was already getting changed out of her uniform and into a shirt and trousers.

"Yes, of course," replied Joan. "Anything serious?" She asked,

245

shaking out her uniform that she had just retrieved from a pile of laundry.

"No, thank goodness. It's chaos though and there are nowhere near enough beds. The windows are all smashed so the shutters are down. We're having to do the rounds with hurricane lamps like we are here. I feel like bloody Florence Nightingale. Some poor chaps are having to lie on the floor! Bloody Japs!"

Brenda laughed and gave her friend a kiss on the cheek and a quick hug as she ran out of the door.

"You're a lifesaver Joan! I'll tell Matron you're on your way. See you later!"

And she was gone. Joan smiled and shook her head. She was like a constant whirlwind! Brenda was spending all her waking hours at the hospital. Joan knew it was because she was sick with worry about Mickey, who was now fighting to defend the Island. Brenda hadn't heard from him in days and was desperate for news that he was ok.

Thankfully, as far as she was aware, Forbes hadn't been called to fight yet. When she had asked about the likelihood of him being called up for battle duty, Forbes had just laughed and said,

"I'm the pay officer darling, if I get shot, no one gets paid!"

Joan rushed back over to the Ward and learned that Sister Kathleen Thompson was being sent over to St Albert's permanently as acting Matron. Brenda had been made Home Sister and Daphne and a handful of VAD's were also going. Joan was glad to be staying at Bowen Road. She had said to Brenda that 'if Daphne put as much energy into actual nursing as she did flitting between wards and batting her eyelashes - she might even get some work done.' Brenda was more tolerant and didn't mind Daphne. She actually found her to be quite good fun.

Most of the VAD's and RAMC nurses were hard working and got stuck in, despite their lack of training. Although, all of the Sisters had agreed that one or two the VAD's were more of a hindrance than help. To say that the sudden influx of wounded and working around the clock was a shock to the system to some was an understatement. Joan found this infuriating and did not enjoy the shifts where she had to 'babysit'. The work was hard enough without having to give constant instruction. It was perfectly obvious what needed to be done. They just had to get on with it. Brenda had told Joan that she needed to be more tolerant, but she was finding it very difficult indeed.

Chapter 21

Joan had hardly seen Brenda since she had been made Home Sister, the extra duties meant that she was responsible for making sure that all the nurses quarters were clean, laundry done, and meals prepared, so hadn't any spare time. Joan had arranged to visit Brenda after her shift had finished and was very much looking forward to a catch up with her friend and her first hot meal in days.

When she had finished her shift, she made her way to the makeshift sleeping quarters in the basement of the hospital to pick up some things to take to Brenda. As she headed down the main corridor she was met by Daphne, who had obviously been running and was clearly distressed. Joan knew instantly that something was terribly wrong. Daphne's face was dirty and smeared with tears; her hands and uniform were also filthy. Her usual calm demeanour was nowhere to be seen.

"My goodness, Daphne," Joan rushed over to her. "What on earth has happened?" She looked Daphne over for signs of blood or injury, "are you ok? Has there been an attack? What is going on? Are the Japs here?" The panic in Joan's voice was rising. She wanted to shake Daphne who was trying to catch her breath.

"Oh, Joan, I am so sorry," panted Daphne, holding her chest and trying to regain some sort of composure, "there has been a shelling over at St Albert's."

She took a deep breath and grabbed hold of Joan's hand, "Kathleen Thomson has been injured," she paused and looked at the floor. "I'm so very sorry…" she could not get the words out. Joan was searching her face for a sign of what she was about to say, "but I'm afraid that Brenda…" she paused again, trying to take deep breaths, her voice catching with the tears that were about to fall again. Joan's blood ran cold and she held her breath, she did not want to hear the end of the sentence. Daphne looked up at Joan, "I'm so sorry Joan, but she was killed outright."

Tears were streaming down her face again and she started to cry convulsively. Joan looked at Daphne in stunned silence, trying to process what she had just heard. Daphne fell to her knees desperately trying to catch her breath in between sobs. Joan slowly lowered herself to sit down beside her. Her head was spinning, she felt like she had been punched in the gut and thought that she was going to throw up. She just sat barely daring to breathe. If she stayed in this moment it wouldn't be real, it wouldn't be true.

Daphne composed herself slightly and sat up against the wall of the corridor with Joan.

"I'm so sorry Joan," she started, "Sister Thomson had gone to meet her and they were walking to the canteen, a stray shell landed between them. Brenda was killed instantly, and Sister Thomson has been badly injured. She's been taken straight to theatre." Her voice went quiet. "There was nothing to be done for Brenda." She turned to Joan and gave her a huge hug. "I'm so very, very sorry."

All Joan could muster was a nod.

"What on earth is to become of us Joan?"

Joan remained silent; she couldn't speak and was fighting the need to be sick. She stared ahead looking at the cracks in the wall and the broken window. Everything had changed in an instant. Her whole world had gone dark. She needed to see Forbes; she needed someone to tell her it was all going to be ok. She wanted to scream, or cry, or both. Instead she got up and turned to Daphne as if in some kind of trance.

"I just don't know Daphne," replied Joan, "but we have a job to do and patients that need us." Her whole body was numb. It was as though she had forgotten how to walk, how to breathe. She had to concentrate hard on each breath, fighting to maintain control. She started to get up.

"Where are you going?" Daphne looked at her, almost in disbelief.

"Back to work. What else am I to do?"

She turned and walked slowly back to the Ward leaving Daphne still sat on the floor of the corridor, looking after her.

Every step was like walking through mud. She had no idea what else to do but work. Matron took one look at her and immediately understood. She briefly touched her arm in a gesture of sympathy. No words necessary. She handed Joan the Ward list and moved on to treat the next patient.

Joan was so grateful. Matron could easily have just sent her back to the dorm out of some sort of sympathetic duty of care. She knew she had to keep working, keep busy, keep her mind from processing the words that she had dreaded to hear. Brenda just couldn't be gone. She just couldn't be. She looked down at the ward list, grabbed the drugs trolley and took a deep breath.

"Now Sergeant Millington, how is that leg looking?"

Joan worked through the night until she was so tired that her body gave her no option but to sleep. Matron had been keeping a close eye on her, and when Joan reached the point of exhaustion she sent her off the ward for some rest. Joan reached the dorm in a daze and collapsed onto her bed. She didn't even change out of her uniform and slept soundly until she was woken by another bomb, which had landed nearby.

When will all this end? She thought to herself. What *is* to become of us? For the first time since hearing of Brenda's death, she allowed herself to cry. She lay there looking at the ceiling and let the tears stream down her face. There was no sound; no heaving sobs, just tears and a pain in her chest that she thought would never go away. She eventually drifted off to sleep again until she was again woken by the sound of bombs exploding.

She lay, bracing herself for the next thud or explosion. She was so tired. She couldn't seem to focus on anything. She was so tired, she didn't think she could even move if a bomb landed on them. She turned to look over at Brenda's bed, in the darkness she could just make out the pile of clothes that she had left out on the neatly made bed and her nurses cap, clearly thrown discarded onto a box serving as a bedside table in her hurry to get back to St Albert's. The pain and the numbness returned as Joan's tired brain reminded her that Brenda was gone. *How could she be gone? What on earth am I going to do without her?*

Another explosion hit, further away this time but the building still shook with its force. She turned away covering her ears. *I don't think I can do this.* The tidal wave of tears and frustration returned. This time she didn't fight it, she let herself convulse into waves of sobs to try and let out the pain in her chest. She drew her knees up and covered her head with her blanket. She lay like that for some time. Her whole body consumed with the pain and sadness of the loss of her best friend. Even when the sobs had grown weaker and her tears had run dry, she still felt the dull, aching pain in her chest, but it was now a part of her, like a constant reminder and she didn't want it to go. She emerged from under her blanket and saw a note that had been left by the side of her bed. It simply read:

Shift covered for today. Matron

She smiled to herself, for the first time she was grateful not to have to get up and tend to the needs of others. She felt the sting of tears again and turned to try to go back to sleep. Within minutes she was fast asleep and managed to sleep all day, despite the constant shelling and the comings and goings of the nurses in the dorm.

She woke late in the afternoon with a start. Where was she? Where was Brenda? It had suddenly dawned on her that she didn't know what had been done with Brenda's body. She couldn't stand the thought of her just being left alone somewhere because nobody had the time to see to her properly. She was still dressed from the night before and ran from the nurses' dorm up to the ward. Matron Dyson was just walking off Ward 2,

"What are you doing Whiteley? Are you alright?" Dyson rushed over to Joan who was still in a distressed state.

"Where is Brenda?" Joan asked, breathless from running. "What have they done with her body? Is she on her own?"

The thought of Brenda's broken body being left abandoned

somewhere, cold and alone was too painful to comprehend. Matron smiled kindly.

"Don't worry Joan, they buried her straight away at St Albert's. Come on I'll take you." She started to lead the shell-shocked Joan by the arm when Gwen appeared.

"I can take her Matron. I've just finished for a few hours so I can take her if you need to stay here." Joan looked at her with a grateful smile. Matron nodded and with a gentle squeeze of Joan's arm walked back to the ward.

"Thank you, Gwen." Joan had started to calm down. As awful as the thought was, she was glad that Brenda had already been buried.

"No problem, come on, we can collect some roses on the way." Gwen put a protective arm around Joan's shoulders and led her out. "We are holding a little funeral service for her later Joan, we can say goodbye properly then."

Joan just nodded as though in a daze and followed obediently. It was as though something inside her was broken and could never be repaired.

Later that afternoon a small group of nurses and doctors gathered at the graveside for a short funeral service for Brenda. The 12 QA's huddled together in silence as the priest gave his final committal. It just seemed so unreal that Brenda was gone. Nobody could believe it.

Daphne had tried to get a message to Mickey, but there was no way of knowing whether it had got to him or not. Joan was desperately sorry that he wasn't there to say his goodbyes. It had all been so rushed, and with the constant background noise of gunshots and screams and sounds of the many battles going on across the water, Joan could not wait to get back to the safety and comfort of the hospital.

When she got back to the nurses' quarters, she folded and packed away all of Brenda's belongings, smiling at the memories some of them evoked. Later, she would take them and pack them away safely in her camphor wood chest back at the Nurses' Mess, and then think about how she would get them back to Brenda's family who, by now, would have received a telegram with the news any family most dreads to hear. Joan's heart ached at the thought of Brenda's parents trying to make sense and comprehend what had happened to their daughter, who was so full of life and had been so excited to be setting out on the biggest adventure of her life. She would write to them and tell them how happy Brenda had been in the last months of her life and hoped that she would be able to bring them some comfort.

Drained and exhausted, Joan sat at the end of her bed trying to gather her thoughts. She realised that she had not had any time to write in her diary. She sat with her pencil resting on the page and soon realised that she had no words for what had happened over the last few weeks.

She simply wrote:

December 1941

Fri 5th Dec

Night Duty

Sat 6th Dec

Bertha's birthday

Sun 7th Dec

War

Dawn Monday

Fri 12th Dec

Mary's birthday

Weds 16th Dec

Brenda Killed

She closed the book and put it back under her pillow. She decided that the only thing to be done was go back to work. She had to keep busy, and being left alone with her own thoughts would do her no good at all.

A couple of days later, Joan got the message that Forbes was outside in the gardens waiting to speak with her. She was so pleased. He had been so wonderful since he had heard about Brenda. She did not know what she would do without him. She ran out to meet him and knew that all was not well as soon as she saw him. He greeted her with a hug, led her to a bench and sat her down, holding her hand.

"Oh god, please tell me. What on earth has happened?" Joan said, the familiar feeling of dread in the pit of her stomach and panic rising in her voice.

"It's Mickey," he took a deep breath, "he was killed yesterday Joan."

His voice was thick with emotion as he struggled to get the words out. "The company sergeant said that he became completely unhinged when he heard about Brenda. He was so upset that he made himself a target and ran at the Japs screaming and shooting. He didn't stand a chance. I suppose the good thing is that he was gunned down straight away so won't have known much about it."

Forbes turned and looked at Joan for her reaction. Initially there was none

"I just can't believe it. That poor, poor man. What can have been going through his mind? He must have been so angry and upset."

"It just doesn't bear thinking about. I cannot begin to imagine how he must have felt. At least they are both together now." He looked at Joan hoping that she might find some comfort in that. Instead her face had become hard and emotionless.

"You know what? They were both fools," she blurted out, her voice quickly becoming angry, "what were they thinking putting themselves in danger like that?! Do you know someone has said that Brenda ran out to save the General's bloody dog?!" She turned and grabbed both of his hands.

"You promise me," she said, squeezing his hands so tightly that her knuckles went white, "you promise me that you do not attempt any heroics. You keep your head down and do whatever you have to do to get through this wretched war." She looked at him, her eyes burning into his to get his agreement. He nodded.

"Of course, my darling," he said, holding her face in his hands, "you know me, not a heroic bone in my body." He was smiling and pulled her close to him. "You need to promise me the same. Lord knows how long this will last. I need you to be strong." He took a deep breath.

"I am being taken to camp tomorrow. Probably Argyle Street, we don't know yet. I don't know how I will be able to get word to you but I will do whatever it takes. You need to be strong and we'll get through this together, whether we are physically together or not. I love you and want to see us get old and grumpy together." He smiled again and pulled her away from him and again held her face. She was now crying, she could not stop the tears as they poured down her face. Forbes going to camp was inevitable, but she couldn't imagine how she was going to cope without him, not so soon. She nodded.

"I mean it Joan. You need to bite your tongue, and keep your head down. The Japs don't care whether you are male, female or a dog off the street. They see this as sport. They have declared all Chinese women as prostitutes and the streets are littered with dead bodies. That's what little regard they have for human life. You and the girls need to look out for each other. We will get through this. I promise." He pulled Joan closer to him and let her cry into his chest.

Her quiet crying turned into loud sobs as her body seemed to suddenly realise the enormity of what had happened. She had lost her best friend in the world, the pain of which suddenly seemed too much to bear and now she was losing him too. Forbes held onto her tightly and let her let it out. He knew that she would not allow herself to do it otherwise. He smoothed her hair and stroked her cheek as she let out the wailing sobs. She had covered her face with her hands, shutting the world out. She was so comforted by Forbes being there. The thought of him being led off to camp tomorrow was almost as unbearable as losing Brenda. She felt scared and alone. Who knew what was ahead of them? She was only grateful that she had her work to keep her mind off things and keep her busy. When she thought of the hospital wards, now filled with wounded and dying soldiers, she realised how lucky she was and that she had been sent there to do a job. She took a deep breath and pulled away slightly, she looked at him and said,

"What am I going to do without you? I think it might send me quite mad not knowing where you are. Do you think you'll be able to get word out to me?" She said, suddenly anxious.

"I will do my very best my dear, where there is a will - there is always a way." Joan nodded and smiled.

"There's my girl," said Forbes softly, wiping her tears from her face. "Don't you worry about me, I will be fine and hopefully it won't take too long to sort out this whole mess."

They sat there in silence for what seemed like an eternity. Neither of them wanted to move as they were painfully aware that once they separated, there was no knowing when they might see each other again. If at all.

When Forbes finally left, Joan thought her heart might break. Every step he took further away from her was like a physical pain. She went to bed that night feeling completely exhausted, spent from crying and the physical pain of losing both Brenda, Mickey, and it seemed Forbes, all at once. It was just too much. Joan lay in the dark again

261

looking over at the silhouette of Brenda's empty bed. She almost expected her to turn up any minute and whisper "Night night, sleep tight." She thought of all the times that she had ignored her and pretended to be asleep, just in case she launched into one of her long stories. She would've given anything to hear one of those stories right now.

The next day, the nurses were all acutely aware that the Japanese were close to breaking through and invading the Island. There was a constant battering of artillery fire and air raid attacks, more frequently, closer and with fewer breaks. The nurses had no choice but to just get on with the job in hand, caring for their patients. This was becoming increasingly difficult with water rations and supplies running low.

Joan had been sent to fetch a drugs trolley from the 3rd floor storeroom. As she was making her way along the long corridor towards the staircase, she heard the familiar high-pitched whistling of a bomb, getting closer and closer. She broke out into a run and tried to reach the relative safety of the stairwell just as the hospital took a direct hit. Joan was thrown from one end of the corridor to the other as the building shuddered and shook with the force of the impact.

As the dust started to settle around her, she found herself in a heap at the far end of the corridor. She held her breath, waiting for the next blast and trying to move to see if anything was bleeding or broken.

She stood up slowly, reaching to her head where she could feel a trickle of blood. Apart from that she was completely unhurt.

She dusted herself down, now more irritated that the precious supplies from the trolley were now strewn all over the floor or buried under rubble. She scrabbled around to retrieve as much as she could, listening for the all-too-familiar sounds of the different types of shells that the Japs were using. Some roared as they thundered by overhead. Others made a blood curdling whistling noise before exploding ferociously into clouds of red hot metal and shrapnel. But they all ended with a sickening thud, and utter carnage.

Joan gathered up as much as she could and grabbed the trolley again just as another bomb hit. It was on the other side of the hospital this time, but still enough to knock her to the ground again. She scrambled back to her feet and ran down the stairs, carrying as many supplies as she could. Her heart was beating out of her chest, and the trickle of blood now felt like it was pumping from the small gash above her left eye. She arrived back on the ward filthy, bleeding, and out of breath.

In contrast to her state of panic, the scene before her was one of relative calm considering the hospital had just been hit twice. She looked around her open mouthed. Freda and Miriam caught her eye as they lifted a mattress that had been thrown over some immobile patients to protect them from the blast. They took in Joan's dishevelled appearance and look of shock and seeing that she was obviously not seriously hurt, they burst into peals of laughter.

Joan could not help but laugh with them. It was either laugh or cry.

"For heaven's sake Joan, look at the state of you. You will give the patients a fright!" Miriam said walking over to Joan and giving her a huge hug.

"Are you alright? Where on earth were you? Are you hurt?" Joan shook her head, still laughing.

"No, I'm absolutely fine but I can categorically say that the 3rd floor is out of action." Joan was trying to clean herself up a bit when Matron appeared.

"Good grief Whiteley, what happened to you?"

"Unfortunately, I was on the 3rd floor when the last two shells hit. I'm absolutely fine though, just a few cuts and bruises." She looked at Matron for a moment; "Strange how this is all just normal now. How did that happen? How is being nearly killed and thrown from one end of the hospital to the other now just all in a day's work?"

Matron just smiled and said, "I think we are now the ones being underestimated. We have a job to do; a few bombs aren't going to stop us. Are you sure you are ok?"

"Yes, I'm fine. I'll go and do the rounds on Ward 2 when I've cleaned myself up a bit."

"Well, be sparing with that hot water, who knows how long we'll have running water for once they land."

19th Dec 1941 - Japs landed

Whilst the nurses and Doctors at Bowen Road worked tirelessly around the clock to care for the sick and wounded, the world outside the hospital walls was becoming more bleak and desperate by the day. The nurses relied on updates from soldiers and whatever they could get from the radio announcements. They knew that the Japanese would land on the Island very soon and did their best to work with the minimum, to make their limited supplies last as long as they could.

They had heard on the radio that torpedo and bombing attacks had sunk both the Repulse and Prince of Wales ships off the coast of Malaya. This was a huge blow to the British fleet and morale across the colony was apparently badly shaken. It meant that there were no reinforcements on the way, that there were now no British ships in the Indian or Pacific Oceans. The Japanese had full control of these waters, a terrifying thought. The colony was vulnerable, abandoned, and everyone knew it.

One of the VAD's had heard an announcement on local Hong

Kong radio that Chiang Kai-Shek's Nationalist Chinese Seventh army was about 100 miles away, on their way to help defend the colony. Hope, at last. The radio announcer also reported that the Chinese guerrilla campaign had been stepped up to divert the Japanese attention from Hong Kong. This was the first bit of good news that they had had since the attack and the morale of the soldiers immediately improved.

"Hopefully that will give them the extra strength they need to sustain their efforts until help arrives." One of the wounded soldiers said as they discussed it on the ward.

Unfortunately, this was not the only news that was reaching them. They were also hearing tales of hundreds of bodies, piled high in Wanchai among the piles of rubbish. One soldier sobbed as he told Joan that he had seen Chinese families begging for mercy whilst being screamed at by the Japanese to shut the children up. Before the children had chance to take breath to swallow their cries, they were shot and their distraught parents led away forced to leave their children dead or dying in the street. Another soldier said he had found a dead monkey in a pile of rubbish, alongside it a baby. Both discarded like general waste.

Every so often, the nurses would open the shutters to let some light and fresh air into the stuffy and stagnant wards. They were soon forced to close them up again as the sounds carried over from the mainland were too distressing for the patients. They could clearly hear gunfire, screaming, shouting, explosions, and the constant sound of soldiers running in heavy boots. It was unbelievable that such atrocities were taking place such a short distance away, just across the narrow channel separating them from the mainland. It was even more difficult to comprehend such chaos and destruction in a place where Joan had spent so many happy days and nights, dancing the night away and exploring. It seemed a lifetime ago.

Now all they knew was fear and dread.

Joan thought of Forbes. She had not heard from him since his visit. She had no idea where he had been taken, but she prayed that he was safe. She thought of Brenda all of the time. She missed Brenda desperately and she wished that she were here to make them laugh and see light in their dire situation, but part of her was thankful that she was now at peace, not having to witness the destruction of the perfect paradise that they had enjoyed for so long. Joan had to continually remind herself that there was no point, and certainly no time, to be maudlin or depressed. Everyone was concerned for loved ones; many had lost someone in the battle already. They had to be brave and strong and very British about what they were about to face. They just had to get on with it with no fuss.

The night that the Japs landed on the Island was, fittingly, shrouded in dark heavy clouds, dumping rain on the island intermittently. This did not stop the determined Japanese from heading straight for the reservoirs and water supplies. For soldiers who had been accused of not being able to 'see in the dark, due to their slit eyes' they were fast and efficient at navigating their way through the hillsides.

The sounds that could be heard from the hospital were deafening and terrifying and every so often the sky would light up as the Japs hit one of their targets. The battalions defending the Island were already exhausted. Their battle had been relentless, offering no relief. No chance for rest and very little food. The Canadian troops had had no training on hillside combat and quickly found it impossible to pose any real resistance to the battle-hardened Japanese. The battle raged on for days, getting closer and closer to the hospitals.

Chapter 22

23rd Dec St Albert's Captured

Following the explosion that had killed Brenda, Miss Thomson had been taken to the Queen Mary hospital. Sister Mary Currie was asked to go over to St Albert's and take over as Theatre Sister and Acting Matron. The QA's had all gathered to say their goodbyes. Joan smiled to herself as she overheard Miss Dyson say to Miss Thomson, "Well goodbye - I don't suppose I shall ever see you again." It seemed that they had all taken it for granted that they may not survive but it was simply taken in their stride.

When Sister Currie got to the converted convent, the work was relentless. The building was sat amongst the hills in an isolated spot - it had been so beautiful in peacetime but was now caught in the crossfire of the furious battle going on around it and was under constant attack. So much so that she immediately forbade any of the nurses from leaving the cover of the hospital.

Daphne was still going to and from Bowen Road with one of the male orderlies to get supplies. It was incredibly dangerous and each time they made it to the safety of Bowen Road, Daphne was reluctant to leave.

"I miss you all so much," she said to Joan and Gwen on one of her visits. "We were all completely exhausted, food is scarce, and the Sisters have to continually move men with immobilising wounds from one side of the ward to the other to protect them from the barrage of shells coming at us from all sides. To add to this, there are continual tracer bullets whistling through the wards which could easily hit patients in their beds," She took a sip of the tea that Gwen handed to her and sighed, "it is making even the most routine ward rounds dangerous. We could be hit by a stray bullet at any time." She looked at her friends. "At least here we were all together. I am no leader but I am finding that I am having to keep up morale and keep the VAD's going. Just this morning I found a poor old VAD, I think you know her Gwen? Mrs Gilbey?" Gwen nodded. "Well, I found her sobbing in a heap on the floor of the Ward, which is obviously not what the poor patients need to see. I asked her what on earth is the matter? – although we all know it could be any number of things!" Daphne smiled as Freda came and joined the group, "The poor woman was just beside herself! She said that 'she just couldn't stand this anymore and that her husband had said that she must not let herself be captured. Her husband had told her 'what they do to women' and she was going to ask Matron for some morphine!" Daphne's eyes were wide, "Can you imagine Matron's response!"

"What?" said Joan, "she was going to ask for morphine and if the Japs take over the convent, she is going do away with herself rather than be captured? Well, I've heard it all now!"

Gwen laughed, "I'd like to have been a fly on the wall when she asked for it."

"I know, that's what I said to her! I said 'and you think Matron will give it to you?! That is just ridiculous. What a thing to say!' To be honest I was quite angry. I said, 'What if all of us just gave up? What then? What would happen to the patients? You would rather give the Japs the satisfaction of seeing how weak you are? They would just step over you. No. This is absurd. You need to pull yourself together. There is plenty of work to do!'"

"Well done you," said Joan, "none of us can blame her for being terrified though I suppose."

"That's the thing though," said Freda, "we are all terrified. But we are managing to keep it together."

"I'm so glad to have you all as friends," said Daphne. Joan looked at her and she had tears in her eyes.

"We just need to look out for each other," she said kindly. "You know, I have even started thinking 'What would Brenda do?' in some situations. I find it actually does help." The three Sisters all looked at Joan. It was the first time that she had mentioned Brenda's name to any of them since the burial.

"Ha," said Gwen, "Brenda would have said, 'don't be so ridiculous, we don't have the morphine to waste!'" The ladies laughed, they all knew it was true.

"I wish I didn't have to go back over there." Daphne said quietly. "I feel so much safer over here with all of you."

"Well it sounds like Matron needs you there to keep the VAD's together." Said Freda. The others nodded.

"I know, she looks as exhausted as the rest of us. She's been asked to keep a diary of the events as they happen. As if she has time for any of that! And where do you even start?"

They waved Daphne off and Joan thought about her own diary. She must make an effort to write in it more often. They were part of an unfolding history, even if they were just a tiny part of it, they should try and capture as much of what the Japs were putting them through as possible.

Back in the dorm Joan and Gwen had just finished night duty. Joan lay in her bed and allowed herself to think of home.

Gwen interrupted her thoughts. "Do you know what day it is tomorrow Joan?" Joan looked over at her, "it's Christmas Eve."

Well of course it was! The last three weeks since the attack had gone by so quickly. No one had even thought about Christmas. She threw her head back on her pillow. How were they going to be able to celebrate

Christmas with the Japs running around all over the hillside? Again, she thought of home. She had no idea what was happening back at home or how safe her family were. All radio communication had pretty much been stopped and the Hong Kong News only seemed to be printing what the Japs told them to print, so reliable sources of any news were scarce.

She closed her eyes and thought of their family Christmas. There was always lots of laughter and music. The tree would be decorated and there would be pots of prepared vegetables on the stove waiting to be cooked the following day. They usually had a small turkey and a huge ham which mother would prepare weeks in advance. She wondered whether they would have a tree this year and whether they would still be able to enjoy a Christmas meal? She didn't even know whether Bill would be able to make it home. Since the attack, there had been no communication whatsoever. She could only imagine what must be running through their minds. They must know that the colony had been invaded?

She then had a thought that made her stomach lurch. What if they had heard about Brenda? They would be out of their minds with worry about what had happened to her and whether she was alive or dead. There was nothing she could do to get any word to them. She had given Forbes her family address, just in case he was able to get letters out. He could at least reassure them that they were both safe. She sighed as she thought of Forbes. She had still had no word since his visit and had heard conflicting rumours about where he might be. It was most likely that he was at the men's camp at North Point. She could only pray that he was safe. A single tear fell as she thought of the world outside and how hopeless it all felt. They would just have to do their best to make the hospital feel festive on Christmas Day. She had no idea how they were going to manage it.

As she was just dropping off to sleep she again thought of keeping a diary and remembered the little red autograph book that Brenda had given to her when they were leaving Liverpool. She leapt out of bed in a panic, praying that she had not left it in the main dormitory. She rummaged through a bag and found it. She held it to her chest in relief. She was too exhausted now but would start to write in it tomorrow.

Chapter 23

Christmas Day, 1941, was a day that Joan would never forget, nor would ever want to repeat. Waking up late, the morning after night duty, she headed straight to the shower block, hoping to get a hot shower before starting her shift. On the way, she bumped into Freda.

"Merry Christmas Joan! Hope you're not expecting a shower. I've just come from there and there is no water at all. The only supply we have working is in the Officer's Barracks and its stone cold." Joan could not conceal the disappointment she felt. This was all becoming too much. "I know. Rotten isn't it. What a very jolly Christmas." Freda said ruefully. "Come on; let's see if we can at least get a bite to eat." Joan turned and despondently walked back with Freda to the Mess. *Yes, Jolly Christmas indeed*, she thought sadly.

As hard as the nursing staff tried to make the day as festive as they could for the patients, all they could manage were a few extra vegetables that one of the medical officers had managed to bring in from Queen Mary Hospital supplies on his latest ambulance run. The patients were grateful, but the atmosphere was a sober one as they all were thinking of home with the usual rumbling sounds of war in the background.

Gwen decided that things needed to be cheered up a bit and

went to find the only radio they now had in the hospital.

"Hopefully, there will be some cheerful music to drown out the guns!" She said as she headed off in search of the precious radio. She appeared back on the ward, holding the radio and looking like she had seen a ghost. There were tears streaming down her face.

"What on earth has happened Gwen?" asked Joan running over to her in concern. Freda appeared and also ran over.

"What has happened Gwen? Are you ok?"

Gwen seemed to be trying to find the words and hurriedly started to plug the radio in at the Sisters' station.

"I was tuning in the radio trying to find a station that was not full of doom and gloom," she said at last, playing with the dials, trying to get a signal. "The Japs have sent a Christmas message. It sent chills down my spine." The radio burst into life and a man's voice rang out loud and clear.

"Christmas message...."

"Shhuuuush!" Joan and Freda said in unison, both reaching for the volume button.

"Turn it down or we'll have the whole ward in a panic." Said Freda. "What on earth was the message?" Gwen nodded towards the radio and the three nurses huddled around to hear the announcement.

"A merry Christmas to the brave and gallant British Soldiers.

You have fought a good fight but you are outnumbered. Now is the time to surrender. If you don't, within 24 hours we will give you all that we've got. A merry Christmas to the gallant British soldiers…" Joan reached out to the radio and turned it off before the message could play again. She put her hand to her mouth and the nurses looked at each other in terror.

"Is that going out on the normal radio channel?" She asked. Gwen shook her head.

"No, I couldn't get a signal on any of the normal stations so I was fiddling and that came on. I don't know where it has come from." Said Gwen, looking terrified. "Do you think we will surrender?"

"Well not from what Hong Kong news said this morning. Apparently, Sir Mark Young issued a message to the troops saying 'Fight on, hold fast for King and Empire.'" Freda said, suddenly aware that many of the patients were sitting up straining to hear what was being said.

Corporal Hughes was in the bed closest to the nurses' station.

"Bloody Japs, they've been sending messages like that through since the attack." He said. "Don't listen to it, it's all part of their propaganda campaign. They are just trying to stir us up that's all. We'll never surrender to them. We'll get help to us from somewhere. I'm sure of it."

Freda looked relieved but Joan wasn't too sure. Outside the sound of gunfire was loud and ferocious. She took a deep breath.

"Well, there is nothing that we can do about it regardless. They may well shoot us as we go about our work but there is work to be done. Come on. Let's leave the radio for a while and get these boys fed." She tried to sound cheerful but she couldn't have felt any more demoralised and downhearted. It was a desperate situation.

Late that evening, Matron called them all into her office. The QA's all huddled together, knowing that it could only be bad news.

"Well, there is no easy way to say this," she said, sounding weary, "but our worst fears have been confirmed and we have surrendered to the Japanese." She sat up straight in her seat, "I have no idea what this means for us at this stage, as we don't know whether the news has reached the whole of the Island yet. All I do know is that we must be extra vigilant as who knows how the Japs already on the Island will react to the news. I don't have to remind you what they are capable of. Our priority is to keep ourselves safe and the safety and wellbeing of our patients."

Joan just wanted to cry. What on earth were they to do? The Japs could appear at any moment and shoot them all dead where they stood. Matron continued,

"The men have agreed to see to the wards and barricade the immobile patients in as best they can. Any able-bodied patient will be expected to help however they can. Please, go and collect your bedding and whatever else you need and can carry. We will spend the night in the shelters. Dismissed."

The nurses scattered quickly, heading downstairs to their dormitory. They threw as much as they could into a bag and gathered their bedding before heading down to the cold, damp shelters. They could still hear rapid gunfire in the distance.

"Why are they still fighting if we have surrendered?" asked Gwen.

"Maybe news hasn't got to them yet?" replied Freda.

"Those poor boys." Joan muttered. The thought of them continuing to fight to the end whilst the white flag was flying was unthinkable. Surely the Japanese would be aware and stop the fighting?

Joan tried to settle for the night but it was impossible. The shelter was freezing cold and horribly damp. They had lit a couple of hurricane lamps but they gave no comfort, they only seemed to suck any air out of the small enclosed space. The shelters were basically cellars. Concrete tombs that would make even the bravest of men feel trapped and claustrophobic. Joan however, decided that this might be the last opportunity for sleep so decided that she would try to get her head down as best she could. Before she did, she pulled out the red autograph book and pencil and wrote:

16th Dec - *A Tuesday. Brenda was killed at St Alberts. Sometime between this day and the following Sat. Mickey was also killed.*

17th Dec - *A very bad day for shelling & bombing.* **_Forbes came to hospital!!!_** *The days following were - well just like passing in a fever of work - sleepless days and hellish nights for me - until the surrender.*

25th Dec 1941 *WHITE_FLAG FLYING – HK surrendered. Nothing but blood, dirt, rush and the continual noise of shelling and bombing. When we knew that they had landed on the island it just added to the strain as according to reports they were in the hills around the hospital and quite likely to shoot us going about our work. I was off night duty 24.12.42.*

25.12 Surrender. Words can never describe what that feeling is like. One night spent in shelters under hospital.

She couldn't think of what else to write. What else was there to say? Things were so confused and uncertain. Any moment now, the Japs could take over the hospital. What would happen then? The familiar feeling in her gut returned, or was that hunger? She couldn't actually remember when she had last eaten. She gave out a sigh and hid the book in the lining of her pillowcase and tried to get some sleep.

The night passed with no disturbance apart from one of the VAD's, a young nurse from Birmingham, being violently sick. Probably from fright— they all felt sick with worry about what was going to

280

happen.

During the day, life went on in the hospital as normal. Joan was amazed by the resilience of the nurses and the morale of the patients. She had thought that some might secretly be relieved that the Hong Kong had surrendered. At least the fighting would stop and they would be protected by the Geneva Convention. They had been told that, as medics, they would be protected and so they must wear their Red Cross armbands at all times. It was their only saving grace. She reached and patted it on her arm as though making sure it was there, like a security blanket.

As she was clearing away some soiled dressings during her rounds, there was a commotion at the Sisters' station and she was called over to help.

"Joan, two medical officers have just been brought in from St Albert's. It would appear that they have escaped and are hysterical." Matron explained. "One of them has a bullet wound to his left shoulder but otherwise seems ok. The other has injuries to his leg. It may need surgery. Go and do an assessment of the leg injury and report back to let me know if we need to open up another theatre."

Joan nodded and ran towards the sounds of shouting. She found Sister Murphy and Freda busy working to stop the bleeding from the bullet wound.

"We're ok here, Joan." Freda said pointing to the second

Medical Officer who was writhing around on a makeshift bed on the floor, moaning in agony.

Joan rushed over to him, grabbing a pair of scissors to cut off his trousers to get at his wounded leg.

"I know that it hurts," she said calmly, "I'll get you something for the pain as soon as I can." The young Medical Officer tried to give her a grateful smile as he winced in pain and looked down at his leg, which just looked like a mess of pumping blood and exposed flesh. Joan went to work quickly, stemming the spurts of blood with gauze whilst cleaning up the wound as best she could. She soon found the source of the wound. A jagged piece of metal jutting out from his inner thigh, just below his groin. Under normal circumstances Joan would have referred him straight to surgery, but there was no time. He was losing too much blood. She looked around to see if there was anyone that could go for help. Seeing no one, she grabbed the young man's hand and told him to press firmly on the wad of gauze on his leg. He yelled out in pain.

"What is your name," she asked as she ran to the nearby supply cupboard for morphine and more dressings.

"Oliver," he replied, "Oliver Newall."

"Where are you from Oliver?" she asked, turning his head away towards the wall to stop him from looking at his gaping wound.

"I'm from South Shields originally." He said grimacing with

pain.

"I've never been to South Shields." Joan said working as fast as she could. She was worried that the piece of shrapnel had severed his femoral artery, which meant that he was at risk of losing his leg if he lost much more blood. She drew up a small amount of morphine and injected it into his arm.

"Now then Oliver, I need you to lie really still for me. There is a piece of metal in your leg that I am going to remove. As soon as it's out we can clean you up and get you a nice cup of tea." Oliver nodded earnestly. Joan looked over at Freda who caught her eye and raised an eyebrow as if to say, are you sure you know what you are doing? *NO!* Joan thought, *I don't!* She took a deep breath and poured water onto the wound, clearing the blood and giving her just enough time to see how deep the wound went. She took a small pair of forceps from her medical kit and quickly pulled out the jagged piece of metal and stuffing the open wound, which was now spurting furiously with blood, with more gauze. Oliver yelled out in pain.

"It's ok," soothed Joan as though it was something that she did every day, "it's out now. I'm just going to clamp this artery and clean you up." Joan was relieved that the artery seemed to only have a small laceration as opposed to being completely severed. She clamped the vein with the locking forceps and continued to dress the wound around the clamp. The pumping of blood stopped and she was able to stitch up some of the gaping flesh.

"Well, well Doctor Whiteley, very well done." said Freda looking over Joan's shoulder at her handy work. Joan took a deep breath of relief just as Mrs Begnate, a VAD, appeared and asked what she could do to help. *Well, about bloody time!* Joan thought with more than a little irritation, but she curbed her response,

"Could you please go and find Dr Southly for me?" She was still slightly out of breath after her efforts and looked down at her uniform to see that her apron was covered in blood. She pulled it off and threw it into a corner. Mrs Begnate nodded and hurried off, soon returning with Dr. Southly who immediately set to work closing the damaged artery and stitching up the rest of the wound.

"Really well done, Whiteley," he said. "The boy may well have lost his leg if he had lost any more blood."

Joan just nodded as she started to wash the blood from her hands, which were now shaking. Once the doctor had finished, they managed to find beds for Oliver and his colleague, Richard, and moved them up to the ward. Richard had been hit by a bullet that, luckily, had passed straight through his shoulder without causing any damage to the bone. He was sitting up in bed and seemed to be in good spirits, obviously hugely relieved that they had made it safely. Freda asked

Richard how he came to be shot and why he hadn't stayed at St Albert's for treatment.

"Didn't you know," he said. "The Japs took St Albert's a few days ago, its complete chaos over there." Joan and Freda looked at each other in horror.

"What do you mean by they took St Albert's?" Joan asked, concerned for Daphne and Sister Currie. "Are the nurses all ok?"

"Yes, yes they are all fine. The Japs were more interested in looking for any of our boys that might be hiding in the building." Richard said, "Actually your Matron Currie was quite the hero of the hour."

"What do you mean?" Freda asked.

"Well, it all happened so quickly but the buggers arrived at the crack of dawn, yelling and screaming. No one had a clue what was going on. All of a sudden there was so much sniper fire around the hospital that one poor chap got shot in the face just lying in his bed."

Sister Murphy put her hands up to her face in alarm.

"Don't worry, he'll be fine, but it was complete chaos. Matron Currie had been assisting in theatre, she heard shouting that the Japs were here and that was it, she was off, she immediately tore off her gloves, grabbed her tin hat and went running downstairs to make sure her nurses were all ok. We tried to stop her, telling her that she would be shot. She just said, "There are young nurses down there, I must make sure they are alright."

"That sounds like Currie" Freda interrupted.

"She didn't seem frightened at all. I was shaking in my boots! I went running after her, the Japs were running around and shouting as we got downstairs. As soon as they saw us they had their guns pointed right at us. They rounded all the medical staff up, dragged us outside and tied us up, leaving us just sat there on the lawn out front. We were shouting, telling them that it was a hospital, but soon shut up when they started threatening us with their rifles and jabbing their bayonets at us. They didn't seem to believe us and spent hours going through the building looking for soldiers. I don't know whether they thought the wards and patients were some elaborate cover up? But they were definitely agitated about something." He winced in pain as he took a mug of tea from Joan.

"It was actually quite funny when one of them came running out in temper, knocked off all of our tin hats with his rifle then went running back into the building shouting. It was a bit like a child's tantrum. Anyway, they left us there for hours. It was about 4pm when they came back out to us. One of the soldiers tripped over Matron's leg and turned and gave her a good blow with the butt of his rifle."

"They did not!" Joan was shocked.

Richard nodded, "Well, that didn't go down well at all and she lost her temper. Started shouting at them about the Geneva Convention and that they had no right to treat medical staff in that way. She was a sight indeed, but we were all praying that she would shut up so she didn't get us all shot! So then, a Jap officer comes marching over to see what all the commotion is about saying he speaks English and demanding to know who had mentioned the Geneva Convention. I'll be honest with you; I thought we were all done for there and then. There was no doubt in my mind that he was going to give the order any minute. He spoke good English, said that he had gone to Oxford and had heard of the Geneva Convention. He started to go on about how the Japanese Imperial Army subscribes to all humanitarian principles, etc, etc. But instead of keeping her mouth shut Matron just said, 'Then you should know better than to let your soldiers treat us in this way, especially since this hospital has been at some pains to honour Japanese dead.'"

Joan could not help but feel proud of her friend and colleague standing up to the Japs. She must have been terrified.

"What did she mean by honour the dead?" She asked, "Surely they don't deserve that?" Joan could not comprehend why any of those monsters should be honoured in death.

"Well you see, the day before, a Japanese General had been brought in. He'd been seriously wounded. He'd had most of his backside shot away actually. Half of his buttocks had gone. We did all we could, blood transfusions, the works, but he didn't make it. Apparently, when they were laying out the body, one of the young VAD's asked whether there were any traditions for Japanese military dead. Somehow Matron knew that they all carried a Japanese flag with them and that Officers' bodies were wrapped in the flag before burial as a sign of respect. So that's what she did."

Joan was shocked at the care, not sure if she herself would have taken the time for someone who'd just been shooting at them.

"She cleaned him up like he was one of our own, and wrapped him in the flag and pinned his insignia of rank and his medals on his chest. I wouldn't have done it myself but I'm very glad that she did, otherwise I don't think any of us would have lived to tell the tale."

He looked over at Oliver, who was stirring and moaning slightly in his sleep. He looked like he may be coming around. The two nurses were completely enthralled in the story, unable to believe what they were hearing.

"Well I'm not sure I would have done it either. What a thing to do?" said Freda. Joan nodded in agreement.

"No, I'm quite sure I wouldn't, but do go on."

"Well, the Officer's ears pricked up at the sound of Japanese dead and when she told him about the General and he demanded to be shown the body. She was dragged up and told to lead them to the body. They were poking her and pushing her forward with their guns. She showed not one ounce of fear. Eventually they emerged from the hospital with the body on a bier with Matron on one side and the Officer on the other. They looked an odd pair as she was at least six inches taller than him," he said with a snort of laughter.

"Anyway, long story short, after lots of jabbering amongst themselves it turns out that this General was a good friend of their Commanding Officer. Matron was hauled in to speak with him. He spoke through the Officer who interpreted for him. Apparently, he was weeping and he said that she had been very good to the General and that she could ask a favour in return. She asked to be released so we could look after the patients. He said no, she then asked that the English-speaking officer stay at the hospital with her and her nurses until his troops were withdrawn, to make sure that the Japanese troops were kept in order. They eventually came back outside to us and they started to untie us. The Jap turned to Matron and said, 'Do English women never cry?' and do you know what she said? I couldn't have been prouder. She said 'Not when they have work to do.'"

"HA!" laughed Joan. "Good for her! Quite right too. So, is the Officer still there?"

"He is indeed. I have no doubt that right there and then, she saved those young nurses from the same treatment the poor women got at Nanking. They have now been allowed to go about their work and look after the patients, even if it is with guns pointing at them the whole time. There is still lots of fighting going on in the hills though. It's hell on earth."

"So, how did you and Oliver end up here then?" asked Freda.

"Well, we'd heard that there were lots of British casualties on the hillside that were just being left to die. We decided that we would get out to try and see how bad the situation was and try and get some of the poor buggers to the hospital." He paused to drink his tea and said with a smile. "Turns out it was quite bad, as I got myself shot and Oliver here got the fallout from one of the shells. We couldn't get back to St Albert's and, luckily, were picked up by some soldiers who brought us back here. We'd have been dead if they'd not come across us. I'll be honest, I didn't think that my friend here was going to make it." He nodded over at Oliver who was still twitching and moaning in his sleep.

"Well, it's lucky for you both to have been brought in, or there would have been two more dead on the hillside." Joan said as she started gathering up her things to take back to the ward. "Now you get some rest, we are going need the help of as many able-bodied men as we can if we're going to get some of the patients moved from the second floor, downstairs."

She turned and walked back to Ward 2, thinking about the story that she had just heard. Her stomach was flipping with butterflies, for the love of god, is that what we've got ahead of us. She wondered how Daphne was coping. She smirked, when she imagined how Brenda would have coped. She'd have probably got herself shot by not knowing when to shut up! The familiar pang of pain returned and the sting of tears sprang up behind her eyes. She missed her desperately. Thinking of Brenda made her write the next entry in her diary.

26.12.42 All female staff to sleep top floor Barrack Block. Just in bed 10am nobody asleep, up comes some man who tells us to creep into hosp. What a nightmare journey. Down the stairs – back again – down again. RAMC men at various points. Bright moonlight of course (Sybil blind as a bat) all carrying our bedding, eventually we arrived Ward 3, large holes in ceiling. Boarded ourselves in best way we could. Slept on floor.

Working Ward 9. Staff Renate, Joan Wood, Mrs Begden, Mrs Q Jeraige. Wonderful work. Nursing as it is dreamed about, working til you're fit to drop.

Whilst the days continued in relative normality at the hospital. They continued to receive news from across the Island as the fighting continued and the Allies were forced back towards Stanley. None of the news that reached them was good. The stories of what the Japanese were doing on the mainland was enough to turn your stomach. Joan was grateful once more that she was in the relative safety of the hospital.

She desperately tried to find out if anyone had any news of Forbes. No one did. All she had heard that he was still most likely interned at North Point Camp where more of the Officers had been taken. She had to just pray that he was safe and would be able to get word to her soon. She had also made enquiries about Dickie. She had not seen or heard from him since the attack, and thought it unusual that she had not heard from him following the news of Brenda and Mickey's death. He surely must know. She had been asking the RAMNC's that had been posted to protect the hospital. No one seemed to know anything other than he had joined the Sapper Field Squadrons with Mickey and had been fighting on the last defensive lines protecting Victoria.

Whilst going about her rounds Freda came to find her looking frantic. "Oh Joan…" Joan's heart lurched, her immediate thought was Forbes. She held her breath.

"I have just been talking to some of the soldiers just brought in. One of them knew Dickie," she continued. Joan's back straightened, waiting for the inevitable bad news. "Apparently, he had led a section of the Royal Engineers in Wanchai. They were involved in the street fighting and he was shot." She paused for dramatic effect, "on Christmas Eve. His men saw that he was still alive but clearly in agony. They went back to get him but they were too late. They saw him being dragged into a house by the Japs. There was nothing they could do for him." She took a deep breath, "I liked him very much Joan. I know he was a good friend."

Joan was still letting it sink in, horrified that her friend was hopefully dead rather than tortured.

Freda continued; "Well, there're not many left from our merry little band from the Viceroy is there? We may be the last ones standing at this rate." As soon as she had finished, she realised what she had said. "Oh no, Joan, why did I say that? Brenda...I mean...I'm so sorry. I didn't mean…" Her eyes filled with tears and she reached out to grab Joan's hand. Her words had struck Joan like a blow but she resisted the urge to berate Freda for her thoughtlessness.

Instead she took her hand and squeezed it. They had all lost people they cared about and were all worried about friends and loved ones. Who knew what the right thing to say was at a time like this.

"Don't worry Freda. How very sad about Dickie. Such a great shame. I liked him very much too. I hate to think of him left to die in the street like that."

Her heart suddenly felt very heavy in her chest. She gave Freda a short hug. "We just all have to look after each other until this god-awful thing is over." She handed Freda a tissue and smiled.

"They'll be having a right old party up there somewhere." Both women smiled and went about their duties.

Joan fought to hold back the tears as she thought about their little foursome on the Viceroy and how irritated she had initially been by Dickie and his constant jokes. The thought of him being left to die in the street like an animal was beyond comprehension. She was indeed the last one standing. The thought made her want to cry out in pain and anger, but instead she took a deep breath and took out her ward list. The last thing the patients needed was one of the nurses weeping and wailing around the place.

Chapter 24

Sadly, the news did not get any better as the day wore on. Joan was just about to finish her shift and was looking forward to being able to get some rest for a couple of hours when she was called to the Matron's office. What on earth could have happened now? When she got there all the other Sisters were there along with some of the VAD's. Joan scanned the room and recognised a young volunteer nurse called Marie Paterson sat with a cup of tea looking visibly distressed. Joan was confused for a moment as the nurse had been stationed at another hospital, what was she doing here? Matron motioned for Joan to take a seat. She caught Freda's eye who gave her a rueful smile.

"Again, I am to be the bearer of bad news, but it is important that you know what is going on outside of these walls. The Japs, it seems, are running riot. Many of them are drunk and clearly looking to cause mayhem. As soon as we leave this room, I want every drop of alcohol poured down the drain. I do not want them coming in here and finding anything that could fuel their loathsome and depraved behaviour." She turned to Nurse Paterson.

"Unfortunately, Nurse Paterson here has witnessed first-hand what they are capable of and very bravely managed to escape from Happy Valley to get help." Happy Valley was a temporary hospital with one QA and a handful of volunteer nurses. Joan had heard that since all of the Chinese doctors had left, they had pretty much been left to their own devices.

Matron continued, "The nurses at Happy Valley have been repeatedly raped and attacked by Japanese soldiers." Joan's stomach tied in knots and bile rose in her throat.

"I don't think it serves any purpose to try and play down what has happened. We have sent help, and the nurses and patients will be taken over to Queen Mary's. We simply don't have the room here." Matron looked tired and drawn.

"It leaves us in a tricky situation as the Japs will no doubt be upon us at any moment. We must remain vigilant and stay in pairs. At no point must any of you move around the hospital alone. Make sure that you stay together. I am so proud of all of you and how you have conducted yourselves over the last few hellish weeks. You are a credit to our profession. It does seem though, that many of the Japanese seem to be disregarding the protection that our armbands should give us, so I can only imagine that things are going to get worse before it gets better. I want to rearrange the wards so that we are all working closer together to avoid too much toing and froing. I will speak to you later about how we can do that. In the meantime, this young lady needs to get herself cleaned up and a hot meal inside her. Joan and Gwen, can you please show her where everything is?"

They nodded and Gwen grabbed a blanket and put it around Marie's shoulders and led her towards the makeshift Nurses' Mess. Neither of the women wanted to ask exactly what had happened, they didn't really want to know the truth. They left her to clean herself up and found her some clean clothes to wear. Eventually Joan had to ask. "What on earth happened? Is everyone ok over there?"

Marie nodded and smiled. "Yes, everyone is fine, or at least they were when I left. Just badly shaken and completely terrified. It has been a complete nightmare since the men left. The Chinese doctors just didn't come back one day and since then Japs have been turning up and taking away the poor Chinese girls. Some of them are only teenagers." She stifled a sob and continued; "There was nothing we could do but wait for them to be brought back and then comfort them as best we could. One of them didn't come back. The awful thing is that I can't even remember her name. Her friend came back completely hysterical. When we finally calmed her down she told us that they had both been taken to a room with three soldiers. They took it in turns to rape them both. The third soldier was clearly very drunk and couldn't 'perform' properly so took out his sword and used it to slice the poor girl to make it easier for him. They just left her there to bleed to death."

The young nurse burst into tears. Joan could not believe what

297

she was hearing. These men were nothing but animals. Forbes was right. They had no regard whatsoever for women, whatever their race. They clearly thought they had the right to do what they pleased.

"We had no idea that the colony had surrendered. We had made up some beds in the corner of the ward to that we could stay together. We lay there and heard the Japs singing and cheering. They were clearly celebrating something but we still didn't know what. The next thing we knew a group of soldiers appeared on the ward, shining torches in all of our faces, as though they were picking out which of us they liked best. It was just awful. Four of the British nurses were dragged out of their beds. The Japs were shouting 'No come, kill all.' The poor things had no choice."

Joan quickly drained a cup of tea, fighting to keep from being sick.

"Matron was completely helpless but she leapt up and said one of the girls was very sick and shouldn't be taken. Thankfully they shoved her back onto her bed. This went on all night. We just had to lie there and pray they didn't take us. There were 12 altogether who were raped repeatedly throughout the night. I couldn't take it anymore. I didn't know what I was going to do but I knew I had to get help. We had been using old coats as blankets so I grabbed one and made a run for it as soon as I could. I only hope that we get help to them before one of them is killed."

Joan and Gwen looked at each other, unable to speak. It seemed Marie had run out of tears and was clearly exhausted. They made her up a bed and let her rest. Joan was in shock. Just when she thought it couldn't get any worse. It did. It seemed all the more poignant and terrible that it was Christmas Day. A day that she had always looked forward to and celebrated. Joan wasn't sure that she would ever be able to celebrate it again.

She decided to head back to the ward to see if anything needed doing. For once, Ward 2 was calm and quiet. It was dimly lit with hurricane lamps and those patients that were awake seemed in good spirits. A couple of them were even sat up and playing cards. Joan smiled to herself thinking it was the smallest and simplest of things that made people able to cope with the worst of situations. She hoped that she would remember that once she got home. She stopped short in her tracks. If she ever got home.

Chapter 25

Sadly, this wasn't to be the worst of it. The next day they were still unaware of what had happened over on the other side of the Island at St Stephens College. Late on 26th Dec Sister Molly Gordon and three VAD's were brought in from St Stephen's. Molly had been sent there from Bowen Road just weeks before the attack. When Joan first saw her saw on the ward, she was initially pleased to see her and went rushing over. She stopped short in her tracks as she realised that something was very wrong.

Miriam was sat with Molly and looked at Joan, shaking her head in disbelief. Molly was clearly in a state of shock but a VAD nurse Elizabeth Fidoe had been telling them of the horror that they had endured over the last 24 hours. She spoke with very little emotion. It was almost like it had all happened to someone else.

The Allies had apparently been pushed back to Stanley on the far side of the Island and had mounted their machine guns in the grounds of St Stephen's Hospital as a last stand to defend the Peninsula. When the news finally reached them of the surrender, the Japs had already broken into the liquor stores and had embarked on what was to be a rampage of looting, rape, and murder.

The medical officers and nurses in St Stephens had watched with horror as, what looked like hundreds of Japanese were reeling and staggering towards the hospital. They saw them vomiting in their drunken state by the roadside and could do nothing to stop them.

Mrs Fidoe said that as the drunken soldiers approached the hospital, Dr. George Black and Captain Whitney of the Royal Army Medical Corps bravely tried to stop them from gaining entry to the wards. Dr. Black was immediately shot at point blank range before being dragged away, leaving the ward to be overrun by the alcohol fuelled Japanese Captain Whitney was also shot despite walking towards the Japanese Officer in charge carrying a white flag plus a Red Cross flag; they were still wearing their white hospital clothing and Red Cross armbands.

She told of how they rampaged their way through wards, screaming and shouting and ripping off bandages and field dressings from the wounded. They then proceeded to bayonet 60 of the 90 severely wounded who had lain helpless in their beds. One young Chinese nurse was bayoneted after throwing herself on top of her patient as she tried to protect him. Others were hiding under beds or in laundry trolleys or anywhere they could take cover. Then, the Japs started to round up the medical staff. Four Chinese and seven British nurses were put in one room and about one hundred orderlies, doctors and stretcher bearers were herded into another room.

"There was no room to sit down, so the wounded were forced

to stand, jammed against each other like sardines in a can. During the afternoon, the Japs would come to remove a number of the men. Each time the soldiers would scream and demand that the men kneel whenever they entered the room. As there was no space to kneel, the nearest to the door were hit with a rifle or leather strap. The prisoners were taken out, two or three at a time, and were dismembered limb from limb. They chopped off fingers, sliced off ears and noses, cut out tongues, and stabbed out eyes before they killed them, some were allowed to escape. The Japs taunted them to tell the Stanley defenders what was happening. We could all hear the men screaming. There was nothing anyone could do to help them."

Mrs Fidoe paused, staring at the wall for a few seconds. Her voice was oddly low, monotone. Like she was in a dream. Joan became aware that she had tears streaming down her face. The room was completely silent. Joan held her breath, waiting for her to continue. She could not believe that any human could be capable of the things that Mrs Fidoe was describing and she had a horrible feeling that the worst of the story was yet to come.

Mrs Fidoe continued, "Some of the men were driven to try and jump out of the window to escape. As soon as they did, they were shot. We were in the other room. The nurses were all screaming; many were tied down on beds of corpses and raped. The rest of us were forced to watch. We were completely helpless. One nurse was dragged from the group by the hair, screaming and shouting. To stop her screams the Japanese soldier took his knife and began to knock out her teeth. There was blood everywhere but she would not stop screaming until he smashed her face with the butt of his rifle, knocking her unconscious. He used his bayonet to rip open her clothes and raped her, calling to his half naked colleagues to come and rape her before she woke up and started screaming again. They had turned the hospital into some sort of macabre, hideous playground where they could do what they wanted. They were shouting, 'You belong to the Japanese now, you are ours.' They did not see any of us as anything other than sport to entertain themselves with."

She took a deep breath and Molly collapsed into tears.

Miriam was holding her, silent tears streaming down her face. It was like they were listening to someone talking about a horror film. It was all just too awful to be real.

Mrs Fidoe said that the Chinese nurses suffered horribly. They had even heard that one poor girl had been sliced open and laid on her side next to a fire, her organs baked and eaten with the soldiers all taking their share shouting 'life is life'. She would have been alive for long enough to know what was happening to her.

Joan could not believe what she was hearing. It was far worse than any horror story she had ever heard.

Still with very little emotion Mrs Fidoe told them that most horrific was the murder of a female British nurse who would not give in. She had been beaten and raped but remained defiant. This had apparently enraged a group of three soldiers who then used a bayonet to try to detach her legs from her body, splaying them open to reveal her to them. They then thrust the bayonet deep inside her causing her to scream out in agony, she tried to grab the bayonet to remove it but the soldiers were now in a frenzy and cut open the poor woman and used the bayonet to pull out her intestines and internal organs, leaving them overflowing from her body onto the ground. They began pointing at the body and screaming that the same would happen to the rest of the nurses if they did not behave and do what they wanted.

Miriam got up and fled from the ward. Joan could hear her stifled sobs just outside of the door. She reached over and put her hand on Mrs Fidoes shoulder, "You don't have to say any more if you don't want to. You can just get some rest." Mrs Fidoe shook her head.

"I don't think I will ever rest again, I need to tell you what happened. You need to know what they are capable of." Joan nodded and gave her shoulder a gentle squeeze. Mrs Fidoe continued, "Apparently whilst all of this was going on, a nurse was being raped on the ground in front of the hospital. She was being held down but managed to bite off the soldier's nose. In a fit of rage, he dragged her and had her tied to a pole where he first cut off her breasts before cutting her open and with apparent expertise removed her uterus. Still in a state of complete fury he forced the sack of the uterus over the poor woman's head and left her to suffocate, screaming at her the whole time. Apparently, it took her hours to die." Her shoulders started to shake and she broke down into uncontrollable sobs, "it was the sun, it shrank the uterus sack and it eventually suffocated her. Patients were forced to watch through the windows of the wards. Many were sobbing and sick at the sight out of despair and horror. There was just nothing that they could do." She was now inconsolable. Miriam had composed herself and returned to the bedside. She soothed the now hysterical young woman and convinced her to lie down on the bed to get some rest. Joan was tightly holding Molly's hand; she turned to her and said, "My dear girl. Were you hurt?" The look in Molly's eyes told her that they had endured something terrible. "Did they hurt you at all?"

Molly looked over at Elizabeth Fidoe who was still sobbing. She squeezed Joan's hand and continued where Elizabeth had left off.

"We had been separated and locked in another room. We were forced to sit and listen to the screams of the men and women, not knowing what was happening in the rest of the hospital. Eventually we were taken out one by one and raped." A sob caught in her throat but she continued, "This happened continually throughout the night. Each time we were brought back to the room another was led away." By now Joan and Miriam were also crying. How could this have happened? Her poor friends had been through something completely unthinkable.

The atrocities over at St Stephen's had apparently gone on into the night until eventually more Japanese Officers arrived and saw that their soldiers had clearly crossed a line. It was then that they released the terrified nurses and ordered them to clean up the hospital. Joan shook her head. "They made you all clean the hospital??" She didn't know how much more she could take. Molly nodded.

"The corridors and stairs were strewn with dead bodies. The able-bodied wounded waded in blood as they gathered the corpses from the execution room to prepare them for burial. They were then told that there would be no burials and were told to pile the bodies to make a huge bonfire. They tried to retrieve name tags for loved ones but were forbidden and beaten when they tried. They clearly wanted all traces destroyed. Mr Begg, one of the RAMC's had been trying to find out where his wife was - he was led to a heap in the grounds by a Japanese soldier. Under a pile of blankets were the mutilated bodies of three nurses that we had all been looking for. There was his wife, her head was severed from her body and she had been dumped like rubbish. They had to carry the poor man away in a hysterical state. His screams could be heard throughout the college. I will be haunted by his screams for the rest of my life." Molly bowed her head, unable to continue.

Miriam finished the story for her. Apparently, the next day, the surviving nurses and doctors were ordered to tend to the patients that needed immediate care. The shell-shocked nurses worked as best they could until a medical officer arrived at the hospital, completely unaware of what had happened, with a new patient. Molly, Mrs Fidoe and two other nurses immediately begged him to take them to Bowen Road. They had to get out of the hellhole that had been their prison for two days. The four women sat there for a long time. Joan and Miriam just holding the stricken nurses whilst they let out their sobs.

Joan would never forget the look in Molly's eyes. Gone was the happy go lucky young nurse that they had met when they had arrived in Hong Kong. In her place was a haunted looking woman who would relive the last 48 hours for the rest of her life. Joan could hardly believe what she had heard, and was grateful that Brenda had been spared any of it. It was enough to break even the most cheerful and purest of souls.

Chapter 26

For the rest of the day, there was nothing else that the nurses could do but try to continue as best they could, getting on with the care of their patients. They all feared the worst and the atmosphere was tense as they went about their duties, expecting the Japanese to arrive at any moment to continue with their rape and murder spree. Joan was completely exhausted. The stress levels amongst the nurses were high, especially amongst the younger ones. They had tried to spare them of as many of the gory details as they could, but the rumours and gossip were impossible to stop. The only comfort was that the constant sound of gunfire had stopped. They could still hear the sounds of shelling but could not determine where it was coming from.

Late on 26th December, a small group of Japanese soldiers arrived at the hospital. To the immense relief of the entire hospital they asked to speak with the Senior Medical Officers and spent a long time discussing the running of the hospital under Japanese command. It would seem that they were to be spared the barbaric treatment that their poor friends had endured. Joan could have cried with relief.

Her relief was short lived. Within a couple of days, a perimeter fence was set up around the hospital and the nurses found themselves to be under guard the whole time. There were guards on each ward, every exit and patrolling the grounds. They later found out that the fence had

been electrified to prevent any escapes. They were told that there would

be no more leaving the hospital to replenish dwindling supplies, and that

their food and water would be rationed by the guards. Joan was working

alongside the Canadian nurse Kay Christie on their rounds. The supplies

and dressings were already desperately low.

"How on earth are we going to look after these men?" Joan

asked. "They are going to have to let us have access to more supplies.

Most of these men won't survive if we can't treat them properly."

"I think all we can do is our best Joan. I'm sure Matron and the

Senior Medical Officer's are negotiating to get us more pain relief."

"Why would they agree to that?" Joan said, sounding angrier

than she had intended. "They don't give a hoot that these men are in

agony. Why would they put themselves out to bring them pain relief?"

Kay didn't say anything. "Soon all we are going to be able to do is hold

their hands and comfort them as they die in their beds." Kay couldn't

disagree.

"Well, if that's all that we can do, that is what we will do. In the

meantime, how about cutting up some of those sheets to make

bandages?" Joan smiled and nodded. She liked Kay very much. She liked

her no nonsense, roll your sleeves up and get stuck in approach. It was

refreshing and comforting to have someone there as a voice of reason. It was too easy to allow yourself to get into a state of despair.

Their conversation was brought to an abrupt end when a Japanese soldier at the end of the ward shouted at them to get on with their work. They both bowed and got on with the rest of the round in silence. Joan hated that she had to bow to these vile creatures. Vile actually didn't cover it. The contempt that she felt for her captors was all consuming. There were times when it took all of her self-control to stop herself from shouting back at them and refusing to bow. Unfortunately, a few of them had learned the hard way that refusing to bow, even to the lowest ranked soldier, would result in a beating. It didn't matter whether you were male or female, Army or patient. If you didn't bow in submission you were sure to be slapped in the face or beaten with their rifle or whatever else they could lay their hands on.

Forbes words were ringing in her head. *Keep your head down, don't draw attention to yourself.* She longed to hear his voice again. She missed him so much. Not knowing where he was, was torture. She had now found out that some of the men had been taken to a camp at Argyle Street and it was likely that he would be there. She had no way of knowing. She didn't even know whether he would be able to get any kind of word to her now that the hospital was under guard. She couldn't allow herself to think about it. The thought of losing him was unthinkable. And whenever she thought of Forbes, she thought of home. What on earth must they be thinking? She prayed that the horrific stories from the colony weren't reaching them. Her mother would be sick with worry. No. She couldn't allow herself to think of any of it. One day at a time Joan, that's all you have to do. One day at a time.

Within days of the surrender, the Japanese seemed to be doing a lot of reorganising of the hospitals and prison camps. It was becoming increasingly difficult to keep track of where friends and loved ones were.

Matron called them for a staff meeting and informed them that they would be receiving patients from both St Albert's and Queen Mary Hospital over the next few weeks. The nurses looked at each other. Gwendoline spoke up.

"How on earth will we feed and care for them? We don't have enough supplies or food to look after the patients we have already."

The other nurses nodded in agreement.

"Well, with the patients will come supplies, I have been assured of that. As for the food rations, we are now down to our last batches of tinned meat. The Japs have promised supplies of rice and vegetables but they have not yet materialised. We need to make sure that the patients are getting what they need. We will have to make do with what is left over until more supplies arrive. Rest assured that I am making a nuisance of myself with the Japanese Commander. I am hoping that he will get so tired of me that he will give in to at least a couple of my requests." She smiled at the nurses who all sniggered quietly.

"I am hoping that with the patients will also come some of our nurses. It would be a great comfort to me to have all of our Sisters under one roof, but as yet I don't know. That is all." She dismissed the group and asked Joan and Freda to stay behind.

"There is a soldier that will be joining your Ward as soon as he is out of surgery. I want you to do your best to get him as comfortable as possible. He has suffered horrendous injuries and was brought in by Selwyn-Clarke so I want to make sure that we give him the best care that we can. He's had a rough time and, by all accounts, is the only survivor from the attack on the Salesian Mission. It's a miracle the poor chap is still alive. I will come and check on him myself this evening. There are also a few men on your ward who are fit to be released to camp. Our instructions are to give them clean clothes and 2 army blankets. They will be collected in the morning."

Joan and Freda walked back to Ward 2. They had heard about the attack on the Mission but didn't know any of the details.

"I wonder what happened to him?" Freda asked. "I didn't think that there had been any survivors at all. Poor chap. He must have been through quite an ordeal." Joan nodded absent-mindedly.

She was thinking about the poor mutts that were to be handed over to go to camp. They were barely fit. One had been suffering from an infection of a bullet wound to his leg. The other was a leg amputee. He hadn't even been out of his bed since he lost half of his leg. How was he to cope in camp? Freda seemed to read her thoughts.

"I'm assuming Matron was talking about Teddy and Norman? I wonder which camp they will be taken to? Poor buggers. I suppose this is how it is to be now? Get them fit and ship them off?" Joan sighed and nodded.

"It would seem so my dear, it would seem so."

Chapter 27

When they got onto the ward, the soldier Matron had mentioned was already out of surgery. Renate and Mrs Begnate were with him, helping Dr. Anderson to transfer him from the theatre bed.

"Good grief," Joan exclaimed. "What on earth happened to him?"

The Dr. turned and said, "He'd been practically decapitated. Only had a few nerve endings keeping him together. No damage to the spinal cord, thankfully so he should be ok with no permanent damage apart from an impressive scar. I have no idea how he survived for so long without medical attention. Someone was looking out for him that's for sure... He'll be coming round soon. We gave him as much anaesthetic as we could but nowhere near enough for this type of injury. He'll be in a lot of discomfort when he wakes up. If we are able to spare some extra morphine, we should. The poor bloke has been suffering with these injuries since the attack." The doctor left and Joan looked at the young soldier's notes. She read out:

"Corporal Norman Leath, Royal Army Medical Corps." She looked over at him as he slept off the anaesthetic. The dressing barely concealed the wound that looked like it covered half of his face and neck. "What did they do to you?" She said as she placed a pillow next to his head to stop it from lolling forward and reopening the wound. He groaned slightly as she moved his arm. He started to try to move. Joan held his arm firmly to stop him from lifting it in his unconscious state.

"I'll stay with him," she said to Freda. "It looks like he'll be coming round soon. I need to make sure he doesn't move this arm and cause any more damage."

Freda nodded and moved on to the next patient, quite relieved that she didn't have to redress the wound. She had seen lots of ghastly injuries, but that was definitely one of the worst.

Joan didn't have to wait long for Norman to wake up and the doctor was right, he was immediately in a huge amount of pain. Joan gave him a shot of morphine. A young soldier on the bed next to him looked over.

"The poor fella can have my share too; he looks like he needs it more than I do." A voice from across the room chimed in "and mine." This echoed around the ward as soldiers happily gave up their pain relief to help their new roommate. Joan felt a swell of pride. The human spirit can never be truly broken, she thought. The men were prepared to endure pain and discomfort themselves for this young soldier who may not even last the night. She smiled gratefully at them all.

"We'll keep an eye on him and see how he gets on. I'm sure he'll be very grateful."

The morphine kicked in and Norman tried to sit up in bed. Joan leant over to help him get comfortable.

"Well," she said, "your guardian angel was certainly looking out for you, wasn't she?"

Norman gave a tired laugh, "I'm not sure about that. I had been put on draft to go back home just before this happened. That'll teach me to mind my own business in future." Joan looked confused but smiled at the young soldier.

"How about a nice cup of tea? If you want to talk about it, I'm all ears. It sounds like you've had quite the adventure."

Norman smirked, "You could say that and yes a cup of tea would be lovely. My mouth feels like my throat's been cut. Oh wait! It very nearly was!" He laughed again at his own misfortune. Joan laughed with him.

"Well at least you haven't lost your sense of humour."

"No, that's the last thing those bastards can take from me." Joan shot a look over at the soldier guarding the door of the Ward. Thankfully, he was dutifully staring at the ward and seemed not to have heard.

"Shhhhh," She said quietly, "I'd keep your voice down if I were you. This one is ok, but a couple of the others would think nothing of beating you in your bed for any 'disrespect'." She nodded over towards the guard, Norman nodded his understanding and gratefully took the mug of tea from Joan.

"So, you are my own Florence Nightingale then are you?" He said, wincing as he lifted the mug to his lips. Joan smiled, "Well I don't know about that, but for the moment you are stuck with me. How does the dressing feel? Do you want me to redo it?"

"No, it feels fine at the moment. I must look a sight."

"Well, you do seem to have won the award for the grisliest looking injury on the ward so far." Joan sat on a chair next to his bed. "What on earth happened? Do you want to talk about it?"

"Not much to tell really. Did you hear what happened over at the mission?"

"We heard that it had been attacked and there were no survivors amongst the male staff." Norman nodded.

"Yes, that seems to be what everyone has heard. There were actually two of us that survived." Joan raised her eyebrows in surprise and let him continue, "There were 27 of us there at the Mission. The medical store had previously been in Kowloon, in an old rope factory but after the attack they decided that it was too vulnerable a position. We had a year's worth of medical supplies that were to cover both the British and Indian Medical Hospitals. It was too much of a risk to let the Japs get hold of it, so we moved the store to St Albert's."

At the mention of St Albert's, Joan immediately thought that he must have met Brenda. She said nothing.

"Then they thought it would be better to move us to The Salesian Mission at Shau Ki Wan. The monks were still there and so we assumed that it was the safest place to keep the supplies. A couple of days before we were attacked they had also set up a Medical Aid Post. A Canadian, Major Banfill, was in command. We were aware that the Japs were on the Island but we were fairly isolated so the Major didn't evacuate. As the night went on it became fairly obvious that the whole of Lye Mun was in enemy hands. In hindsight, we should have evacuated as soon as we knew the Japs had made it onto the Island but we thought we would be protected as we were all medical volunteers, we all had our Red Cross armbands."

Norman looked into the bottom of his mug and then closed his eyes as he told the rest of his story.

"By 6.30am the next day we were surrounded by them. There must have been 250. We were outnumbered at least 20-1. We were told not to resist. You wouldn't have got any resistance from me. Straight away they killed two Rajput Soldiers who had only arrived the day before and were waiting for an Ambulance transfer to the hospital. They were shouting at everyone, it was all a bit of a blur. They all had guns pointed at us; we had no choice but to surrender. They made us all line up outside and forced the men to strip off down to our underwear. Tunics, shorts, boots, the lot. They then made us hand over all of our rings, any other jewellery and watches. Thankfully they didn't seem interested in the women but were shouting that Colonel Tanaka had ordered for all prisoners to be killed. They just left us there like that for half an hour 'til an officer arrived and took charge. The poor girls were terrified. I can only imagine what they thought they had in store for them. The best I could hope for was a bullet in the back of the head.

They tied Major Banfill's hands behind his back and led him away. They took him inside and made him watch as they bayoneted some of the patients inside. The rest of us were marched off along Island Road and then up along a path onto Mount Parker. We must have marched for 10 minutes before they stopped us at a clearing next to a mullah, one of the main drainage ditches. I thought I was a goner for sure. They lined us up and made the 5 doctors kneel. They just shot them in the head. There was no warning, no shouting. Just shot them and kicked their bodies into the ditch. The rest of us they started to bayonet and decapitate.

There would have been three St John's Ambulance Men, eight Canadians and ten of us RAMC's. As the men fell they were kicked into the ditch. I felt a blow to my neck and fell to the ground. I was surprised I was still alive if I'm honest. I thought, the only way I'm going to survive this is to play dead, so I rolled myself into that ditch with the rest of them. I was lucky because anyone showing any signs of life were finished off with a bullet. I suppose I must have passed out with the pain. Probably saved my life." He paused and looked at Joan. She was hanging on every word, reliving the story with him, amazed at how normal these stories were now becoming.

"How on earth did you escape from that ditch?" Her eyes were wide in amazement, "you most certainly should be dead!"

"I know, I suppose I just lay there. Once the Japs were satisfied that we were all dead they headed off down the hill. Anyway, I just lay there. For hours. I was too scared to move. I didn't know the extent of my injuries but I knew it was bad. Eventually I got myself up and crawled along the ditch and into the tunnel. I crawled along there and heard a whistle. I tell you, I nearly had a heart attack there and then. It was Dr. Osler who'd been 2nd in command at the mission. I didn't know him very well. He'd been shot in the back. He wanted me to stay with him. I knew that I had to keep moving whilst I could. I was losing a lot of blood. I convinced him to keep moving and we crawled through tunnels and out on the other side of Mount Parker. He wanted to make a run for it back to St Albert's, I wanted to get back to the mission to see if anyone else had survived so we went our separate ways.

I have no idea what happened to him but when I got back to the mission, the monks told me that the nurses had been let free and no harm had come to them. I was so relieved. They gave me some food and let me rest there for the night. It was too dangerous for them to hide me for much longer so I left early the next day and eventually came across an abandoned house. It had been badly shelled but there was water and shelter in the cellars. I hid out in there until the day after the surrender. I guessed we'd surrendered as all the gunfire stopped."

"How on earth did you survive for days on end with just water and half decapitated?" Joan was stunned, "and how on earth did you get here?" Norman just smiled.

"I headed towards North Point Camp, thought I would be safer there than wandering around waiting to be shot. There Selwyn-Clarke found me and took me back to Queen Mary hospital. They have no beds and it is over run, that's why they transferred me here."

"So, you were there for 8 days before coming here?"

"Yes."

"So, why on earth did no one see to your injuries? You could have died." Joan was incredulous that he had just been left with no treatment. Norman just shrugged.

"Doesn't really matter now does it?"

"No, I suppose it doesn't but still…" Joan got up and took the mug from him, "you must be exhausted. Why don't you try to get some sleep and I will check on you later."

"Thank you, Sister. I am very grateful to you." His eyes were already heavy with tiredness, and it was not long before he was fast asleep.

Joan continued her duties, unable to get Norman's story out of her head. She was quite sure there were many more out there that had similar stories to tell. Again, she prayed that Forbes wasn't one of them.

Before she finished her shift, she checked in on Norman again.

"He's been asleep since you left." Said Renate who was busy changing beds. "Shall I let you know if he wakes up?"

"No don't worry, I'll check again in the morning. Good night Renate."

"Good night Sister."

Joan lay in her bed that night unable to sleep. What sort of a world were they living in where people could do such horrific things to each other? She reached for her diary, thinking that she should start to write at least some of it down. Try as she might, she could not think how she would even begin to write down what the last weeks had been like. Instead she just put the diary back under her pillow and tried to force herself to go to sleep. As she was drifting off she remembered what Norman had said about being drafted back to the UK. Why was he still here? What had happened to make him stay? She must ask him in the morning.

Chapter 28

Joan woke early the next day to find Renate sat on the edge of her bed in tears.

"What is wrong Renate?" Joan rushed out of bed to her side. "What has happened?" She almost dreaded the answer. They just seemed to be going from one horror to another.

"Joan, it's all just so horrible." said Renate, gratefully taking the hanky Joan had handed to her; she looked over nervously at the door of the dorm, knowing there was a guard on the other side. "I was on the night shift with Freda, I find it terrifying here at night. They sneak around in their rubber boots and just appear. Sister was writing up her notes last night and one of the Japs crept up behind her and just stood there watching her with his bayonet pointing at her back. She pretended she hadn't seen him and carried on. He must have got bored and went away but they are silent, you just don't know when they are going to appear."

Joan nodded. Matron had told them that the Japanese Commander had been surprised that there were so many women at Bowen Road. He had told her that they should all be on alert and not put themselves at unnecessary risk. Not very reassuring Joan had thought.

"But that's not the worst of it," Renate continued, "as he walked away he was making these awful slurping noises. It made my blood run cold. Then we heard all of this shouting from outside. They were all shouting at each other. We looked out of the window and saw that they had about three Chinese as prisoners. They had tied them to the trees."

She started to cry again, "Matron came in and told us to come away and put the shutters down before a guard arrived and shot us all. She was so cross. It was just awful; we heard all of this screaming and shouting." She paused and looked at Joan and held her hand. "And then there was the smell. It was the smell of burning flesh Joan. The animals had cut open the Chinese and were burning their insides. Whilst they were still alive!"

"How do you know all of this Renate? How do you know they had done that? Surely they wouldn't do that in the hospital grounds, in plain view of everyone." She thought back to what Molly and Mrs Fidoe had told them about what happened at St Stephen's and knew that they mustn't put anything past them but this she found unbelievable.

"Well one of the patients told us that that is what they did. It was an act of superiority. 'Life is life' he had said. They eat the organs to make them stronger warriors. Can you believe that such a thing exists? Anyway, we didn't believe him. Then there was more shouting. I'm surprised you didn't hear the commotion."

Joan had heard shouting but this had just seemed normal to her after the events of the last few days. She had been so exhausted she must have just gone back to sleep.

"Their Commanding Officer arrived and it seems he went berserk. The soldiers were led away and then an officer arrived in the hospital and ordered Lt Fletcher and Marshall to go and cut the bodies down and bury them. When they came back they told us what they had seen. The bodies had been completely mutilated. I'm so frightened Joan, they just seem to hate us Chinese and think they can do what they want with us."

Joan gave her a hug, "I know, I don't think any of us are immune to their hate if I'm honest. We just have to look after each other and be strong. This will all pass soon I'm sure of it."

Joan waited with the young nurse until Freda and Gwen arrived after their harrowing shift, they saw Renate and went over to comfort her.

"Is it true?" Joan asked.

"I'm afraid so," said Freda, "completely horrifying. They are just sub-human. Animal is too kind a term for them."

"Why don't we push the beds together and we can all get some sleep? We might sleep better if we're together?" Gwen suggested. Renate nodded gratefully and the women started to move the beds around. The guard burst into the dorm to see what was going on. He shouted and pointed his rifle at them all. He seemed to be satisfied that they weren't making any trouble and walked out. The women just looked at each other.

So, this is what it was going to be like from now on. Constant fear of being shot, or worse, at the hands of their unpredictable and seemingly unstable captors.

Joan left the nurses to get settled and get some much needed rest. She headed up to the ward to check on Norman and see how the previous night's events had affected the patients.

Matron was already on the ward and told her that she needed to stop the young nurses from becoming hysterical. They just needed to carry on as normal.

"I am meeting the Commander this morning. I will ensure the safety of my nurses, don't you worry. In the meantime, we all need to keep our wits about us and keep our heads. Literally." She gave Joan a wry smile. "How is your patient doing?" She nodded over towards Norman. Joan was looking through his notes from overnight.

"He did remarkably well yesterday after he came back from theatre and it looks like he had a fairly peaceful night, all things considered." She looked at Matron, "he will need more pain relief, we are dangerously low. Are we going to be given more supplies? I'll check on him now and see what he needs and report back. Do you want him moved to Ward 3?"

"No, he can stay where he is for now. I have been told that we are likely to be getting our new arrivals in the next few days so we will look at space once we are clear on numbers. I am going to ask the Commander for more antitoxin and morphine. I am not expecting anything but a 'no', but I will continue to ask. Thank you Sister Whiteley."

Joan went about her ward round as usual. The patients were definitely unsettled by the night's events and spoke about it in hushed tones so as not to draw the attention of the new guard on duty. Many of her patients were immobilised by being trussed up in Thomas Splints, many suspended from Balkan beams. They were her main cause of anxiety. How on earth would they move them quickly if the Japs decided to turn on them? She tried to take comfort from Matron's reassurances that the guards on duty were too well disciplined to go against their orders. She had been assured that her nurses and patients would come to no harm. She reassured her patients as best she could. Not really convincing herself as she did so.

When she finally got to Norman, he was awake and again seemed in good spirits.

"So, what is on the menu for us this morning Sister Whiteley? Bacon and eggs? Smoked salmon?" he joked as she checked over his dressing.

"Ha, you'll be lucky," Joan replied. "I think this morning we have bread, tinned pineapple chunks and weak tea."

"You make it sound so appetising." Norman chuckled. "So, how am I looking then? Have they done a good job in patching me up?"

"You do appear to be a miracle of modern medicine lieutenant." replied Joan as she peeled back the dressing to reveal the wound.

How they had managed to sew him up so neatly amazed her. The wound was a long and wide as it was deep. This made it very difficult to dress without half strangling the poor man. One of the VAD's appeared at her side with a trolley containing a bowl of tepid water and fresh bandages Joan smiled gratefully and started to redress the wound as best she could.

"There was a bit of excitement here last night I believe?"

"I believe so," Joan replied, "best not to think about it. The Japanese CO has apparently assured Matron that it won't happen again. We have to trust that he is right."

"Well I wouldn't put anything past the sly little bastards," Norman whispered, "and neither should you."

"No of course not." Joan said officiously. "Now you get some rest. Mrs Begnate will be round with some tea for you shortly." She turned to continue on her rounds when she remembered that she had meant to ask him why he had stayed.

"So, you didn't tell me why you didn't get on that boat."

Norman laughed. "No, I didn't did I. It all seems so silly now. We had a farewell party on the ship before we were due to leave. One of the corporals got a bit handy with his fists after too much drink. He started a fight and I had to keep him under close arrest. He was court martialled and I had to give evidence and watch the ship sail away without me. Like I said, should have minded my own bloody business." He smiled and looked at Joan, "but just think if I had gone, I would be missing bread and pineapple chunks for breakfast."

"Indeed you would." Joan smiled and turned to continue her rounds. As she made her way to Ward 9 she was intercepted by one of the medical officers.

"Joan, Garstang has got his radio working, they are talking about moving some of the RNO's to North Point camp. I'm assuming that Forbes will be going with them. Will come and find you if we hear anything else. The Japs are apparently rounding up all of the civilians and taking them off to Stanley."

"Stanley prison?" Joan asked.

"Yes, looks like they are going to be using it as the main internment camp. Will keep you posted on Forbes."

Joan's heart stopped at the sound of Forbes name. She was constantly terrified of getting the worst news. If he was being moved with the Royal Naval Officers, she could only hope that they were being treated well. Everything seemed to be happening so quickly. She could hardly keep up. She had to keep track of what was going on, she made a mental note to write it in her diary.

Despite the chaos going on all around them, the nurses settled into their new routines relatively well. The main problems they faced were the now desperate food rations. It was becoming increasingly difficult despite Matron Dyson's constant demands of the Japanese C.O. The nurses were exhausted but worked tirelessly to care for their wounded and sick. At night they would huddle together in their crowded dorm and try to keep each other's spirits up with tales of 'the champagne days' as Gwen called them. They would talk of loved ones and their families. It was hard not to become overcome by the situation but they all knew that in the grand scheme of things, they were in a better position than most.

The hospital was starting to feel more confined and they were more restricted in where they could go. Most of the residence buildings around the hospital had been taken over. They had also set up a guardhouse right outside the nurses' dorm. This was the cause of much fear and distress amongst the nurses. After the incident of the three Chinese prisoners, they had been assured that there would be no repeat of any such scenes of violence, but they should have known better than to trust the Japs.

Kay, Joan and Miriam had been working long days and had been looking forward to getting back to the relative safety and calm of their dorm. They were immediately aware of a lot of activity outside at the Guardhouse. They turned out all lamps and crept up to the window. They could see a number of soldiers standing around a group of four or five men in a slightly different uniform.

"Kempeitai!" Miriam exclaimed in a loud whisper. Joan's stomach lurched at the sound of the name of the Japanese Secret Police. What on earth were they doing here? The four women held their breath, not daring to move a muscle. They would most definitely be killed if they were spotted. The group of men were dragging two prisoners out of the guardhouse. It was impossible to see in the fading light whether the prisoners were Chinese or white. The prisoners were thrown to the ground and one of them held down whilst a Jap forced a water hose into his mouth.

They watched as the poor, unfortunate man had water forced down his throat until his stomach was full and severely bloated. The other prisoner watched on, clearly distressed and aware of what was happening. With a lot of shouting the soldiers stood around were forced to hold the man down and cover his mouth whilst the rest of the soldiers stamped on his swollen stomach until water was forced out of all orifices. The tortured man was then beaten and left on the ground. They turned and grabbed the other prisoner, dragging him back inside the guardhouse.

The nurses looked at each other in utter horror and revulsion at what they had just witnessed. May opened her mouth to speak, but Joan but her finger to her lips, nodding towards the door as they heard footsteps. Instead of their Japanese guard, Freda and Gwen walked in. Seeing their shell-shocked friends, they rushed over and pulled them away from the window.

"What on earth has happened now?" asked Freda.

"Kempeitai" Kay repeated.

Gwen's eyes widened.

"Kempeitai? Here?"

"Yes, in the guardhouse. They are obviously using it to torture prisoners."

Freda looked confused. "What do you mean Kempeitai?" She asked.

"Shhhhhhh!" The nurses all hissed, pulling her over to the beds. Miriam looked nervously over towards the door but there was still no sign of the guard. He was probably one of the ones that had been outside sticking the boot in.

"You've heard of the German Gestapo?" Gwen said to Freda in hushed tones.

"Yes of course," Freda replied.

"Well these guys are much worse. Japanese secret police are beyond evil. I can't believe they are here using the hospital."

"Well, from what we have just seen they certainly enjoy their work." Kay said and proceeded to describe what they had just witnessed. Gwen and Freda looked suitably horrified.

"Well, I am glad that we have moved all beds together." Said Freda, "I don't think I will ever sleep soundly again if I sleep alone. What's to stop them breaking in here and murdering us in our beds?"

"I don't think they are that interested in us to be honest," replied Kay. "They seemed extremely focussed on the job in hand." They all held their breath and listened again for sounds from the guardhouse. There were none. In fact, it was eerily silent.

They all huddled together. No one wanting to be the first to go to sleep. Joan went and lit one of the hurricane lamps and spotted the guard. He stood silently inside the door of the dorm, just watching them. He gave her such a fright she almost dropped the lamp. In a moment, he was gone again. They all looked at each other and shook their heads. The guards were like ghosts! It was almost eerie how they would suddenly appear and disappear. It was most disconcerting.

They had almost got used to the quiet, almost silent shuffling sounds of the Japanese guards as they moved about the hospital and despite the menacing glint and constant threat of their bayonets. But so far, the Japanese C.O had kept his word and no one in the hospital had come to any harm.

"Don't you feel like a goldfish in a bowl sometimes," said Gwen, breaking the silence and obviously wanting to think about something other than what might be happening over in the guardhouse.

"I'm sick of having one of them peering at me everywhere that I go. It's like being surrounded by a bunch of mute peeping Toms! And what is the fascination on the wards, it's like they've never seen sick people before! I hope the bloody Governor and his henchmen are nice and cosy in their camp. I'd string them all up for giving in to these poor excuses for human beings!"

Joan chuckled. Gwen was prone to a good rant, usually with good reason and she was glad of the distraction.

"I do fear for the safety of the Governor if you ever got hold of him." Joan said with a quiet laugh.

"Well, he'd get a piece of my mind, that's for sure." Freda looked over at Joan and rolled her eyes.

"Do you know when they are sending people to Stanley?" Freda asked. Gwen shook her head.

"No, the last I heard was that people had been moved to brothels and hotels down near Queens Road. They put a notice in the Hong Kong News that all enemy nationals were to assemble at Murray

Street Parade; only not many people saw the notice and only about 1000 turned up. The Japs were not happy but made them march for miles carrying everything that they had down to Queens Road. I'm not sure the Japs really know what to do with us all. The conditions down there are pretty horrendous from what I can gather."

"How on earth do you know all of this?" Joan was always amazed by Gwen's ability to know what was going on before anyone else!

"Renate's sister got word to her via one of the Indian runners. They are all caged up like battery hens down there, all sharing bathrooms, if they are lucky enough to have one, and no clean water. They've been there for days already. I assume they will be there until they round up everyone else." She lowered her voice slightly. "There's a chance that Renate will be forced to go with her family. Because she is Chinese and under age, I don't think they'll let her stay here. They are all being shipped off to other camps."

Joan was very protective of young Renate but feared what Gwen was saying was true.

"Who knows where we all might end up?" Freda said glumly. "I suppose we should count ourselves lucky that we are here and have each other. I think I may have gone quite mad without you girls keeping me sane."

The young nurses all nodded their agreement. They did feel like the lucky ones, despite the lack of food and privacy.

"Anyway, busy day tomorrow," said Freda. "Apparently, the patients from St Albert's are coming here. Lord knows where we will put them!"

The nurses groaned and settled themselves down for the night. All huddled together for warmth and peace of mind.

Chapter 29

Joan realised how lax she had been in writing her diary. There was either no time or no energy to bother writing anything. She sat down now in the Nurses' Quarters with her back to the door to hide the diary from the ever-curious guard. Miriam was getting herself ready for night duty.

"Keeping a diary Joan?" she asked.

"Well, that was the idea. It's just so hard to remember what has happened and when. I find that every time I sit down to write in it, all I want to talk about is food. What we have eaten, what we might eat tomorrow. I have become obsessed."

Miriam laughed. "I think we all have. I wonder what delights are in store for us today?"

"Rice and beans." They both said in unison and laughed.

"I'm going to have to dash Joan, are you going to be ok here until Freda comes down." They still had to be vigilant about not putting themselves in vulnerable situations and avoided being alone at all times. This in itself was a challenge and when tiredness and hunger reared its head, tempers could become frayed. Joan nodded, she was actually glad of some time alone. Even if it was only for five minutes.

"I'm fine," she said, "you go. I'm going to try and remember what has been happening over the last 2 months." Miriam smiled and was gone.

Joan stared hard at the little book. What on earth could she write? One of the doctors was keeping a secret record of all patients and surgeries. She had nothing of any importance to write down. In the end, she wrote;

10th Jan 1942 – *(approx date) Naval Hosp to St Alberts. Patients from Queen Mary's to us. Patients from War Memorial to us. Patients from St Albert's to us.*

25th Feb 1942 - *St Albert's over to St Theresa's*

She thought of Daphne and Matron Thomson over at St Theresa's and what a nightmare they must be having. One of the VAD's, Miss Draper from St Albert's, had fallen ill and been brought over to Bowen Road. The stories that she told of the conditions they were working in and the state of the patients made Joan's toes curl.

She had told her that the Japs had apparently decided that they wanted to use St Albert's for their own wounded and had given the nurses one hour to get themselves and their patients to leave. Kathleen Thomson was now back in charge, despite her injuries. She was given three lorries to load with anything that they needed. The nurses and RAMC's had hastily collected linen, medical supplies, mattresses, food, anything that they could lay their hands on and load into the lorries. Patients were prepared for transfer to Bowen Road. After precisely one hour they were told to stop. They had no time to say goodbye to their patients and within half an hour had found themselves on a coal barge to Kowloon.

Miss Draper said that, when they arrived on the mainland, they were herded like cattle into wire pens with other POW's and left there for hours. It was raining and cold and the poor nurse said she had never felt more like crying but Matron Thomson kept them all going.

"Don't let them see that they have broken us." she had said. "Keep your heads held high, we have done nothing wrong. We are Queens Army Nurses. It is the Japs who are being dishonourable." The nurses all raised their chins and stared over the heads of the group of jeering Japanese nurses that had now gathered. One of the QA's said under her breath, "Now I know what it's like to feel like an animal in a zoo." Matron Thomson had merely straightened her back and looked even more determined. Eventually two out of three of their lorries arrived and they were taken to St Theresa's Convent.

What they were presented with horrified them all. It was like something out of the dark ages. The nuns had done their best but they

341

had been given no medical supplies and the food situation was clearly worse than at St Albert's. The VAD had chuckled as she described a menu that had been written in pencil and put in the kitchen.

Breakfast -   rice and spinach.

Dinner -   rice and turnips.

Supper -   the Lord will provide.

Miss Draper had gone on to describe the state of the patients. They were desperately ill, on the verge of starvation with dark, sunken eyes and cheeks. Their skin was so thin that it was almost transparent and looked like it had just been draped over their protruding bones. The nuns had only rice to feed them and as many of the men were suffering with severe dysentery, this was just not enough. So many of them died in those first days, and then more arrived from Shamshuipo. Busloads of them, many of them died on the way. Matron made the medical officers take away the dead before we admitted the patients.

Joan had held her hand as she was telling her story. Her strength bolstered by the first half decent meal in months and she seemed relieved to be talking about what was going on in the hospital.

"There was always the dread of finding one of our loved ones amongst them." She said. Joan's thoughts immediately went to Forbes.

She hadn't heard a word from or about him in weeks. She prayed again that he wasn't amongst the poor, unfortunate souls that had ended up at St Theresa's.

"They wouldn't give us any more food to give to the constant stream of patients. Sometimes the nurses could only have a cup of hot water before bed. Some of us were becoming as poorly as the patients." She had stifled a sob as she said that Mrs Gimley had died. She was in her late 60's and had worked right up until the end but simply could not go on. "I have to say." She said pulling herself together. "I have never come across two braver women than Matron Currie and Matron Thomson. They deserve a medal of honour when this thing is over."

"Why do you say that?" Joan asked.

"Well, the French Nun who had been running the convent was obviously terrified of the Japanese. Major Saito was in charge and Matron Thomson just kept on asking for supplies. He kept on refusing but it didn't stop her. He was living in the house next door and we could see boxes of serum had been piled high in one of the rooms, obviously brought in from one of our hospitals. When the first case of Diphtheria arrived, Miss Thomson just lost her temper. She demanded to see the Major, telling him that we would soon have an epidemic on our hands. We had nothing to be able to deal with diphtheria, no disinfectant or protective clothing. She was more concerned about the nurses getting the infernal disease. She was amazing. We isolated the top floor. More cases came in. We had to use the sun as a disinfectant, hanging clothes and sheets out of the windows, hoping the heat would kill at least some of the bacteria. We just had to hope and pray that we didn't get it. Thankfully none of us have so far. Things just got worse. We did what we could. It was like going back 50 years. All we could do was rinse their mouths out with tepid water and hold poultices to their necks. It was just awful.

In the end, in most cases we just had to hold their hands and comfort them as they died the most horrible of deaths. Matron did not give up. She went every day and demanded the serum. Every day the Major threatened to shoot her. In the end, she wore him down and he threw a packet of the antitoxin over the fence at her. He had screamed, 'There, do not ask me for anything else, or I will have you shot!' She had just smiled and nodded graciously. No fear in her face at all. I think this infuriated him even more."

Joan smiled at the thought. They were joined by Gwen who had brought Miss Draper some tea.

"Tell Joan about the garden party." Gwen said. Miss Draper laughed.

"Oh my goodness," she said, "I don't think the Japs knew what to make of us at all. Like I said, the Major lived in the house next door. He had commanded a group of orderlies to clean up the garden so he could have a garden party for his lady friends. Sergeant Houston had been livid, and was ready to refuse. Said he'd rather die. Matron convinced him that they would only take it out on the patients if we didn't do what they asked. The next thing we know we hear singing from the garden. Houston and one of the privates had found some clothes in the cellars of the house and were dancing and singing around the garden with rakes and spades." Miss Draper was laughing at the memory, tears falling down her face.

Joan looked at Gwen in amusement.

"He'd found a long georgette dress and a wide brimmed hat. The private was in a bathing suit. They were singing 'Daisy, Daisy give me your answer do…' It was just what we needed; it cheered the whole hospital up for days. Thankfully the Japs were so bewildered by the whole thing; they just watched and let them get on with it."

Joan and Gwen fell about with laughter.

"Can you just imagine their faces?!" Joan said. "Well thank you Miss Draper, you have cheered me up no end. I'll leave you to your tea." Joan continued her rounds with a smile on her face. Even in the worst of situations, they still couldn't beat our sense of humour from us.

Joan was still smiling as she thought of the story. When she heard footsteps outside and quickly put the diary away. Freda came bursting into the dorm waving a newspaper around.

"Can you believe the Japs are telling the world we are missing in action?" She hissed as she pointed angrily at the newspaper, trying to keep her voice down.

"What do you mean?" Joan said, grabbing the paper. The front cover was filled with stories of Japanese rule and superiority and their reorganisation of the colony. There was an article about them doing their utmost to find the nurses and QA's currently 'Missing in Action.'

"Our poor families, they are going to be going out of their minds with worry." Freda said. She had clearly got herself into a lather about the whole thing. "Anyway, Matron wants to see us about it."

"Well I'm sure it can't be as bad as all that," said Joan. "Last week it said that all the British Women were in Jap hands. Hopefully they are only getting news through reliable sources back home."

She could only imagine what must be going through their minds. Hopefully the War Office would be in touch with the families to alleviate concerns.

The QA's all gathered together in Matron's office. Joan looked at them all. Everyone looked so tired and thin. Mere shadows of ourselves from this time last year she thought, feeling more despondent than ever before.

Matron did her best to boost their morale.

"I'm sure you've all seen the paper that has been floating around. I just wanted to let you know that the War Office has written to me and sent me a copy of the letter that will be going out to all of our families. Hopefully this will give them some assurance that we are all safe and as well as can be expected."

She read from the letter:

Dear...

I enclose herewith a copy of an assurance given by the Japanese, which may help to relieve your anxiety during the anxious time of waiting for news of the Q.A.I.M.N.S and the T.A.N.S. serving in Hong Kong and Singapore. You will be informed at once when any news is received.

Queen Mary, who is the President of Queen Alexandra's Imperial Military Nursing Service and the Territorial Army Nursing Service, commands me to convey to you a message that she is sharing in your anxiety and feels deep sympathy with you as well as great pride in the Nursing Services.

The British Red Cross Society is being approached with a view to making the necessary arrangements for parcels of food and clothing to be sent to all our Members. In the same way as to all other Officers and men of the Army in enemy occupied countries.

The thoughts and prayers of all their colleagues will be with them. May I also offer my personal sympathy.

Yours sincerely

K Jones

Matron-In-Chief

"Well I'm not sure that will alleviate any anxiety at all." Piped up Gwen. "Surely they must know where we are?"

"The Japanese have moved personnel around so much since the surrender; I don't know how they can know where anyone is. I suppose they are waiting for absolute confirmation before informing our families." Matron shot Gwen a silencing look as she continued to read out the statement from the Japanese regarding prisoners of war.

You will be glad to learn that we have at last received through the Argentine Government the reply of the Japanese Government as to their attitude towards the Prisoners of War Convention. It is to the following effect:-

'The Japanese Government have not yet ratified the Convention and are therefore not bound by it. They will, nevertheless, observe its terms "mutatis mutandis" in respect of English, Canadian, Australian, New Zealand and Indian prisoners taken by them. As regards the feeding and clothing of prisoners, they will on a basis of reciprocity take account of their national and racial customs.'

All of the nurses started to talk at once. What on earth did all of that mean? That was no comfort to anyone.

"Ladies, I would remind you that, above all, we must keep our heads and not get over excitable about things that are not within our control. I completely understand your feelings on this matter, especially as we know the harsh reality of what they are capable of, but we have to trust that our government and the War Office are doing everything that they can to help us. All that we can do is continue to do our best under the most difficult of circumstances. Every single one of you should know that your families would be bursting with pride had they witnessed how you have worked and pushed through these dark times with the fortitude and strength that has been noted and admired by our Army. We must continue to be brave and resolute in our principles and never let those buggers get us down."

The nurses looked at Matron in surprise at the unusually derogatory description of the Japs. She just smiled and said.

"That is all, ladies."

Just as the nurses filed out, Matron called Joan back. Joan's stomach did the familiar lurch of dread. Please tell me it is not bad news she thought to herself.

"I've had some sketchy reports about the movement around the Officers' Camps." Matron said, "Forbes name was on the list of RNO's to be sent to Shamshuipo in the next few weeks."

Joan held her breath. Suddenly, very confused as to how she should be feeling. Matron continued, "I think that can only be a positive thing. We now at least know that he is still alive and that he is obviously strong and well. They are only moving fit and healthy over there from what I can gather."

Joan tried not to think of Miss Draper's stories of the poor men taken to St Theresa's from Shamshuipo. Her heart felt like it was going to burst with relief that he was ok. Just to hear that he was alive was enough.

"Thank you so much for letting me know Matron, I am very

grateful." She couldn't wait to get back to the dorm and tell the others. She left the Matron's office and had to stop herself from running down the corridor. When she got to the dorm she was disappointed to find it empty. They must have all gone straight back on duty. She got out the diary and wrote.

Spring 1942 – Forbes moved from North Point Camp to Shamshuipo

The next few weeks were tough. One by one, all of the nurses became ill with dysentery. Hardly surprising, as the lack of hot water and medical supplies made it almost impossible to keep the wards hygienic and sanitary. It was only a matter of time before they all fell ill. Joan knew it was inevitable and, despite her best efforts, she started with the appalling symptoms and was sent to the women's ward. Joan could not remember ever feeling so dreadful. The lack of food and nutrition made it all the more difficult to fight it off. She spent two long weeks on the ward before being allowed back to the dorm to convalesce. She was not allowed to go back to her normal duties for another two weeks. What on earth was she to do with herself for two weeks!

Sister Christie and Freda were in the dorm when she was brought back from the ward. They were so pleased to see her back.

"There she is!" said Kay. "How are you feeling? You really had it bad."

"Come on, let's get you into bed. We've put clean sheets on for you and everything," said Freda, leading her by the arm like an infirm patient. Joan smiled at their kindness and concern. She was pleased to be back in the relative comfort of the dorm.

"Here you go, some reading material for you," said Freda, handing her a printed newsletter, "I don't know where they found the time, but it is really very amusing." Joan took it from her and read the title, The Snake and Staff? What on earth?" She laughed for the first time in weeks and started to flick through the pages.

"Shall I go and get you some tea?" Asked Kay. Joan pulled a face, "I'm not sure we can call that stuff we serve on the wards tea."

"Oh no no no, my dear, I completely agree. I will get you a proper cup of tea, made from proper tea leaves." She gave Joan a knowing wink. "It's not what you know round here these days." She said with a chuckle as she headed off. Joan turned her attention back to the newsletter. It was dated January 1942. Freda was right, where on earth did they find the time but it really was just the ticket for cheering her up.

Joan spent a frustrating few days confined to her bed. She felt so guilty watching the others going backwards and forwards. It was obviously very busy on the wards. She was itching to get back to it. Renate had given her some good news. It seemed that Norman Leath was making a great recovery and had now been put to work in the Hospital Administration Office. Joan was so pleased. That boy had had such a lucky escape. In fact, she was feeling increasingly guilty about how she had come through the war so far practically unscathed in comparison to some. She knew it was silly to feel like that, but when she thought what others had endured it was a sobering thought.

Just then Gwen popped her head around the door.

"How are you feeling Sister Whiteley? Feel like some fresh air?"

"Oh boy, do I?" said Joan, already throwing the blankets off her bed and pulling on some slacks. Gwen looked at her in amusement, "I'd brush your hair and pinch your cheeks if I were you, you'll be scaring the patients." Joan laughed and pretended to be insulted but did as she was told and felt instantly better. Despite being a bit wobbly on her feet, it was good to be up and around. Gwen offered her arm, which Joan gladly took.

"Where are we off to? Anywhere nice? The beach? A picnic?" she giggled. Gwen just smiled. "I have a little surprise for you." She led her straight to Ward 9. Joan was confused. Did they need her to work?

"We've just had some patients in from North Point camp that need looking over."

Joan looked at her suspiciously, and turned to look around the ward. And then she saw him.

There he was, sat up in bed with his arm in a sling and a big smile on his face. Her legs nearly went from under her but she managed to break into a run before throwing herself onto his bed and throwing arms around his neck. A huge cheer went up from the rest of the ward as the men clapped and cheered for probably the first happy moment in months.

Joan didn't want to let go in case it wasn't true. Eventually she pulled away and put his face in her hands.

"You look thin." She said.

"Well, the new chef is appalling," joked Forbes, and then looked at her with an intensity that made her want to faint. "You are indeed a sight for sore eyes. How are you my dear? How have you been? I have been going out of my mind with worry. All of the stories…" Joan stopped him and shook her head.

"Don't worry, I'm absolutely fine." She looked around, "We've actually been very lucky. How about you? Why are you here?" It suddenly occurred to her that he must be ill or injured. She jumped back off the bed and looked at his arm. "Oh my goodness, I'm so sorry, did I hurt you?"

Forbes laughed, "No, don't you worry. It's just a scratch. I managed to put a rusty nail through my hand whilst we were trying to fix up the huts in the camp. The camp doctor thought it might have gone septic, but it's fine. But even if it wasn't, it would have been worth it to come here and see you. I should have done it months ago!" They both laughed and sat for hours catching up on the last months until the light faded and Gwendoline was lighting the hurricane lamps around the ward.

"How's the patient?" She asked as she got to Forbes.

"Faking it I think," smiled Joan. "Don't be fooled by that Scottish charm."

"Well it's nice to see a smile on your face Sister Whiteley. I will leave you to it but just be warned, Matron is due any minute. She'll shoo you straight back to bed if she sees you."

"Yes, you'd better go," said Forbes. "I don't want to get you into any trouble. I'll still be here in the morning. We can hopefully get more time together before I have to go."

Joan reluctantly left him to sleep and went back to the dorm in a daze. She didn't even feel hungry anymore! The relief of seeing him was more than she could ever have hoped for. She went to bed that night with a big smile on her face, sleeping soundly for the first time in months.

She got up the next morning and went straight up to the ward. When she got there his bed was empty and he was nowhere to be seen. She panicked and ran over to Sister Murphy who had been on night duty.

"Don't worry Joan, he's only been moved downstairs. We need his bed." She looked at Joan's faced as it relaxed with relief. "He's likely to be taken back later today or tomorrow though. I'd make the most of it whilst you can." She said softly before going back to her report.

Joan went downstairs and found him sat on a pile of mattresses talking to some other 'able bodied' patients. She thought again how thin he looked but other than that quite well. She walked over and one of the men made room for her to sit on the mattresses.

"Good morning my dear," he said, squeezing her hand.

"Good morning, how did you sleep?" she asked.

"Well, much better than I have in a while to be honest."

"When do you have to go back?" She didn't want to hear the answer.

"In about an hour," he said quietly.

"Oh," Joan didn't even try to hide her disappointment, "I thought you might be here for a few days at least."

"I know, but as there is not a great deal wrong with me, I'm not sure how I can drag it out for much longer unless I put another nail in my hand." Forbes pulled her towards him. "We'll be together forever as soon as this is over." He whispered in her ear, "Have you managed to stop them from getting your pearls?"

"Yes," she smiled. "They are tucked away for the moment. I think they have lost interest in us all a little bit to be honest," she said, looking over at the scruffy looking soldier on the front steps of the hospital. "They don't even prowl the corridors and wards any more. They just hang around in groups about the place."

"Well, that's a relief at least. They got my watch. It wasn't worth much, but dad gave it to me before I came out here." He changed subject, "have you heard from your mum and dad? Are they ok?"

"No, they've not allowed any letters in or out of the hospital." Joan said sadly, "I have no idea how any of them are. How about you?"

"No, much the same. The men have said that the Japs are going to let us send telegrams out soon, so hopefully I'll be able to get word to you that all is well."

Joan nodded and had to gulp back tears as the ambulance pulled up outside to take them back to camp.

"Now don't be sad, I am just thrilled to have seen you and that we are both safe. Remember our promise; keep your head down and no heroics." Forbes held her with his one good arm. "At least I've had a bath and have some clean clothes!" He said, trying to keep his voice jolly. Forbes leant over and kissed her on the check and handed her a folded wad of Hong Kong Dollars.

"Forbes, I can't take this." She tried to give it him back.

"You can and you will." He said as they were herded outside. "I will send more as and when I can."

Joan just gave a grateful smile as once again she tried to hold back the tears as the Japanese driver started to shout and push them towards the ambulance. Forbes was the last to get in. They drove away and Joan stood, rooted to the spot until she couldn't see the ambulance any more. She couldn't believe he had gone again so soon. It now all felt like a bit of a dream. When would she see him again? She headed back down to the dorm, her heart heavy once again. But at least he is alive she told herself. To distract herself from the tears that were stinging her eyes, she pulled out the diary;

22.4.42 Forbes arrived hospital. I was still convalescing.

A few days later she wrote;

23.4.42 Forbes went to camp. A few miserable days until I got used to it.

It was months before she felt able to write anything else but after a period of nothing happening, all of a sudden things started to happen all at once.

15.6.42 back a couple of days. Quite suddenly we were being told that 3 people were to be exchanged from Stanley – Ms Greaves, Ms K Stark & Mabel Redwood left in afternoon – Marion Lee, Mrs MacKenzie & Jester arrived. Much chattering, as this was the first time we had really had anybody from Stanley or outside anywhere – into our place. We learnt that 10 had been exchanged from Theresa's &

the ones from there were all ill – some more than others - Miss Thomson has complete paralysis of left arm! We are all agitating to go over to Theresa's to help but it is no good. They have an epidemic of Diphtheria in Shamshuipo

21.6.42 Duty on Ward 9 back to my old haunts

27.6.42 The Americans left and I'm more than pleased to feel that the Refo's and others are away. Mrs Weilandt also – First letter home – month fades out & the news from what we can gather is desperate

4th July 1942 - Great air of tension in the place - waiting for something to happen. Poor mutts that we are!

5th July 1942 - A very amusing 'mock court'. Money matters much conversation – haven't had a cent since Forbes went – apart from odd dollars leant to me so am more or less confined to rice, Yam & cucumber. An odd tin of marmalade still must say that I'm much more contented than those that have much! This feeling probably won't last!

17th July 1942 'A Big Day!' all except 12 sisters received money from Argyle Street. I had 50 Yen from Forbes. Thank god for him. The days pass – they are mainly meatless days now

8th Aug 1942 - terrific tension Colonel Shackleton & Colonel Simpson and Cmdr Gleave leave for Argyle St (sent message to Forbes). Something else in the air. We are told by Matron at lunchtime that all sisters & VAD's are going to

Stanley on the 10.8.42. Feverish packing, terrific depression amongst staff and patients.

Chapter 30

"So, Forbes must have gone back to Argyle Street and not Shamshuipo then?" Said Gwen as they all opened their much-anticipated envelopes. It had been hard to survive without any kind of pay, especially now that a thriving black-market community had been set up in the colony.

"Yes, I suppose he must have." replied Joan, "I must say I'm glad, looking at the state of some of them coming in from Shamshuipo."

The Sisters hadn't received any pay since the surrender, as the Japanese did not recognise them as Officers. The food in the hospital Mess had been rationed and then rationed again. The only things they seemed to get these days were rice and vegetables and often the vegetables were unidentifiable. The hospital staff were so hungry that they forced it down, but any opportunity that they had to get their hands on some proper food, they took.

A couple of the medical officers regularly risked their lives to get more supplies. Usually from some of the more enterprising Chinese. Some of the braver of the Chinese would come to the perimeter fences with all sorts of luxuries like marmalade and tinned meat. Without the money sent through to them from the camps or that they were able to borrow, the Sisters had no way of getting hold of any of it.

The arrival of the money from Argyle Street or the arrival of packages from the other side of the electric fence soon became the focus of their existence.

Days blended into nights and the rumour mill continued to turn. There was talk that the Americans had bombed Japan in retaliation to Pearl Harbour. It had been on a much smaller scale but they had targeted the factories and more worryingly for the Japanese, they had got close enough without being detected. This caused all sorts of rumours. Would it make the Japs angry and want to take it out on their American prisoners or would they enter into negotiations with America to free their POW's? Nobody knew for sure but all of a sudden people were being moved from the hospital. They didn't know whether they were being repatriated home or just moved to a camp. Not knowing was torture. Joan had long since stopped believing all that she heard or read. All that she could do was to take one day at a time.

After months of waiting for something to happen, even though they didn't know what, it was a tremendous shock when Matron told them that they were to pack up and that they would be moved to Stanley in a matter of days. This threw the young nurses into a complete state of panic. Apart from the fact that they had no idea what lay ahead for them but they were also leaving the hospital with no nurses. It was to be run with the current medical officers and doctors and two orderlies. With the constant stream of seriously ill patients and so few supplies, this felt like another act of cruelty by the Japanese.

Joan shuddered to think how they would cope. She knew they probably wouldn't. Even more troubling was how on earth would Forbes know where she had been taken? There was no way of knowing whether any messages were getting through or whether they were getting any kind of communication at all. This had Joan in a complete panic. What if they couldn't find each other? The thought of their brief meeting at the hospital being the last time she would ever see him was too much for her to bear. The thought of being completely alone yet again without anyone knowing where to find her was terrifying. She had sent messages with Colonel Shackleton and Commander Gleave as they were taken to Argyle Street. She just had to pray that they would be able to get them to him.

The day they were to leave Bowen Road, they were to be ready for their bags to be inspected at 8.30 a.m. They spent the morning saying their goodbyes and finally in the early afternoon they were told they were to leave. The whole of the hospital staff and any patients that could stand, all came out to wave them off. Joan thought her heart might break. She found Norman Leath and gave him the greatest hug. No words were spoken. Joan didn't trust herself. She feared that once the tears started, they would not stop.

She would not give the Japanese the satisfaction. Some of the other nurses were not so worried about what the Japs thought. The sound of sobbing from both the nurses and the staff was enough to set the strongest of men off. They were herded on to 2 buses. All of a sudden, there was a real sense of urgency to set off.

As Joan boarded the bus, jaw locked against the fear burning in her throat, one of the medical officers climbed to the top of the steps and began to sing.

"Should old acquaintance be forgot, and never thought upon" One by one, all of the nurses, patients, and doctors, both on the steps and loaded on the bus, joined in the verse. The old ballad affected her in a way no amount of terror or hopelessness could. This moment, singing with all of these people whom she'd shared both her fondest and most horrible memories with, was the most beautiful moment of her life. Voice catching as hot tears rolled down her cheeks, she finished the verse, holding Gwen's hand, "we'll take a cup of kindness yet, for auld lang syne." Never prouder of her countrymen, Joan pressed her hand to the glass, knowing in her gut it was the closest she'd ever be to these friends again.

The bus pulled away…She could bear it no longer and broke down in floods of tears. She looked out of the window and wondered how many of these people, whom she had grown so fond of, she would ever see again.

Waves of nausea came over her and she wasn't sure whether the sickness she was feeling was out of hunger or foreboding. They stopped at Queen's Pier and were told to get out of the bus. It was now mid-afternoon and the sun was at its fiercest. They were forced to line up and just wait. This is it Joan thought, I'm going to be shot. This is where they get rid of us all. Beads of sweat were trickling down her back and all she could hear was the sound of her heart thudding in her chest. She tried to take deep breaths to calm herself down. It was no good. She realised that her whole body was trembling. *Please do not faint*, she said to herself. Then, to her horror, she saw Colonel Tokunaga arrive on his horse. She had never seen such a repulsive looking man.

He was known throughout the colony as 'Fat Pig' as he was so obese, but he was better known for his cruelty and disregard for western life. He was the Commander of all the POW camps in Hong Kong.

Joan thought that her legs were finally going to give way from under her, when Gwen gave her a dig in the ribs. Another bus had just arrived and out poured the nursing staff from St Theresa's. They all looked deathly pale and thin. Joan strained her neck to look for Daphne and Miss Thomson. She finally spotted them as they were being forced into line with the rest of them. They were all commanded to bow to the Commander and look ahead only. Anyone seen to be looking away would be shot.

So many things were running through Joan's head. She thought of Forbes, she thought of Brenda, she thought of her family. She wanted to scream, she wanted to scream until she had no breath left in her body. She thought back to what Brenda had once said to her. *What is to become of us Joan?* Now, as she stood here in the blazing, intense heat of the afternoon sun, with the Japanese Prison Commander in front of her, she thought a bullet would be a blessing. She only hoped it would be quick, and they would all be shot at the same time. She braced herself, certain that she would hear the command given at any moment.

Instead, she heard Colonel Tokunaga, speaking through his odious looking interpreter, congratulating the nurses on their bravery and thanking them for their hard work and tenacity. He welcomed them and said that they were now to enjoy the hospitality of the Japanese Imperial Army at Stanley Internment Camp. The last words she could remember were,

"You are going to Stanley and your stay will <u>not</u> be short."

Thank you for reading my book!

I really appreciate all of your feedback, and I love hearing what you have to say.

I need your input to make the next book even better.

Please leave me a helpful review on Amazon letting me know what you thought of the book.

Thank you so much

Jo Price

Acknowledgements

I could not have written this book without the following:

The Hong Kong War Diaries website - meticulously updated by Tony Banham, who was also always at the end of an email if I needed any information.

The Superstar Launch Team who helped me spread the word about my first novel to allow this part of history to stay alive. Thank you to each and every one of you!

And finally my lovely mum, Alison MacLeod and her sister Jean MacLeod who have supported me every step of the way, dredging up long forgotten stories and handing over the precious suitcase and its contents, without which, this story would not exist.

Thank you.

The following books were an amazing source of information and detail:

The Fall of Hong Kong by Philip Snow

The Battle For Hong Kong 1941-1945 Hostage to Fortune by Oliver Lindsay with the memories of John R. Harris

Sisters in Arms British Army Nurses Tell Their Story by Nicola Tyrer

Grey and Scarlet edited by Ada Harrison

Grey Touch With Scarlet by Jean Bowden

Quiet Heroines by Brenda McBryde

.

About the Author

Jo Price lives in Didsbury, Manchester with her two teenagers Luke and Alyssa, and house full of pets. Always an avid reader, she aspired to be a writer from a young age and it has taken until now for her to share her story.

Jo started working on this story 10 years ago after having her children. It was a story she had always wanted to write and keep alive for her children and generations to come. Her fascination with her Gran's diaries and other memorabilia from her time in Hong Kong during the 2nd World War, led her to research the period and uncover a little known piece of history that she became passionate about keeping alive, not only for her Grandparent's but for all of those who fought and suffered at the hands of the Japanese.

It became a study of human endurance and a labour of love, but a story that had to be shared. This is the first in a series of novels, telling their incredible story.

24219891R00217

Printed in Great Britain
by Amazon